this book belongs to

J. Soltysiak

3527

GRIEVOUS ANGEL

Also by Irene Lin-Chandler

The Healing of Holly-Jean

GRIEVOUS ANGEL

Irene Lin-Chandler

HEADLINE

First published in 1996
by HEADLINE BOOK PUBLISHING

10 9 8 7 6 5 4 3 2 1

British Library Cataloguing in Publication Data

Lin-Chandler, Irene
   Grievous angel. – (A Holly-Jean Ho mystery)
   1. English fiction – 20th century – Chinese authors
   I.   Title
   823 [F]

ISBN 0-7472-1495-6

Typeset by Keyboard Services, Luton, Beds

Printed and bound in Great Britain by
Mackays of Chatham PLC, Chatham, Kent

HEADLINE BOOK PUBLISHING
A division of Hodder Headline PLC
338 Euston Road
London NW1 3BH

In loving memory of Arthur Stanley Chandler

Acknowledgement

Many thanks to good friend Stevo Chiang of the B.U., Taipei

Chapter 1

Strolling ahead to the schnapps stand on this snowy night in Volkspark, Schiedam, Holly-Jean experienced a sudden jolt. Elbowing aside the mob, she reached the bar and knocked back a celebratory double shot of clear Genever. Unless she was deluded, that jolt – a surge of well-being from littlest toe-nail to longest split end – signified glad tidings. The tiger had awoken. *Mended.*

Holly warmly surveyed the crowd of stubbly Turkish pimps, drunken Dammers, shy Filipino seamen counting guilders to buy blue-eyed heat, rowdy Brit artic-drivers, wide loads hanging from their belts, and the frocked-up angels of every gender, race and age. There were Moluccans, Thais, Dutch . . . and stunning East European girls, beautiful stragglers from liberation. With the beatific serenity of intoxication, Holly sauntered off. The snow was falling fat and irresistible, Chinese lanterns hanging from the fir trees casting a cosy glow over the carnal commerce. Volkspark after midnight – Ed's sensimillian idea – was a Christmas card straight from Hieronymus Bosch. Hey, feeling *this* good made her nervous.

Which was the precise moment when a one-legged woman gybed on a single chrome crutch out of the dark and her cellphone began to bray.

Startled, Holly swore in Hakkanese. '*Diao ni-ah mei tze-bai!*' No passer-by understood the colourful things she said in that ancient language. In this case: 'Do

1

something unspeakable to the rear end of your nearest relative.'

Naked but for a platinum wig, white fur coat and one diamanté-studded high-heel glinting in the red light, the prostitute caressed her single thigh, beckoning. '*Kom!*' she whispered.

Mouth agape, swaying, Holly remembered her manners. 'Um, not tonight, thanks.' She extracted the nagging phone. 'Yes?' – her eyes mesmerised by the snowflakes falling on the bloom of silky pubic hair at the top of that one shapely limb.

'Is that you, Miss Ho?' The voice was well known to her, ditto the sinking feeling.

'Yep, Holly here, Mrs Howell-Pryce. What's happened?'

'Terrible news. I'm sorry to inform you of the death of Elfa Ericksson.'

Holly-Jean spun away, sending a flurry of snow to dance madly in the wind. 'Tell me!' she exhaled steadily.

'As you requested, when you're abroad the office answer-machine is re-routed to my house. I went to Wales for a couple of days, got back home late from Paddington Station and have just played through the messages. You'd better listen for yourself.'

Holly heard the crackle of her answer-machine, the beep, then a husky voice: 'Elfa Ericksson just got herself killed . . . *Giri.*'

Mrs H-P fretted, 'I've listened to it over and over again, but I can't make out that last word. Is it "jeery" or something?'

'It's Mandarin,' she said simply, and killed the thing.

I wan gwei! Ten thousand devils! One blister on her brain: young Elfa dead. And some monkey invoking *giri*, the ancient Chinese concept of duty – an unavoidable obligation that bound the invokee to unconditional service. But why her? And who was the monkey?

2

She looked at her watch. Schiedam to the ferry terminal at Hoek van Holland was only twenty minutes away at this time of night. Add another twenty minutes for the heavy snowfall. She should just make the night-crossing. She ran a mental checklist: passport, cash, credit cards, notebook PC and shopping were all in the Peugeot. First rule of the globally mobile: keep the wherewithal to hand.

'I do you both for a special price,' called the woman, arching back over the bonnet of a BMW. Both?

Ed van Schrempft, her chemically challenged friend, had staggered up on the ice. '*Houd Verdommer!*' he pointed. 'Only one leg? S-surreal.'

'She's real,' said Holly drily. 'Look, I'm sorry, Ed. Something's come up. Gotta make the night-boat. I'll drop you at Schiedam Noord Station. Let's bail!'

Ed's pupils were like burn-holes; snow coated his straggly goatee. Transfixed by the unusual offering, he lurched closer. The woman raised her knee, stroking herself '*Isch hot heer! Upkom!*'

Baby-arms out, Ed shuffled towards the beckoning steam. 'Think I'll s-ss-stick around, Holls.'

Holly didn't have time to get through to wherever Ed's head was at. 'Suit yourself, Eddie. See you.'

The woman deftly snagged him into the blazing comfort of the fur coat.

Back tyres sliding on fresh snow, Holly-Jean tooted the horn as she passed the BMW. Lamp turned orange-for-occupied above the city-ordinanced parking booth in Volkspark, Schiedam, west of Rotterdam city centre, this freezing Wednesday night, late January.

Fifty metres down the wooded lane, the Peugeot fish-tailed through a gang of Feyenoorders – Rotterdam football supporters – brandishing bottles and scarves. She heard enraged yells, and a bottle smashed on the roof. She accelerated, weaving all over the lane.

Crossing the junction with the main road that ran through the park, she glimpsed the dark shape of an approaching vehicle, fast, no lights. Reflexively she stamped her foot and the brakes locked, spinning the car 180 degrees into a sidewards surf towards the snow-draped treetops of the precipice on the other side. Heart pumping adrenaline, Holly forced herself not to grab at the wheel. With light taps on the accelerator, fluid steering, she just managed to finesse the car's momentum along the straight and away from the edge, when the Peugeot was sideswiped by the oncoming car; it careened across the snow and with a deafening scrunch, wrapped the passenger door round a concrete lamp-post.

In the sudden silence, Holly sat through the serotonin reaction, chest heaving. Mixed emotions of joy to be alive and livid rage at the other idiot. Smelt petrol and quickly switched off the ignition. She jumped out, shaking broken glass from her leather jacket and jeans. She looked down the road. No sign of the other car. Flashbacked glimpse of a black four-wheel drive RV. Maybe a Commanche Jeep or a Discovery. Whatever. They hadn't stopped. Which meant it was either a drunken maniac or deliberate. She surveyed the damage. Tyres, wheels, axles: all intact. Frockuvan ugly dent, but driveable.

Holly stepped over to the edge and looked down. If it hadn't been for the lamp-post ... She came over goose-pimples. *Chi-pi*. Chicken-skin, the Chinese call it. Looked at her watch. She'd have to hurry to make that night-boat. She climbed back in, crossed her fingers and turned on the ignition. The car started up first time, and Holly point-turned by inches till the Peugeot was free of the lamp-post and facing back in the right direction.

Passing by the entrance to the red-light lane a second time, she heard a strange *whump!* looked to her left and saw a white flash deep in the forest; hesitated, shrugged, drove on.

4

Holly-Jean rolled the leased Peugeot onto the two a.m. Harwich ferry just as the last of the big artics was being chained down for the crossing. The deckmen had refused to take the sorry-looking Peugeot at first, and Holly had to give a quick demonstration drive round the empty car park to prove the damage was purely superficial.

She sat in the airplane-style recliner sipping espresso as the North Sea bucked beneath the tin. Too wired up, from the near-miss accident – if that's what it was – and Elfa Ericksson's death, on top of two nights of no-sleep fooling in Rotterdam. A thought kept tickling the edge of her brain. Unable to access, she let her thoughts float, hoping to catch a wave.

The last time she'd seen the girl of whom the Fashion Editor of *Harper's* had written: 'These kind of incandescent co-ordinates don't come around very often', had been a one-off fashion shoot at the Highgate *dojo* last November. The German photographer, a right charmer in black latex fetishist gear and an odd name Holly couldn't recall, had wanted 'der starker Kontrast' and got it. Holly-Jean, in Taekwondo black belt. Tiny, dangerous, sweating. Chinese hair its usual spiky crop. A single swipe of brushwork from the make-up woman to highlight her best feature: those eyes dark as pools of blood. Bean-pole Elfa, fully made over, Hepburn-hep, a long-necked princess in Tomasz Starzewski evening wear.

After the shoot, the two girls had dumped the German and exchanged a few chapters of life at Marika's Wine Bar down the hill in Islington. Describing her life of public exposure that had begun with baby commercials as 'one great big very lucrative joke, thank You, God,' Elfa seemed a perfectly normal twenty-year-old supermodel, hardly a hint of precious. They'd a natural bond wrought from experiencing the wrath of the anti-miscegenists. They'd both had their share of shit for the crime they'd committed at birth; diluting the Caucasian division of mankind.

Holly's mix: Chinese Hakka mum, English dad.

Elfa's mother was Swedish. She and Marika, who owned the wine bar, had been 1960s au pairs. Elfa's stepfather was a Tory MP for somewhere, but she'd dropped that subject quickly. Her real dad had been an Ethiopian one-night stand – which fleeting conjunction had created magic: cappuccino pigmentation, ice-blue Nordic eyes, and limbs that flowed out of Africa. Elfa did triathlons when not modelling, and in the *dojo* shower, Holly-Jean had been awed by that female perfection of the genus *homo sapiens*. Elfa unabashedly used that blessed body to further her ends – sinful in jealous Britain; the tabloids whinged spitefully about £10,000 waking fees and other colossal earnings from endorsements and accessories. Now that she was dead, thought Holly, sadly blowing on her hot cup, the slugs would no doubt rake the muck so very diligently.

A sudden squall smashed into the side of the ferry, sending trays sliding and provoking a sudden cheer from the bar, where the truckers were playing three-card brag amidst bottles of Carlsberg Elephant beer. Holly-Jean looked out at the North Sea's churning white-tops, lit up by the passing ferry-boat. Not far distant, an oil rig twinkled its lonesome light through the lashing rainy night. This old stretch of water had seen so much and wouldn't know what the world was going to miss. Would the fish care? Probably not. Holly raised her cup: Elfa Ericksson, zapping that dreary winter day, now switched out. Shine on in that other place and on that distant shore.

Holly ordered fresh espresso with a shot of Genever from the waitress. When it came, the spiced coffee's smooth fire warmed her cockles, thawing the chill of bereavement a little. She took out her notebook PC and began to do her expenses for the three-day business trip to Holland. Sorting through the mess, she came across the receipt from tonight's

6

dinner with Ed at the Sumatra Rijstaffel restaurant on Westewagenstraat. It listed thirteen dishes, five different satays and three bottles of champagne! No wonder her brain was a fog. (Holly deemed it churlish to factor in the previous dawn's night-clubbing with her other Dutch friend, Rita Wineberry.) Ed van Schrempft was always fun ... if you consider three-day hangovers fun. Ed had worked at the Dutch branch of her previous job, previous life. He had declared unilateral lust at a sales conference in Brighton; she'd kindly turned him away and they'd ended up friends. Nowadays he was vaguely self-employed and indecently rich. With his leaky nose and constant trips to the men's room, it didn't take a genius to figure: Holland. Funny money. *Oxy*-you-moron.

Not that Holly disapproved; you choose the choice, you live the life.

But with his mind on toxic idle and body puffing out more each year as poison drip-fed the sack, she worried about his health.

Ed was loyal and dear and going to live to a very ripe young age.

The Hieronymus image of the one-legged woman returned now, and with it, a bizarre vision of Ed going for glory. Judging by the wary looks of the passengers opposite, Holly had obviously failed to suppress the giggles.

Just then the ship's horn blared and her own fog finally cleared. During the Rijstaffel, Ed had asked after 'my mate Elfa'. It was the first Holly'd ever heard of a connection between her two friends. Knew it was irrational, but she felt betrayed.

'What the hell's "Old bull eats young grass" supposed to mean?' Ed had protested. 'Holly-Jean, you've got the typical dirty mind of a Confucian puritan.'

'Oh, just good friends, are you?' she'd said, peanut and sambal oelek dripping from her skewer of monkfish.

7

Tapping his index finger on his nose, Ed had replied obliquely, 'For an ultra-bimbo, Elfa's a smart kid. Definitely understands the essentials.'

'And how does the crystal logic of your unsullied mind define "the essentials"?'

Ed had declared with gusto, 'Why, what else, my girl? Sponduliks, dinero, gelt!'

Now Elfa Ericksson was dead and for some subconscious reason back there in Volkspark, Holly had kept the news from Ed.

On the seat beside her the cellphone chirped. Holly wondered who knew she was out here in the middle of the North Sea at five in the morning? Then she answered her own dumb question: *they don't.* Damn cellphones – can't live with 'em, can't work without 'em.

'Consider this: your fine yellow ass, my honed silver blade.' Male. Neutral accent.

Across the water the cranes of Harwich loomed out of flat misty East Anglia. Awake for the second dawn in a row, in quiet, measured tones Holly-Jean finally vented her night's sarin of rage.

'So you'd like to test your blade? Fine. You're welcome any time. My rotor-disposal can shred a severed dick in three seconds flat. Organic, right? We can recycle.'

But only the eerie moan of an electronic ghost answered from the ether.

Chapter 2

Holly came off the M25 at the A11 into North London, bang into the neverending morning rush-hour. It was past ten and yet the traffic was still inching its colubrine way into the city centre a dozen miles away. As usual, after even the quickest visit to somewhere like Holland, the metropolis looked shabby, backward, downright filthy. Wind picked up detritus from the pavement and blew it across the Peugeot's bonnet. There was a miserable freezing drizzle, not enough for a decent rinse, just enough to smear dirt across the windscreen.

By the North Circular the Peugeot was out of washer and Holly out of her mind with frustration. Lack of sleep and the bloody traffic had made her boiling-point irritable, and for once her *chi* breathing techniques failed her. Who could she call and annoy? A debate with Ho Ma-ma on the perils of singledom would have been perfect, but Ma was living in Taiwan these days. Good friend Marika would be at her morning yoga class – besides, the subject of Elfa was bound to come up and after last year, Holly had made it a rule never, ever to mix her work with her personal life.

Which left no alternative to getting down to work.

With an exhausted yawn, she called Mr Hua. As usual, she was given another two numbers before reaching him. He listened as she spelled out her proposals for the Convention in Den Haag – the purpose of her trip to Holland.

He sounded pleased. In typical arcane Mandarin, he

pronounced, 'Some people say Little Sister Ho is confused. Too confused to trust. Doesn't know whether she's Chinese or English. They call her a banana: yellow skin, but white inside. Easily squashed.'

He paused. Holly said nothing. She'd heard it all before.

'Others say Little Sister Ho is like an egg. Yellow inside, but brittle white shell. She'll break if dropped and the yellow will run away.'

Another pause. Another no response.

'But I tell them, they're all wrong. Little Sister Ho is a passion fruit. Her skin's as tough as rhino-hide, but inside she is bursting with pink juice and sweet ripe passion. You free for dinner?'

'Nice work, but not tonight, Joseph.'

Two cars ahead someone somehow had crunched a bumper – must have fallen asleep – and the discussion between the drivers looked to turn nasty. From behind came a deafening cacophony of horns – everyone letting rip their frustration. Holly joined in for a second or two, relishing the insanity of the moment. Then she pounded her notebook PC on the passenger seat and found the number for 'Princess of Sheba Models', the agency that had set up the Highgate *dojo* shoot with Elfa Ericksson. If she was going to find out the truth about Elfa's death, the first place to start would be the girl's model agency. She'd call them to offer her services.

Sitting in the stop-start crawl within sight of Manor House tube station, Holly-Jean was about to call the agency when she spotted a newsagent. She'd had the radio tuned to the 24-hour news station, but so far there'd been no mention of the supermodel's death. She pulled on the hand-brake, jumped out with an apologetic smile at the grim faces lined up behind the Peugeot, dashed inside and bought a couple of tabloids.

She needn't have bothered. As she was re-clicking her

seat-belt, she spotted the newsagent's felt-tipped poster: *Heroin OD of millionaire model.*

Holly said aloud, '*Lywan-jang!* Crap. Bilge. Utter bollocks.' She mashed the phone buttons angrily.

'Sheba's, good morning, Reception,' intoned a female.

'This is Holly-Jean Ho of H-J.H. and Associates.'

There was a short pause, followed by, 'Miss Ho, please wait a moment.'

A second later, a male voice burst onto the line. 'Is that Holly-Jean Ho? Joel Unmack here. Thank God you called! Her Bitchiness has been throwing royal tantrums all morning. How soon can you be here?'

Holly had intended merely to fix an appointment with the agency to offer her services as an acquaintance of Elfa's and as a professional PI. See what their response to the supermodel's death would be. She would far rather be heading home for shower and sleep, but the campy urgency had her intrigued.

'Never, if I sit in this traffic,' she said, spotting an NCP sign in the middle of a row of traveller's hotels. Manor House station was still in her rear-view mirror. 'Look, I'll dump the car and get the tube. Eleven-thirty OK?'

'Do that, and I'll be yours till eternity.' The man oozed relief like post-coital dribble.

Holly reached the model agency in South Molton Street at eleven-forty. Muttering to herself, 'Glamour is an attitude, not something you can just put on,' she entered a room full of gorgeous hopefuls of both sexes clutching their black portfolios. For a brief moment, they gave her their best profiles, until with a communal glance they realised she'd come about the cleaning job and communally glanced away.

Holly rudely stuck out her tongue in response, licked her fingers and ran them through her spiky black hair. Announced to the Sloaney receptionist in pearls and blue cardy that she was the urgently awaited Miss Ho.

How do they do that smile with just the lower lip, she wondered, as the receptionist murmured into a phone.

A door at the far end of Reception burst open.

'Don't know how or why, but thank the Lord you're here! I'm Joel.'

Joel Unmack was thin, tall and very camp in bottle-green velvet top-coat, loosely tied silk Burgundy bow, ruched white shirt, black tights and brown riding boots. His hair was long and loose, and of a dark navy that matched the shadow applied beneath the eyes.

'Shelley, right?' said Holly. The assembled beauties, perhaps sensing their error, went very quiet.

'George Gordon Noel, the Sixth Lord Byron, puh-leeze,' said Joel foppishly as he ushered Holly past the communal re-offering of best profiles and through the door. Holly tugged him to a halt and whispered frantically, 'Wait a second! Am I just slow on the uptake today or what, Joel? You were expecting me, right? I mean I was about to call you and offer my services but you lot seem to have pre-empted me.'

'It's a twisted story, darling, and all my fault. I cocked it up if you really want to know.'

'But why me?'

'Oh you come highly recommended, my dear.'

'By whom?'

'Oh never mind that, there's no time now. Her excrescence is waiting.'

Leading off to the left of the short corridor was a large hectic office. Joel steered her through the door to the right.

'Holly-Jean Ho,' announced Joel.

Everything about the woman who rose up from behind the huge glass desk was big. Big body. Big head. Big crimson hair. Big brassy voice. As for that nose...

'So relieved you could *finally* make it. Coffee, Joel!' she yelled. 'De-caff?'

12

'Espresso,' said Holly, mustering a facsimile of brisk confidence.

Big nipples poking through a white Calvin Klein T-shirt, big legs encased in black suede Gaucho chaps, the woman strode from behind the desk, taking in Holly's dishevelled leather jacket, jeans, balding Air Jordans and clutch of Dutch shopping bags with a gaze at once disdainful, askance, bemused. Wishing fervently she'd gone with the hot shower option, Holly pointedly eyed the woman's enormous left-cambered shnozz likewise.

'Aramint de Lache.'

Holly took the proffered hand. 'Holly-Jean Ho.'

The woman had a grip like a prop-forward. Maintaining the clasp, Holly found a secret pressure point with her index finger and gave a slight prod. Ms de Lache whipped away her hand as though electrocuted. Her eyes narrowed in rapid reappraisal; the bark seemed more respectful. 'Good to meet you. I trust you're fully prepared, Miss Ho? Speed must be your first priority.'

Holly smiled casually. 'Actually, a hot shower's my first priority. I've just come off the night-boat from Holland. This is about Elfa Ericksson, isn't it – or am I missing something?'

'You didn't get our message? Fucking hell!' Aramint de Lache pressed a button. *'Jo-el!'*

A harassed-looking Joel re-entered with a tray bearing coffee cups, and darted a beseeching glance at Holly.

'Oh, wait a moment,' Holly lied, already experiencing deep aversion towards the big woman. 'My office system went down yesterday – no one could reach me.' She took the espresso and acknowledged with a wink Joel's silently worded, 'Thank you.'

'Well, you're here now and that's what counts,' said Aramint, pacing. 'We want you to put an immediate stop to these lies about Elfa.'

Holly said, 'Yes, I imagine the scandal would hardly be good for the agency.'

'Complete disaster,' agreed Aramint, hurriedly adding, 'of course, that's not the point here. We simply must do all we can to protect Elfa's good name and reputation. That's your job, Miss Ho, and we've wasted far too much time already.'

Holly's nostrils flared. A definite warning sign to those who knew her. 'Actually, my services aren't on offer,' she said coolly. 'A couple of answers and I'll be on my way.'

Aramint sniffed disdainfully. 'I'd have thought it more appropriate to negotiate the fee with a little less indecent haste. But have it your way. Standard *per diem* plus bonus?' In a practised move, she extracted a slim cigar from a silver Art Deco case, inserted it into an ivory holder, lit up with a lighter concealed in the corner of the case and exhaled a twin ski-jump of blue smoke.

Waving the smoke from her face, Holly-Jean decided, in the interests of non-violence and the promotion of world peace, she'd better leave immediately. But she had one more question. 'Might I know who I was recommended by?'

'By *whom* I was recommended,' Aramint corrected her with a patronising smile. Gingerly adjusting her big hair she said airily, 'Oh your name came up. Who was it now? Oh yes, that's right, wasn't it um, Melanie Wand? You know, uh...'

'The fashion editor at *The Face*?' Melanie had been at Camden School For Girls with Holly-Jean. The Old Girls Network. Nice of her.

'Yah that's right. She'd called to commiserate when the news broke. I mentioned we might need to hire a trouble-shooter to sort out the truth from the lies and innuendo. She unhesitatingly endorsed you.'

Aramint's next words reminded her of why she'd come.

14

'Miss Ho, you know as well as I do that Elfa Ericksson was a perfectly healthy young girl. Positively brimming! The world was at her feet, she had everything to live for, and nothing will convince me she took drugs willingly.'

'You definitely rule out suicide?' said Holly. She hadn't really known Elfa that well, and besides, she wanted to gauge this loud, flailing creature's reaction.

'Utterly, absolutely perish the thought!' Aramint semaphored frantically to some distant vessel beyond the wall.

'So we might be talking murder.'

Ms de Lache took her time answering. She sucked on her cigar, blew two perfectly concentric smoke-rings, and while admiring them, mussed her big crimson hair. '*Murder?*' she said archly. 'God only knows. I'm not the detective, you are.'

A voice from the desk speaker-phone said, 'Mariella's on hold, you want to speak to her?'

Aramint swore. 'Fuck the woman! No – put her on. *Ciao*, darling! Nadja? Not a hope. Don't be silly, darling, it's the middle of *Fashion Weeks*!'

Holly looked out of the window at the falling rain and the peacocks parading down South Molton Street in designer rainwear, and recognised one certainty in her life. One epistemological truth, one deduction of logic, one *categorical imperative*: she would do without the Aramint de Laches of the *fin de millénaire*. The gorgeous denizens of this Cute and Lovely Dark Age.

Aramint was finishing up, 'Milan and Paris on the same day? You got whacky baccy in your pipe, darling? *Ciao!*' She turned to Holly. 'Well?'

Holly stood up. 'On reflection, I've decided the case is beyond my scope. I recommend leaving the matter in the hands of the authorities.'

She gave her regular spiel. H-J.H. & Associates specialised in intellectual property (IP) copyright violations in electronic software. 'We also undertake, on an individual basis, other investigations, such as: character and background assessment, criminal and civil record search, credit rating, personality profiling, missing persons and aberrant behaviour inconsistent with standards expected in significant relationships.'

Aramint gaped. 'Screwing around, right?'

Holly nodded sagely. 'Right. Matters involving violence and death remain outside our heavenly mandate.' She didn't add – unless she wanted the job. In which case, no method yet devised by man would stop her. Holly-Jean Ho hadn't been born of a Hakka mother in the Year of the Tiger for nothing.

'The autopsy should disprove the heroin rumours,' she concluded. 'If there *is* any foul play, the police investigation will uncover the facts.'

'Piffle and you know it!' snorted Ms de Lache. She began to pace again. 'So you won't take the case. I'm surprised. Not what I heard about you at all. The story goes you care, you really care. Well, I suppose you don't want to get your fingers grubby. Can hardly blame you.'

She shouldn't have smirked.

Especially with Holly being so tired and irritable.

But then she didn't know Holly-Jean Ho. Didn't know about the stare.

Holly had gone very still. Her eyes locked into Aramint's as she summoned her *chi* and projected it, laser-like, in the way the Chinese call 'lancing the mirror of the soul'. The big woman stopped smirking, froze mid-pace, tried to look away, her big crimson hair twitching with the effort.

After a moment Holly relaxed, a wistful smile, distant and sad, flitting across her lips. Aramint seemed to have shrunk. 'Um, perhaps it's all for the best . . .' Her voice trailed. She seemed to have difficulty with the clasp of the cigar case. The lid sprang open and the cigars fell all over the floor. She

16

scrambled clumsily on all fours, revealing tights on inside-out.

Don't blame Holly, she can't help it: the tiger has a big heart. Besides, every bone in her body was telling her Elfa Ericksson's overdose was neither accidental nor intentional, and to dig for the truth she would need the Princess of Sheba model agency's professional endorsement.

She said, 'Elfa Ericksson didn't do drugs, had everything to live for, thus no cause for suicide – and if anyone had a hand in her death, I'll find them.'

They agreed terms and Holly turned to leave. As she reached the door, Aramint drawled out in an oh-so-casual tone that to Holly's geiger ears was spitting radiation, 'You might want to start with that pretty little beach bum of hers.'

Holly turned. 'A boyfriend? I didn't know Elfa had a regular relationship.'

'I'd hardly call Paddy Fistral regular, would you?'

On the way out Holly stopped by and spoke to Joel Unmack for a while. As she eventually made her way out into South Molton Street and the rain, she was lost in thought.

The last forty-eight hours had been one hellacious rollercoaster ride. Now the name of Paddy Fistral had cropped up. The legendary Britpopster-cum-world-class-surfer, whose pretty baby face stared down from the walls of countless pubescent bedroom walls.

She stepped out into the throng of peacocks, and made her way back to Oxford Street. Waiting for an empty cab Holly-Jean said aloud to herself, 'Looks like you've got yourself into a major manic maelstrom, kiddo, and only one thing's for certain: it's gonna be a very strange trip. As they say.'

Chapter 3

Exhausted and ready to kill for that hot shower, Holly cabbed it back home to Camden Lock but was greeted at the big v-junction at Camden Tube by some kind of public demonstration.

'Sorry, ducks, can't go no fervour.'

Cursing foully in Hakkanese, Holly paid the nervous-looking cabbie and stomped off on the half-mile walk home.

Reclaim the Street said the banners. 'Hah!' said Holly-Jean.

Despite the freezing drizzle, assorted-flavoured Camden-ites – cyclists, ecofreaks, New Age Travellers, punks, hippies, and a tourload of ecstatic Japanese tourists – had assembled in carnival atmosphere.

Despite everything, Holly began singing in the rain. An adaptation; 'A world without cars ... just couldn't be. Only a fool would say that...' A group of Celtic inebriates enjoying the hullabaloo from the vantage of a rich-smelling puddle, raised their cider bottles joyfully at Holly's ditty. The sight of the returning migrant plonkies warmed her. She'd lived all her life in this neck of North London. Seen all the changes. And now Camden had come full circle.

Fifteen years back, the High Street was awash with piss, vomit and ugly brawling. Then came the Eighties, the property bubble and media trendies to gentrify the area.

19

Pubs were dolled up, dress-codes enforced – anything but hard-hats and fresh wounds. Miles Davis replaced Philomena Begley and the Treetop Boys. Draught Guinness disappeared as urgent-eyed lucre-grubbers sipped fancy imported beers and made deals.

They tried, and for a while, succeeded in making Camden Town look like Europe. But the hard wind of the nineties had chipped away at the façades. The cider fraternities returned. Nature reasserted herself. Cue Disney sound-track...

Holly reached Camden Lock. On the cobblestones below the iron staircase leading up to her office-studio, waited the male in her life. GiGi, the three-legged, neutered seal-point Siamese tom. As usual, he was so overjoyed to see her that his single front paw was unable to brake in time and he cat-apulted into a fat, ivory-fur tangle at her feet. '*M'row!*'

'Hello, my sweetestheart!' She nuzzled his neck, while he dribbled ecstatically, purring like a Hilti drill. 'Just met another limbless cat in a white fur coat, but don't get jealous – she was none too choosy about granting her affections. Not like you, my loyal friend.'

It was good to be home.

Mrs Howell-Pryce, the Unmerry Widow of Pontypridd, Holly's excellent part-time assistant, must have heard the commotion, for she appeared on the third-floor iron walkway to welcome her home.

'You made it safely back across the water, then?'

Grey hair, severely disciplined by plait and pin, charcoal cardigan buttoned to the top, dark-green skirt, brown tights and shoes. The quintessence of Welsh school-mistress vanquished by gigantic purple titanium-rimmed glasses.

'Thanks for coming in on your day off, Mrs H-P. Love the new specs!'

20

'Ahem.' Behind Holly a throat was cleared. The smile of welcome frosted on Mrs Howell-Pryce's face. GiGi tensed rigid in her arms and Holly offered up a prayer to the skies: make whoever it is disappear!

'Miss Holly-Jean Ho, formerly Deirdre H. Jones?' Shit! The law. Two of them. White. Male. Large. Plainclothes. She was flipped the badge twice. Two different varieties. And to really rub her nose in it, they were still referring to her old given English name. Strange to hear that relic of her previous identity, her previous life. Seemed a lifetime ago that she'd changed all that by the simple expedient of officially taking up the Chinese name her mother Ho Ma-Ma had given her. In fact it was only two years ago. But for Holly-Jean it was still a lifetime. 'What?' she snarled.

'A few words. May we come up?'

Holly's bitter response, 'Rhetorical question, right?'

In silent procession they climbed the steep iron staircase. Mrs H-P stood at the front door ramrod erect, glaring as the two policemen trooped by. Inside, the old warehouse was divided in two. The purple spray-painted door to Minty's studio, reminder of happier times, looked hard shut. Been that way since Christmas. He was going through a dry patch. Holed up in Devon.

Holly sat the policemen at the kitchen table near the entrance to her large L-shaped space and ordered them not to smoke.

Out of earshot, Mrs H-P brought her up to date in her hyper-efficient way. Then, with a gaze so withering as to lead the casual observer to speculate on whether the policemen were knowing carriers of the Ebola contagion, she exited, leaving Holly's workstation neatly piled with memos.

Holly stashed her perishable goodies from Holland, made three cups of espresso, cut a piece of precious chorizo and fed it to a slavering GiGi, then sat down opposite the men.

The tall blond handsome one with the battered face of a rugby back-row spoke first. 'Excellent espresso. Dutch?'

Holly nodded. *And so are you, tulip. That Dutch-English accent is unmistakeable.*

'You've just returned from Holland, that is correct?' he continued. 'On behalf of a client?'

Without thinking, Holly said, 'Privileged information.'

The other policeman – greasy dark hair, military moustache, bad skin and malodorous Barbour jacket – a far less palatable prospect compounded by a treacly Brum accent, said, 'Leased Peugeot, registration number J456 CYD. Night-boat to Harwich, loik?'

'Special Branch, loik?' Holly feigned nonchalance, but warning bells were clanging. *She must guard against the debility of exhaustion.*

The Dutchman handed Holly a name card and she read aloud the English flipside. 'Captain Her Preesman, Special Security Office, Criminal Intelligence Division, Royal Netherlands Police. Very impressive. Why me?'

'Miss Ho, three members of the public have placed you and your car in Volkspark, Schiedam, West Rotterdam at around one o'clock this morning.' The Kriminalpolitie officer consulted his notebook. 'Quote: "The *verdommernt* woman-driver nearly hit me, so I made sure the number-plate stuck in my mind." Unquote.'

Holly smelled something fishy and it wasn't GiGi's breath. 'It was pitch dark and those monkeys were too drunk to stand, let alone memorise a passing car number.' *Tamada!* Too late she bit her tongue. *Not enough sleep, dammit!*

Preesman smiled casually. 'The number was traced to the car-leasing company. The rest was quite straightforward. We already knew your identity at three o'clock this morning. I flew in at nine, my colleague from Scotland Yard's anti-terrorist unit, DI Beezer here, kindly met me

22

with a car at Heathrow. We've been waiting outside for more than an hour.'

Anti-terror? Holly felt an icy trickle deep down. 'So, we've established I was in Schiedam last night,' she said. 'What's the problem?'

Preesman continued, 'Sometime after midnight last night, a timed *plastique* device was attached to a parked car, a BMW, in the area of Volkspark, Schiedam, set aside by the municipal authorities for the purposes of adult recreation. The vehicle and occupants were subsequently blown to pieces.'

'Poi-ella, the way I heard it,' offered Barbour sardonically. Holly buckled in her chair.

'We were eventually able to make a positive on one of the occupants,' said the Dutch officer, reading from his note-book. 'Edward van Schrempft, resident of Berglostlaan 9, Rotterdam. Would you confirm that you know this man and, in fact, were in his company immediately prior to the explosion?'

Despair drilled her heart. Dear Eddie caught with his pants down one last time. 'Yes. It was Mr van Schrempft,' she whispered.

Not quite surreptitiously enough, Beezer picked his nose and deposited it under Holly's kitchen chair. 'You must have left in a roight hurry to make that boat. Or was it a huff, loik? Snowing heavily. Your friend without transportation.'

Holly felt like ripping off the moustache. 'You know perfectly well he'd met someone. It didn't matter. It wasn't like that between us. Eddie and I ... we were just old friends.'

Her sorrow bled out of her like a drift-net, but she would not cry in front of these men. Instead a migraine flared like an igniting purple Bengal match one half-inch behind her eyebrows. She excused herself and went to the bathroom.

23

While she peed, she reached for the Tiger Balm and scooped a thick smear onto her forehead. Rubbed in violently, the freeze-burn blotted out the ache and set her mind afire. Jumbled thoughts, questions without answers.

First Elfa, now Ed. Dead within a day of each other. Were the deaths connected, or the timing pure coincidence? Her two friends had known each other, but never mentioned the fact to her until Ed's reference to Elfa at the restaurant. Intentional subterfuge or chance omission?

Holly stopped rubbing. Looked at herself in the mirror.

Had her brain not been so mangled by hangover, trauma and sleep deprivation, she'd have seen it sooner – the possibility of target error, mistaken identity. Could it not have been a Flying Eagle come out of the snowy night, talons sharpened for *Ho Shao-lan* – Holly-Jean Ho? Had she herself thus been the cause of it all: the deaths of two friends? *Wo-dr Tyan!* Dear God. She shivered, shook her head, and snuffed that one.

Back in the kitchen, the Dutch officer said, 'Any information you think could help is vital, Miss Ho. If it hadn't been for luck, the carnage would have been far greater.'

'Luck?' said Holly faintly.

Preesman's face was grim. 'On detonation, the car became a firebomb and literally rocketed into the forest, narrowly missing a mobile café which was crowded with drivers and transients at the time.'

Holly pictured again the cheery throng, the smell of smoked sausage and Genever.

Preesman held up three fingers. 'We have three scenarios. One, a random attack on the red-light corner of Volkspark in the middle of a snowstorm in January – in which case we are dealing with a maniac. Two, it was aimed at the working woman in the BMW. Possible, but she's an unlikely target.'

He paused at the third finger. 'And then there is your friend, Mr van Schrempft. We need a motive, Miss Ho. Volkspark is a well-known drug-dealers' hangout.'

Holly shrugged. 'Holland is a well-known drug-dealers' hangout.'

'Perhaps the pair of you had a mutual interest in the exotic erotic?'

Holly didn't dignify Beezer's comment with a response. Instead, she reached for the wall-phone. 'I think I'd better phone my solicitor.'

'I don't think so,' said Beezer, hand snaking out to rip the external jack from its housing. Holly was already up, locked into defensive stance, her chair tumbling backwards across Ma's old Chinese carpet. Beezer had gone grey at the gills.

The Dutch officer raised his hands placatingly. 'Please calm down! Both of you.'

Still glaring, Holly released her guard and picked up the chair. 'In my home he behaves, unless he fancies singing soprano at the Masonic Ball.'

'I'm still curious,' said Preesman mildly. 'Edward van Schrempft has no criminal record.' Holly kept still – Kripo must be sleepwalkers not to have a jacket on Ed. 'Though there are certain questionable areas with regard to his lifestyle.'

'The Cessna, loik, the Lamborghini, loik.' This guy sounded more foreign than the Dutchman. Holly wished them both gone.

'You want to eliminate Ed as a target? Easy,' she said. 'Here's the chronology as best I can recollect. We met at eight o'clock last night outside the Sumatra Restaurant on Westewagenstraat. After dinner, about nine forty-five, we entered Roots smoke bar, a few doors down, where we watched the live band. Towards midnight we walked back to my car and drove around Rotterdam Centrum till we decided to go to Volkspark, arriving there at, say, twelve-fifty. That bomb couldn't possibly have been intended for Ed van Schrempft.'

'Why not?' demanded Preesman.

'Because ours was a spontaneous, spur-of-the-moment decision to turn the wheel and drive out to Volkspark. To hit specific targets, bombers need exact time and place. Your bomb was either aimed at random or someone else entirely.'

Preesman shook his head. 'I'm afraid it isn't that simple, Miss Ho,' he explained. 'First, perhaps your friend made a habit of visiting this particular lady on a regular weeknight. Understandably, out of embarrassment, he would have disguised the fact from you. Secondly, were you with him the whole time in Volkspark? It gets pretty busy there at nights, quite a crowd. Couldn't he have made some discreet transaction without your noticing?' Holly's face showed no reaction, but she recalled vividly her happy walkabout wondering where Ed had got to.

Preesman continued; 'And thirdly, devices are now widely available on the open market which feature advanced electro-magnetics. They can be attached to a metallic surface by the gentle touch of a blindfolded child and detonated by remote electronic communication within any timelapse desired and from up to considerable distances.'

Beezer spoke now. 'It's entirely possible that someone followed you from Rotterdam, watched, waited, then slipped from the bushes to attach the device to the chassis under the BMW once they were sure your friend was inside the car and otherwise occupied.'

He smiled unpleasantly and his tone became silky. 'Of course, there is one other possibility we may have overlooked. That you, Miss Ho, were the intended victim. Tell us again what you were doing for three days in Holland?'

26

Holly was furious with herself. From the very beginning she'd underestimated these men. She'd been sorely lacking in diligence! The slightest hint of Dutch police involvement and the Societies would cancel the Convention. The slightest hint that she was the cause and they'd cancel her.

Heart going like a steam-hammer, she began a frantic ad-lib in the calmest of voices, 'Business, pleasure – a bit of both. I have this really great friend in Rotterdam—' Holly's convoluted fantasy about setting up a financial consultancy with Rita Wineberry was not totally off-the-cuff. Eighteen months previously, they really had considered such an idea, and Holly was able to recall enough of the feasibility research to go into mind-numbing fiscal minutiae. After ten minutes, the policemen's eyes began to glaze over.

Judging they were about done, she finished up breezily, 'You can check all this out with her – Marguarita Wineberry, Apartment 6-D, 150 Van der Helm Straat.'

Preesman wrote in his notebook. Then flipped back a page and read, 'And the client whose privilege you referred to earlier?'

Wan-ba Dan! Tricky bastard!

'You might as well know. It won't make any difference now. My client was Mr van Schrempft,' she lied. 'I helped with his English legalities.'

'Didn't realise you had a loicence to practise law,' Beezer remarked nastily.

'I don't,' replied Holly. It was time to blow one last cloud of smoke. 'However, as a member of the British Association of Private Investigators, in accordance with the Established Code of Practice, I can choose to invoke client-privilege. For your further information, I have a licence to legally operate an investigation agency within the London Borough of Camden, and since we specialise in IP Copyright Protection, our area of practice is extended internationally, bound only by the limitations of foreign laws. We are a

27

limited liability company registered at Company House. The paperwork's all here, actually, if you want to check. I might add that all my taxes and contributions, national, local, personal and employee are in order. I am also fully up to date with utilities, cable, electronics. And cat licence.'

The two policemen exchanged weary nods. 'We'll be in touch,' said Preesman.

Beezer leant over and scribbled a phone number on the name card. 'Don't be leaving the country, loik.'

Holly looked at him. 'Until my passport is confiscated, I'll go when and wherever I like.'

Beezer replied darkly, 'Don't push it. Things can easily be arranged.'

At the door Preesman said, 'Miss Ho, you're not a bad liar.' He seemed to hesitate. 'There is just one more thing. We're having difficulty identifying the second occupant. It's very strange . . .' He appeared embarrassed. 'The lady apparently bore the brunt of the explosion, being – ah – underneath your friend at the time of detonation, and thus her injuries were far more extensive. Yet already the forensic people insist parts are missing.'

'Parts?' said Holly.

He looked very uncomfortable. 'Body parts.'

So Holly told him.

When they'd gone, Holly sat looking out of the window for a long bleak while, GiGi's warm weight, purr and dribble her comforter as the winter afternoon dimmer-switch turned steadily outside. The ache seemed maternal, almost. Elfa had been worldly-wise, but she was still just a kid.

Eddie was Peter Pan. Never had grown up.

Suddenly she needed to know if it had been a simple trick of fate that had led them to Volkspark, or had there been cause and effect? She re-ran the movie of *Last Night in Rotterdam*.

28

After the Rijstaffel, Ed had insisted – 'for the digestive purposes' – on dropping into the nearby smoke bar called Roots with its five-pointed leaf sign beckoning. The small club wasn't too crowded, midweek. They'd stood at the bar.

'Give me something won't get me completely out of my head,' Ed had said.

'Completely-out-de-head 'ming right up.' The bald-domed waxed-mustachioed smoke-tender had reached down to a lower cabinet.

'No, no, I said *won't* get me completely out of my head.'

'OK. No sweat. Try this. What I smoke all day when I'm working.'

The machine-rolled joint came from a glass humidor on the bar. Watching the excellent Dammer-Jamaican reggae band, Holly'd had a single toke for old time's sake and within five minutes was a cabbage.

The stuff was so strong, Holly so unused to it, that they'd driven around city Centrum for an hour in absolute hysterics, and when Ed suggested a detour to Schiedam – 'to see our world-famous night-ladies' – Holly'd thought it an utterly hilarious idea and spun the wheel.

Surely nobody could have followed that zonked-out zig-zag. Her and Ed's state of advanced intoxication precluded any possibility of pre-planning. The trip to Volkspark was pure chaos theory and Ed van Schrempft's final excess was truly Hieronymus Bosch come to life. Bizarre? Highly. Undignified? Definitely. Appropriate? Entirely.

As he himself would have said: '*Way to go, Ed!*'

Holly abruptly dropped GiGi to the floor and stood up. Fine and dandy, Holls! Good job! You really dove-tailed that one neatly.

She paced by the window, her thoughts as brooding as the black clouds over Chalk Farm gasworks. Who was she kidding? No matter what Mr Hua might say, when it came to

29

likely targets, how could she possibly discount herself? And what about the black RV sideswiping her Peugeot? The threatening phone call on the ferry crossing?

Holly laid her head against the icy window pane. She knew to pursue that one might lead to madness.

'Meow.' GiGi stared up at her, tail erect with worry. He always understood her moods. Holly scooped him up and wiped the salt from her eyes on his fur. She drew the blinds, stripped off and stepped into the shower.

Holly-Jean's shower, as at other such times, was a great deal else besides. She got the washing part over fairly quickly. Cleansing the body to her utter satisfaction was a vitally important part of the process, and certain ritualistic patterns had to be followed.

After thorough use of shampoo and soap – today she was using natural aloe gel – she loofahed vigorously till every inch of skin tingled. With meticulous care she rinsed her entire body, inside and out. Next, she stepped over to the mirror and flossed her nasal passages with a silver chain. A tricky job whereby a silver chain is passed, weighted end first, through the nostril, scooped out of the back of the throat, and by gripping both ends, tugged back and forth. She repeated the exercise on the other nostril, stepped back in the shower and aimed the jet of water to flush out both passages.

Back at the mirror, she used her tongue-scraper, a narrow metal strip, to rake the furry deposits off her tongue. As usual, she was amazed at the quantity of scum accumulated. Next, she Q-tipped carefully inside both ears. Brushed her teeth diligently for three minutes, then flossed between every molar. Finally, she finished the job by gargling with rosewater.

Five more minutes under the hot-water jet. Two more under the ice-cold.

When she was dried, she put on loose-spun cotton

30

pyjamas and went to stand on the *tatami* mat. Though meditation had begun with the act of cleansing, and the clatter in her brain was already beginning to cease, Holly knew that this much grief would require all her esoteric skills, those much-misunderstood skills that had come out of history and used just two instruments: the body and breath. *Chi-kung*.

First, she stilled her brain, emptied her mind. Drip-fed that silence into every capillary. Until nothing was left and everything was there: Holly became her body. Through directed breathing, touch, pressure and motion, she began to nourish the network of energy centres as laid down on the ancient body map. Reconnecting them one by one. Till she had fully replenished her *chi*.

Historic Chinese healing: since modern science hasn't yet progressed far enough to test its theories, you either accept or reject. Those in the know wear ten-league boots. The pooh-pooh-ers can pour themselves a treble scotch and hunker down in front of the TV.

The phone rang. 'It's me,' said Mrs H-P. 'Just checking. Those men cause any trouble?'

Holly said, 'No problem, Mrs H-P. Thanks for calling, though.'

'Well, *you* sound cheerful enough.'

'Yep! Just fixed my National Grid after the hurricane knocked out the power lines. All the lights are back on.'

'Been at the Alsace more like,' sniffed Mrs H-P.

'Kind of.' That would be the next item on the healing menu. Some might label Holly a hypocrite, a wine-swilling, meat-eating ascetic. She called herself a free spirit. Determined never to be bound by rules.

Her disposition improved a thousandfold, Holly fed GiGi a hunk of Gouda, opened a bottle of chilled Alsace and swigged from the neck, put Berlioz' 'Au Bal' from the *Symphonie Fantastique* on the CD player and called Senior

Officer i/c ALCO Asian-Liaison Crimes Organisation, Detective Sergeant Michael Coulson.

Despite last year's banishment from the Chinese half of her world, she'd kept up, for professional reasons, her connections and good name – to a certain extent – with the law. Though regarding the latter, the admiration extended mainly to Coulson's little outfit – 'ALCO by name, alkie by nature' – the Met's fairly futile attempt at bridging the ethnic gap with the Chinese inhabitants of the capital city. Such goodwill as Holly-Jean Ho had engendered through her efforts at race relations mattered a great deal less to the Metropolitan Police in general, and not at all to those who walked the higher floors of New Scotland Yard. Thereabouts, Holly-Jean Ho knew perfectly well, she was considered a piece of troublemaking yellow shit.

'Coulson here. Yes?' came an harassed-sounding voice.

'You the police-man of my desi-ah. You the one set my heart on fi-ah.' Holly had long developed the knack of twisting Mick Coulson round her little finger.

'Holly-Jean, light of my life!'

'Betcha say that to all the girls.'

'Listen, mate, when you've got the four effs, the ladies don't exactly come crowding.'

'The four effs?'

'Fat, fucked, failed and forty.'

Holly laughed. 'Not to worry, Sarge. You know what they say: "Abstinence makes the frond grow harder".'

He thought about it. 'Frond as in dangling leaflike organ? Hey, naughty but clever. Is that an original? And it's Detective Inspector to you.'

Uh-oh. Dropped a brick. Knowing Mick's fragile ego she'd better finesse pronto.

'Yes, that's one of my very own. So you made it to DI! Well, that's one less "eff" for starters. Congrats, Mick!'

'Don't deserve it,' he said modestly. 'Word only came through a couple of days ago. I was going to call.'

'Any reason, or just plain old hard work?'

They both knew exactly why. Holly just wanted to see Coulson handle it.

'Did a Mandarin course at Berlitz. Might have helped.'

'Blimey, Mick.' No mention of a little help from Yours Truly?

Coulson said, 'Listen to this: *Ching ni gei wo i-ping pi-jou. Sye-sye ni.*'

Holly translated, 'Please give me a bottle of beer, thank you.' Well, at least you've got your communicative priorities right. No matter that nobody in Chinatown speaks anything but Cantonese with a mere smattering of Mandarin, the national language of all Chinese.

'Yeah, well, I was putting my skills in the global context. More marketable, right?'

'Very astute of you.' The ungrateful shithead.

'To tell the truth, Holly-Jean, I just couldn't get my laughing gear round the Cantonese nine tones. Mandarin's bad enough but at least it's only got four.'

'I'm impressed, Mick.' What a tightwad.

'And of course, I have to acknowledge your help in netting the Oxbridge Language Schools connection.'

Now you're talking. 'Ahh, don't mention it,' said Holly, adding, 'still, a favour done is a favour owed, right?'

That last autumn, Holly had handed the police officer, on a plate, the UK end of a worldwide distribution system of illegal aliens, drugs and prostitution. This was the obvious reason for his promotion, and it constituted, as far as she was concerned, a massive IOU.

Coulson sighed, 'Which, I suppose, brings us to the point of this phonecall.'

Too right, boy. 'I need the Medical Examiner's report on Elfa Ericksson, including autopsy, if performed.'

33

'The model who overdid?'

'The same.'

'You gotta be kidding. That's way out of my patch. Besides she's only been dead a few days. The body's hardly cold yet. You won't get an official report for a week or so.'

'There must be something official for the record. Think of all the press coverage.'

'Yeh, the scum always rises at pretty young deaths,' conceded Mick. 'Oh well, I s'pose there'll be some sort of initial post-mortem findings. Since I do owe you one, I'll see what I can do. But this is quits, right?'

'You can do it, Mick. E-mail, if possible.'

'No access.'

'Then sneak some hard copy. Meet you tomorrow lunch at the pub.' Which meant the Nag's Head off Gerrard Street – the only pub in London where you'd find old Chinese gents in battered Shanghai fedoras drinking pints of best and rolling their own Golden Virginias.

'Brace yourself, Holly,' said Mick gravely. 'The pub's gone. Right now there's a bloody great hole at the end of Gerrard Street. They're putting up yet another frigging office block.'

'I don't believe it!' Holly's favourite pub gone. Another bereavement.

'Neither did I. Constable Jones told me. I had to go and have a look for myself. Broke my bleedin' heart. Not a word to us regulars. Bloody outrage, you ask me!'

'Where are the old Chinese boys going to drink?' asked Holly.

'Dunno.'

Didn't care either, the asshole. 'So where shall we meet?'

'How about the Coach and Horses?' suggested Coulson. 'Nice friendly hostelry, down-to-earth.'

34

'Awash with dipsomaniacs, you mean. Oh, all right. One o'clock?'

'Can't promise you—'

'Oh yes, you can!'

Next she dialled up Mr Hua. Three by-passes later, she reached him.

'You did say the *Fei-ying Bang* lien on my person had been rescinded.'

'Correct.'

'Any reason why someone would car-bomb me in Schiedam?'

'Can't think of one off-hand. I'll look into it.'

'Do that.'

Then she remembered to call the leasing company and have them collect the Peugeot. She told the despatcher it should be easy to spot. There'd been a slight accident.

She checked the fridge, stuck two fingers in a jar and fished out a fat piece of goat's cheese from herby olive oil. Washed it down with another swig of Pinot D'Alsace. Then she sat on the carpet with knees tucked under her and read through the tabloids she'd bought during the traffic jam at Manor House. Editing out the hysterical innuendo, Holly tallied the facts.

Elfa Eriksson had been found, clothed in her nightgown, reclining on a rug before the marble fireplace of her very expensive flat in Holland Park, by the Filipina cleaning lady, Mrs Epifania Pangalina, when she let herself in for work nine o'clock Wednesday morning. Having tried and failed to wake her boss, Epifania finally realised Elfa was dead and called the police. Their initial investigations produced little ground for assuming suspicious circumstances.

The doors of the flat had been locked from the inside on the cleaner's arrival, but not dead-bolted or chained.

Epifania was quoted as saying that since Elfa often worked late into the night, and thus slept-in late, they had decided to dispense with the door-chain and dead-bolt on cleaning days so that Epifania could let herself in without waking her boss. It was reported also that there was 24-hour security in the form of a uniformed concierge at the front desk on the ground floor of the 1930s Deco-style block of flats just off Holland Walk. On the night in question,the concierge had neither seen nor heard anything irregular. Initial blood-testing had shown the presence of the controlled substance, heroin. The police were treating the case as suicide or accidental death.

Holly stood and slowly stretched back all the way down to touch the ground behind her. Savoured the arch, dropped down flat. Exhaustion was fighting the combined effects of countless espressos and *chi kung*. She checked the clock – nearly six – then fingered aside the blinds to peer at the windy black night outside. She fed GiGi another hack off the chorizo, let him out to do the Midnight Rambler, did the washing up and hung the chorizo back on a suspended hook alongside a huge twine of herbs and garlic heads brought back from Crete, a wind-dried sweet Chinese sausage, and her muslin-wrapped attempt at home-cured Parmigiano.

Yep, Holly was still weathering the efforts of the growing host of her friends to go veggie. Couldn't fault their arguments, but so far her taste buds weren't listening. It seemed Ho Ma-ma had instilled in her an ineffable yen. Coyly, Holly told 'em: her Chinese genes prevented her.

One last call was to Marguarita Wineberry in Rotterdam. Rit' and she had been fast pals since the summer of '77. Partners on a candy-floss stall and occasional stand-ins for the knife-thrower at Whitelegs West Country Fair. Rit' was Maltese – dark, fiery and smart. A guaranteed giggle with a fondness for gambling which she'd traded up to become an astronomically renumerated *arbitrageur* with Berijl-Ffynche. Whether that stress candidacy had encouraged even further her friend's naturally riotous ways remained a constant puzzle to Holly-Jean. Whatever. Rita Wineberry – ouch! Hangover City. They'd got through two bottles of frozen clear Genever, and that was *before* leaving the apartment on Van der Helm Straat for a night's clubbing down Stadhuis and Meent, where their wild antics on the dance-floors elicited disapproving stares from the locals. Despite their liberal laws and reputation, the Dutch will never be anything but girdle-tight conformists.

The call went through. Holly told her friend to expect a visit from the Kripo to corroborate Holly's story.

Rita said a few kind words of sympathy. Which in Ed's case, Holly accepted gratefully. She knew Rita had never liked him and was jealous of the time Holly spent with Ed when she came over to Holland.

'Rit', did you know Ed and Elfa were connected? Seems I was the last to find out.'

Rita replied, 'I've seen them once or twice with that fashion crowd who hang at Pol Bar on Stadhuis. Mind you, Rotterdam's a bloody small world.'

'And hardly the fashion capital of Europe.' Holly felt queasy. 'Why on earth was Elfa spending time in Rotterdam? And with Ed? Just can't picture those two together. Were they, y'know, intimate?'

Rita snorted. 'Beauty and the Beast? Hardly.'

Holly thought it was time to get real, and quit avoiding what was staring her in the face. She blurted out, 'Rit', I'm getting a really bad feeling about this. Can't help thinking the two deaths are connected. Is it possible Elfa was dealing drugs for Ed?'

Rita's casual response only confirmed her fears. 'Kid, in this world, anything's possible. If the fashion biz demands, someone's gonna supply. Me, I don't know anything about

Ed van Schrempft's private business, but I might know someone who might know someone who might know someone else.'

'Could you ask around? Discreetly?'

Rita was indignant. '"Discreetly", the girl says. You think I just fell out of a tree! Holly-Jean – I hear anything, I'll get back to you. Meantime, Holls, you sound a bit whacked. Go get some sleep.'

Holly put down the phone, inserted her earplugs, curled up under the futon and tried to do exactly as Rita had ordered.

Didn't work. Rita's call had left her mind too cranked. The Ed-Elfa connection looked murkier than ever. Thunder rattled the windows. Wind howled down from Hampstead Heath. Strange old night. Holly thought about the threatening phonecall on the ferry crossing. The black RV's now-seemingly deliberate sideswipe in Volkspark. Were *they* coming for her again?

Her skin came over *chi-pi* and she began to wander the flat with the futon wrapped round her shoulders. The wind had got up outside, a voice moaning at the window pane – *let me in*. Her Chinese half felt the turbulence of the night. Heaven's homeless were out looking for shelter from the cold...

'Bollocks to that,' said her English half, and Holly-Jean opened a fresh bottle of Gewurztraminer and put on an old favourite CD. 'The feeling was bad at home,' wailed Donald Fagen.

Things *really* got peculiar when Ma telephoned, reverse charges. 'Pick me up at Heathrow, Saturday, four in the morning.'

'Whaat?' Holly choked on her Alsace. Today was Thursday. Saturday was the day after tomorrow!

'I've had it up to here with this fornicating heap of monkey-dung. I'm coming home.'

38

'H-H-home?' said Holly faintly.

But Ho Ma-ma was at warp-speed. 'Too many maggoty crooks, testicle-lacking policemen, rotten turtle-egg traffic, humid sweating farting pollution. D'you know, downtown Taipei's got so bad, if you can't stand the place one more second, just scoop a chunk of the air with a spoon, eat it and die! *Ai yo!* And that's not to mention what's really wrong with this place—'

'Wonder what that could be?' murmured Holly to herself.

'Too many dog-fart Chinese!'

'Ma!' Holly put a stop to the litany. 'You're Chinese. Taiwan is Chinese.'

'Perhaps I am. Perhaps I'm not. Perhaps I'm a pimping English, after all.'

After a harangue lasting ten more minutes, detailing the shortcomings of both races, and the inevitable: 'You marrying yet?' Ma managed to slow down enough for Holly, in the interests of financial decorum, to urge her mother off the line. She said goodbye and promised to be there for the British Airways flight at four o'clock Saturday morning.

It seemed very quiet after the call. Holly-Jean liked quiet – the reason why she loved this place at the back of Camden Lock. Ten minutes from the centre of the great metropolis, yet each night, after the crowds from the street-market had gone home, it was as quiet as a rural village. Holly thought about that.

Thought about the fact that they had finally sold the old family house at Parliament Hill Fields. That Ma's share was locked into Asian unit trusts, and she would thus be cash-strapped and without a bed.

Holly sat up and looked at the sofa-bed. Thought of tiny Ma's colossal presence filling this place, her jealously guarded space, symbol of her freedom. She panicked. *What is happening to my life?*

39

But almost as quickly she discerned a buzz of warmth spreading from her lower belly – the source of positive *chi*. Soon followed by a certain quickening of the deadbeat pulse. Felt a smile of silly, ridiculous proportions commandeer her lips. Next thing Holly knew, she'd jumped up, changed the music, pumped up the volume and was bopping and yelling to Katrina and the Waves. 'I'm walking on Sunshine, Yeh-Yeh!'

GiGi's fur looked as if it'd been dipped in polyurethane, but he was smiling. Though she hated to admit it, since Ma had retired 'home' to Taiwan last year, Holly had missed her mother achingly. Ma was her anchor, her one knowable truth in a split-life that embraced two worlds whose logics so often seemed diametrically, stubbornly, opposed.

The music ended. Missing Ma was all well and good, but as for actually living with that awkward bundle ... Holly's euphoria vanished abruptly. Ho Ma-ma, tiny but TNT, in this space? Next stop Prozacia. Come down from that wall, Holls!

She swigged more Alsace and paced the floor to the same song. There was only one thing to do. She'd have to get Ma a job: something to occupy that boundless energy. Humming, fox-trotting, mind awhirr.

An idea began to form. Mad, but maybe.

Chapter 4

She woke at five in the morning, jacked her notebook PC into her huge, village-hall-sized, trestle-table workstation and got to work.

Her business in Holland had been scouting a site for the Friends of Chinese Opera Convention to be held the weekend of 26–28 February. Triads operating in North-West Europe urgently needed to broker a turf-allotment, 'In order to prevent the eruption of all-out hostilities, and the subsequent calamitous effect on business and mortality' – in the BBC phonemes of Mr Plum Blossom, aka Mr Hua, that handsome Chinese gentleman and profligate killer of Holly's acquaintance.

'Heavens! Not a threat to liquidity,' Holly'd said, and agreed to do the job.

Mr Hua, the Societies' PR man in London, needed Holly to assume her former role as the only neutral party acceptable to all cliques, factions and whatever Gangs of Five, Six or Seven had sprung up since the last North-West Europe Triad carve-up. If you asked, Holly would say she was a consultant. Would add her own reality cuff: You don't want to know unless you're into mayhem in a big way.

The phonecall, one week ago, had come as a very pleasant surprise. Holly thought she'd blown, for all time, her credibility with the Chinese community. Her role as go-between, conduit, interpreter of different worlds, had been a cherished one. Long-nurtured since early adulthood.

But that was before last year.

She'd lost so much face over the death of the runaway girl Su-ming, and various ensuing frock-ups in East Asia, she reckoned her *guanchi* – a uniquely Chinese term defining networks, connections, relationships, influence, friends, *power* – was currently about as effective as a Taipei traffic-light.

'You mean to say my *guanchi* hasn't gone down the toilet?' she'd asked Mr Hua incredulously.

'Correct, Ho *Syau-jye*.' Addressing her as Little Sister Ho, at her age (overthirtyish – kind of) was translatable as 'Extremely Unmarried Miss Ho'. 'Due to your face-gaining defeat of the now-deceased Pang Chong-ts and the subsequent lifting of the *Fei-Ying Bang* lien, your *guanchi* is good.'

Holly had taken this confirmation of the rumoured ending of the Flying Eagle Triad death sentence with a surge of serotonin causing temporary breath-loss and dizziness: an effect similar to being winded by a sudden blow to the solar plexus. In this case, a very sweet sudden blow.

She'd barely heard Mr Hua's blather. 'Nowadays your expertise in this unique sphere of public relations is widely admired throughout the Secret Societies.' She was too busy thinking: Ho Shao-Lan *syau-jye*, (Umarried Miss Little Orchid Ho), Ms Holly-Jean Ho, formerly Deirdre H. Jones (see how frocked-up a girl could get?) was back in favour on the Street, Gerrard. Once again a three-way conduit between the folk of Chinatown, the Secret Societies and the Law. Unbelievable news that burst like a new sun through the dark miasma of recently acquired fears. Old: the getting of. Babies: the unbegetting of. And the back-lit one she couldn't shrug off – the sneak fear of a death that might come as suddenly as a delivery of white chrysanthemums.

'I'm relieved to hear it,' she'd finally said.

He'd rung off with the words, 'That I would judge to be a very Mandarin understatement.'

That was last Friday. She'd driven over Saturday. Given free rein to act in her own best judgement – a deadly burden actually, since errors on Society business were normally treated with a fatal lack of tolerance – Holland was her only choice. (Rijstaffel, Rita and relaxed law-enforcement.) Leaving Mrs H-P to hold the fort, Holly had dropped everything.

She could afford to.

For the first time in her life, Holly's balance-sheet was big and black. In December the successful prosecution of an importer of fake holograms made in Guangdong to be used on counterfeit Microsoft Windows packages had netted her a genuine fortune in loss-stemming commission. Ta very much, Delly! Holly's old adversary, that lovable rogue Delvin Barker, had resurfaced yet again with yet another rip-off. Last year, his outfit Intertronics had destroyed Publish-It Software's reputation; the Taiwan fakes contained a virus that erased the user's hard-disk. As usual, by the time anyone noticed, Delly'd disappeared into thin air. Going against the Seattle colossus had proved his undoing. He'd been extradited from Crete, and after three months on remand tending the organic broccoli at Ford Open Prison, Delvin had been fined £40,000 and his only traceable asset, his beloved yacht *Copycat*, had been confiscated. That must have hurt the vain boy.

Holly recalled Delvin's contorted face in the dock. He'd crumpled on hearing the sentence pronounced. Eyes filled with raging tears, he had turned across the courtroom and with pointing fist had screamed at Holly, 'I'll get you for this, you interfering bitch! What harm did I do! What harm?'

He was still yelling as he was led down to do his stir.

43

Must have loved that yacht something awful, Holly had concluded, dismissing the threats.

Meanwhile, other jobs had paid well. Still were. The agency, to Holly's amazed delight, was making money. In fact, she was rolling in enough coin to feel guilty, especially with most of her friends hurting. Not that she was complaining. She had the Chinese respect for cash. As Ma used to say, 'Money'll get you through times of no hope, better than hope'll get you through times of no money.'

By Tuesday lunchtime, she'd found the perfect hotel for the Convention in the diplomat ghetto just north of The Hague on the E19 to the North Sea sand dunes. The Hotel Surabaya, a Dutch burgher mansion, crimson-bricked with white shutters, set in formal gardens, offered the kind of utterly discreet, real-art elegance, only an expense account could afford.

As far as Holly could make out, the clientèle that winter day were either UN freeloaders or *trafikantes*. Her moon-eyed meandering with a book of poetry in hand during afternoon tea discerned five separate species of the latter: Chinese, Latin-American, White Russian, Kazakh and Chechen.

Product: drugs, arms, bonded women and, surprise, surprise: pirated software. She couldn't swear to it, but at one point she was sure she overheard the phrase, 'nuclear-grade zirconium', which was enough to cause *chi-pi* and curdle the milk in her cup of Earl Grey. The hotel was obviously used to secretive pow-wows by the boys.

There was absolutely no objection to sweepers from various factions dropping by a day or two in advance to poke around the plasterwork and unscrew the light-bulbs.

'Normal practice, madam,' said the oleaginous hotel manager. 'Many of our guests favour this kind of precaution. I must stipulate, however; that any damage – structural

44

or otherwise – will be fully charged at the management's discretion.'

'I bet,' said Holly, booking the top three floors using Mr P.B.'s platinum credit. In case you're wondering, the Friends of Chinese Opera bit was homage to Billy Wilder.

GiGi had just come in, and was warming his icy rear end on her shin, mewing hungrily. Holly stopped pounding the keyboard and rolled her neck. Looked at her watch. Seven a.m. It had taken two hours to log in the Convention schedule and draw up a draft of the itinerary.

Some itinerary. Girls, golf and gambling.

She fed the cat and, with great reluctance, turned to the only other major job on the agency's books. COMSEM – the Committee for Moral Supervision of the Electronic Media – a wealthy Westminster lobbying group with whom Holly felt only half-easy (smug Young Tories backed by remnants of the Festival of Light handbag fascists according to Holly's journo *guanchi*), had her tracking a child-pornography scam on the World Wide Web.

Her brief: to dig up hard evidence for presentation to Parliament in support of an amendment to the Computer Misuse Act to censor so-called cyberspace, with a very generous *per diem* and huge cash bonus for any subsequent public prosecutions.

Holly got the picture. The sinisterly prim and their fat pointboys wanted a show-trial with full tabloid frenzy to further their political ends. But single-issue pressure groups are labelled the new Nazis and Holly was into neither witch-hunting nor censorship. Still, the basic premise – fight the kiddy-porners – was sound, and the money unreal. Holly's journo had called back later. Some very big moolah was involved. As to who or why exactly, nobody'd worked that one out yet.

45

So since November, whenever she had nothing else to do, Holly had been dogging a trail of sleazy homepage sites through the total anarchy of the Internet. Usual tools like *New Riders' Official Internet Yellow Pages* or the *Magellan Internet Directory* had proved useless for the 'Connoisseur's rarities' she was seeking. Dreary browsing of the open discussion forums of the sexual bulletin boards and engaging in ever-more sordid discussions with sicko individuals had finally yielded.

The Romans called inhospitable Scotland with its freezing winters and murderous savages, uncivilisable: the end of the world.

Ultima Thule.

This, too, was Holly's acronym for the Net: *Ultra Terrifying Horrifying Utterly Lawless Electronia.* She'd seen enough 'Nuns with Donkeys', 'First-time Fist-fucks' and 'Celebrity Gerbil Graveyards' (work that one out – clue: anal stimulation), till she could stomach no more.

As to positively I.D.ing these people, she was no closer than when she'd started – which for Holly-Jean was very frustrating, since tracing the elusive, some might call it invading an individual's right to privacy, was a routine part of her line of work. Private Lives? History! There was no such thing in today's data-based world.

You need dirt on the competition? Piece of cake. Within hours Holly-Jean could quote bank-account details, credit-card transactions including latest balance (very revealing: like where you went on holiday, which restaurants you ate at, etc), itemised phone bill, car-ownership details, salary and job prospects, income-tax details including tax reference number, National Insurance number, even gas, electricity and water bills.

But this guy's a foreigner, you say? No problem. Illegal access to international data-bases just takes a while longer and costs you more.

46

Holly-Jean reckoned that right now, the 'Personal Information Trade' was a global gold-rush as frenzied as any '49, and to the hacker nothing cyber was safe or sacred. From Cheltenham to the Vatican, stored secrets were being violated and sold. Most useful and expensive were the databases of the FBI, the CIA, the DIA, (Defense Intelligence Agency) and the ultimate: the recently formed DHS, Defense HUMINT (Human Intelligence) Service. With satellites continually eyeing every inch of the planet, the latest surveillance technology – laser-analysis, heat-scan, infrared, and the newest development in prying: electron-photonics – the DHS could afford their proud boast:

'You give us a name, any name, anywhere on the planet and we'll tell you what he or she or it's doing, saying, consuming, watching and listening to, at any given moment in time.'

As the US Embassy official trying to chat up Holly in the Dickens Bar of the Birmingham Hyatt during last October's Surveillance Trade Fair, poetically put it: 'Lady, we can analyse your fart under the blankets from outer space.' Since he'd consumed four gin martinis within the last ten minutes, Holly forgave the lack of taste, but not the sweaty hand which then squeezed the top of her thigh. The lightning-fast poke in the groin went unnoticed by the man's colleagues, who had gathered round in concern at his apparent epilepsy. The technique is named 'Sword-fingers topple the ardour of the unwelcome lover', but that's an approximate translation of the Mandarin.

Anyway, bully for you, Big Brother, and if none of your new toys can stop the hackers from hacking, how the frock was humble Holls supposed to nail these cybernetically reticent species of scum?

Sure it was easy to trace the homepage site to a Web address – big deal. Holly knew it wasn't going to be Scunthorpe anyway, and foreign telecom companies were in the business of growth, not shut-down. Especially in the newly developed economies of Asia – a common homepage site for this kind of 'specialist material'.

Sure you could inform the on-line service company which maintains the Web site that the server was serving up underage porn. Their answer: the material exists purely as magnetic impulses stored electronically along with a gazillion others – why or how should they be expected to police cyberspace? Besides which, should anyone get that close to such a Web site as to threaten it with sanction of some kind, the site-owner would just shut down and open up along the electronic road a day or so later – just as the telephone scams, known as 'boiler-rooms', did before the computer age.

Sure you could try and hack into the Web site and destroy it. The serious purveyors of the type Holly was after would have developed 'firewalls' – buffers between themselves and the Internet – a combination of hard and software, to protect their computer system from intrusion.

In fact, I.D.ing these people in the first place, and then proving in a court of law that a certain individual(s) was responsible for the distribution of imagery across cyberspace was all but impossible.

In a recent lawsuit in the States, an Internet grifter, his scam 'an unbeatable investment opportunity' in imaginary Costa Rican coconut plantations, beat off both the almighty Securities and Exchange Commission, as well as the Commonwealth of Pennsylvania, by simply denying any knowledge of how information about his coconut plantation got onto computer networks...

But even if you did by some magic fluke positively I.D. a source, you'd then have the job of persuading an NDEC government, anxious to encourage their nation's participation in the Internet and thus reap the imagined benefits of the brave new cyberworld, to consider extradition of a citizen

48

for breaking international laws not yet in existence, amid all the negative feedback that would entail. Forgetitsville.

The point about all this is precisely Holly's brief – *no one's breaking any laws!* There aren't any enacted globally. No international law governs the Internet. Back to square one. Get laws passed in the down-loader's country making it illegal for that individual to possess the material. But that would still leave the server, the purveyor of the filth, high and dry with middle finger flipping, and that made Holly-Jean's blood boil.

How to snare these slippery eels? Holly finally decided she'd copy the US government's MO to snag hard evidence against Alphonse Capone in the past and the barons of Medellin and Cali today: *follow the cash.*

There were usually two methods of payment for down-loading the product onto your floppy dick.

One way was to quote plastic – not too cool. It left you, the buyer, vulnerable to official scrutiny and trace. Your fee meanwhile was sucked within a nano-second into the black hole of the financial dry cleaner's that begins in Cayman or Liechtenstein or the Isle of Man and ends wherever. The end-user's account is virtually untraceable unless you are the FBI, the CIA or some other such international heavy-breather able to make these offshore banks open up their secrets.

The preferred way, much safer from all points of view, Holly discovered, was to use the commercial sex-phone numbers that accompanied the offerings. You then could either use the anonymity of a purchased international phonecard or just run up a massive phone bill with no one the wiser as to why. The distributor just closed up electronic shop and changed numbers any time someone got too close to the boiler-room or made an official complaint. The old boiler-room side-step.

Stymied once more, Holly was on the point of jacking it

in. Seemed her only chance at successfully fishing the Net would have to be some kind of magic lure. So in desperation, one last time, she went back to basics. Men had always bought dirty postcards. From the cave paintings on. The only difference today was the advance of progress.

Electronic imaging and the latest cameras provided pristine product.

The Web provided both instant access to worldwide demand and the supplier with cyber-anonymity.

The unequal distribution of worldwide wealth provided the children.

Holly-Jean reckoned supplying sickos with their contraband spike had no hidden agenda; the purpose, like that of any enterprise, was pure and simple cash. Greed was the motivator. So greed would be her *lure*.

She chose a site which offered the category 'Asian chickens' and whose homepage address was *http:/ /www. philibuds.com.tw/prawn/*. Using one of her male alter egos, she placed an order for ten thousand pounds' worth of access time.

The order was instantly queried by the homepage for reconfirmation of the quantity. Holly reconfirmed. The screen went blank. Holly figured automatic security program. *Firewall*. Access denied to cranks, timewasters, protestors and anything that might hint of scrutiny beyond curious.

She tried again, this time requesting a more modest two hundred pounds' worth.

It worked.

She didn't sit and watch while her diskette whirred down its load.

She waited a few days then ordered a thousand pounds' worth of access time – material. This time the order went through immediately. She cleaned the windows. By now there was a growing number of discs and she had someone from COMSEM drop by to pick up the pollution.

Next she placed an order for five thousand pounds and in response the screen threw up a list of personal questions. She answered *n/a* to everyone. The screen went blank.

She tried again and got this: 'Orders of the quantity requested may only be supplied to members of the organisation. Successful applicants should begin by completing the questionnaire.'

Three days after Christmas Holly became Member 000857UK of the Prawn Club and her screen went completely jet black. Dead-centre a tiny red squirming pattern morphed into a blood-red prawn suspended in the black-ink sea of her screen.

Holly watched, skin crawling with *chi pi*, as the red words slowly surfaced on the black, as though some primitive life-form from the deepest ocean trench, ugly, ancient, evil, had entered her home.

An international network for those men who appre-ciate the unique aspects of life in Asia.
The Prawn Club.
Revealing Asia and the Dawn of Life.

She began negotiation of large, regular orders. She demanded guarantees, called for more information, hinting at large-scale cash investment with an end to further expansion in the global market.

So far they'd given her zip, *nichts*, *mei-you*.

The real problem was, Holly could no longer stomach the job and she'd found out one thing: surfing the Web was fine in pristine ocean curl, not quite so in scummy effluent. Which was why she spent the next hour dithering about the flat rather than face the screen. She was just making up the sofa-bed for Ma when she remembered her mad idea from the night before.

Ho Ma-ma might have been born a Hakka peasant in

51

Miaoli County, Taiwan during the fifty-year Japanese occupation, but she was no idiot. She had an intellect as sharp as her tongue. Where Holly got her smarts. Moreover, Ma was highly read. Married life in England with just one child to rear – after Holly, Ma's womb walked off the job, and those were the days before artificial insemination and test-tube babies – was spent either in the local library or at adult education classes. And Ma could talk. 'Incontinent mouth', the Chinese call it. *Dwo-tswei.*

Faced with staggering transfer-charge call phone bills, following Ma's move to Taiwan last autumn, Holly had arranged through her local cousins to get Ma put on-line, and to be set up with a PC and a modem. She'd quickly proved adept and Holly's e-mail was swamped for a time with ongoing tirades. Soon, however, Ma's enthusiasm waned. She started calling by phone again, said she missed the sound of Holly's voice. 'If God had wanted us to talk by keyboard, He'd have put vocal cords in our fingers.' (In translation from the original Hakkanese, Holly deleted all references to rat-penis-brained Chinese male software salespersons.)

The fact remained that Ho Ma-ma was damn good with computers, and Holly reckoned that with a bit of luck she could kill two birds with one crone. She'd set Ma on the trail of the child-porn merchants and at the same time let her deal – Professor Calculus-style – with the odious COMSEM brigade.

A totally mad idea? Maybe. Maybe not.

It was time to head downtown to meet Coulson.

There was sleet over Soho and it was cold enough to freeze the spherical appendages of the zinc-copper alloy primate. Holly-Jean was waiting in the doorway of the Coach and Horses when Mick Coulson showed up at noon, though that was after she'd taken a moment of solemn silence to stare at the hole in Gerrard Street where the Nag's used to be and grieve.

'It's bedlam in there. Can't hear yourself think for all the drunken blather and yakking mobile phones,' she complained.

'Just a pint,' said Mick, brandishing a buff envelope. 'Got your stuff. I'm buying.'

Holly grabbed the envelope. 'God forbid we deny the boy his oral fixative. I'll find a seat. Mine's a glass of Alsace. Make sure it's been opened today or I'll have gin and tonic.'

Inside, the Coach and Horses was its usual lunchtime bacchanal. Hacks, poets, musos, actors, literati and businessmen, Soho regulars and bewildered tourists reading their guide books, stuffed the infamous pub to the gills. It was extremely loud. And fluid. *Very* fluid. In fact, Holly reckoned you could say the Coach and Horses this winter lunchtime was afloat.

A couple moved out and Holly grabbed their seats on a wall-bench. Mick fought his way back with their drinks. In the act of slurping his beer and dipping a huge pork pie in English mustard Mick casually nodded to the envelope and said, 'Don't get too excited about that bumpf. As I said before it's only an informal public release of the initial PM findings. The Medical Officer's official report won't be out for a week or so. So don't read too much into it.'

When a well-connected policeman like Coulson started telling her not to get too excited about something, Holly's antennae shot skywards. She tore open the envelope and began to study the MO's initial release. Following the notification of the death by the cleaning lady at 9.15 a.m. Wednesday, two police officers from Ladbroke Grove Police Station (Holly knew that nick, it was about five minutes away from Elfa's fat on Holland Walk) had been first to arrive and had sealed the flat until detectives arrived and took over. Following initial examination by the ME, the body was pronounced dead at the scene and taken by ambulance to the mortuary at St Mary's Hospital, Paddington.

The time of death was stated to be approximately early a.m. Wednesday.

Holly looked up as a raucous crowd of advertising types spilled in. Gandhi collars, wire-rimmed specs and cell-phones. Sleet was still falling. She went back to the report and shut her ears to the pandemonium.

TOD, early Wednesday ... thus the enigmatic phonecall to her office-machine, re-routed to Mrs H-P's house late on Wednesday was no breaking newsflash; someone had obviously thought first before making the call.

Holly scanned on. Initial bloodtests had shown the presence of a very small quantity of the controlled sub-stance. The ME's conclusion: accidental death possibly due to unlawful ingestion of heroin. Nothing new so far. The newspapers had all that.

Wait a minute. Something caught her eye. 'What's this about 0.07 mm polyethylene low-density stretch-film traces on a set of false eyelashes and left-side pierced earring?'

'No idea,' shrugged Coulson. 'Never heard of the stuff. Probably due to clumsiness when removing the packaging.'

'Packaging?'

'Body-bag.'

Body-bag. The words came with a chill. 'Body-bags are hardly likely to be made of material which leaves traces on the victim, are they?' she pointed out.

'Don't arst me,' said Mick casually. 'Ready for another?'

Holly declined. She watched him fight to the bar.

The bugger knew more. She wrote a note to check the polymer out. The confirmation of heroin in Elfa's blood, albeit a small amount, disturbed her. If she had been a user, what did that do to Holly's theories of a super-healthy

54

Wunderkind? On the other hand, the shit could have been administered surreptitiously.

Or maybe Elfa had a secret. Since she'd entered this line of work, Holly'd found that people mostly did.

'Why do they write "death *possibly* due", Mick?' she asked when he returned with his fresh pint of 'real' ale.

'Wethered's Ordinary,' he announced reverently and quaffed a third, before asking, 'First, why don't you tell me your interest in this police matter.'

Holly looked at him. Talking like a TV cop again. Still, why not humour him? Mick Coulson was the one Met officer she felt she could trust. A rare commodity, to be put to use and not let go to waste.

'I've been retained by the Princess of Sheba model agency,' she explained, adding, 'Also, I knew Elfa Ericksson. Not really closely, but well enough to get very edgy at talk of a heroin OD.' She slapped her palm on the report. 'Mick, she was a triathlete, for frock's sake! You don't get to swim, ride a bike and run a hundred odd miles nodding out on smack, do you?'

'Guess not,' said Coulson, cramming the last quarter of the yellow-smeared gelatined pork crust into his mustachioed mouth.

Holly looked away. Not a pretty sight. Perhaps she'd reconsider the veggie thing. 'Why "possibly" due, not probably or definitely? Leaves it wide open, doesn't it?' she persisted.

Coulson looked at her. 'You'd have to ask the Medical Examiner, but from what I understand, according to the initial path. lab. results on routine bloodtesting, the amount of heroin found in her system was pretty tiny. Not normally enough to kill what is acknowledged to be an extremely fit young woman in the prime of life. Though there could have been an allergic reaction or some unknown genetic aversion.'

55

Whoa! thought Holly, so he does know more. Definite pong of funny handshakes and white boys in drag.

'So what's the Masonic word?' she asked.

Coulson wiped his bristles with a napkin, downed most of the pint and belched with satisfaction. 'Beg pardon!' He looked at her, hesitated, then said, 'All right, just for you, Holly. It seems nobody's that bothered. Word is it'll rest.'

'So that makes the report inconclusive?'

'No,' said Mick, finishing his pint. 'That's how it stands. "Accidental death possibly due..." You know the girl's stepfather is—'

'A Tory politician,' finished Holly. 'I'd have thought he'd be snapping at your heels for a full-on police investigation.'

'Quite the opposite, apparently,' said Mick. 'Wants her to be left in peace. Preserve the name of his daughter, sort of stuff. I can understand that.'

'Oh, so can I,' said Holly, antennae doing the *watusi*. Something wasn't right. 'So what happens next?' she asked. 'Elfa gets buried and forgotten, just like that?'

'Nope,' said Mick. 'Next comes the inquest.'

Though during the last year Holly had been involved personally in two unlawful deaths, she had attended the law's formalities in neither case. One, an uncontested plea of justified self-defence having been accepted by the Crown, the case went no further. In the other, she'd been excused by the magistrate on medical grounds and her testimony as a circumstantial witness was read out in court. Not that her presence would have contributed much.

At the time, her mind had taken a trip up the Kolyma River.

To this day, parts had yet to thaw.

'Hey, Holls! You in there, gel?'

She focused. Mick Coulson was looking distinctly worried.

She shook her head, exhaling slowly. 'Sorry, Mick.'

'Gave me the willies, Holly, like you'd gone somewhere far away.'

Holly smiled, 'You were saying about the inquest?'

Mick still looked concerned, then with a shrug he intoned, 'In all cases of non-natural death i.e. those persons that may have died from violence or accident, there must be an inquest, at which time the ME's report on the initial post-mortem is presented and in most cases accepted. Following which, the Coroner issues a burial notice, the body is released into the care of family for burial and RIP.'

'Unless?' said Holly.

'Unless someone were to challenge the report at the inquest, for example, by presenting new evidence to the Coroner which would warrant further enquiry by the police and stay-of-release of the body. In which case, should the Coroner concur, the body would not be released to the family, further post-mortem tests – that is, a full autopsy – would be carried out, and the police would have to re-open their enquiries.'

He gave Holly the worried eye and added, 'But nobody's about to do that – right?'

Holly finished her glass of Sylvaner. 'Frock knows.'

Coulson raised his eyes to the heavens and said, 'Uh-oh, somebody'd better warn the poor Coroner that fecal matter is poised to conjunct with his rotating cooling device.'

'Ho ho, Coulson,' said Holly drily.

'Yeah, right,' said Mick, watching her leave. 'Ho – frigging – Ms Ho.'

Holly-Jean used the walk over to South Molton Street to try and gather her thoughts. It wasn't entirely an exercise in futility. The sleet invigorated her somewhat.

Aramint de Lache was unbelievably busy, darling.

'That's okay,' said Holly, mightily relieved. 'I only need to talk to Joel for a minute.' Perversely, she found herself

frog-marched behind a trail of cigar smoke into the office
which today was about as tranquil as the Chicago futures
trading pit. Joel and three other women were working
phones. Fax machines spewed up, printers clacked like
mallards on crystal meth.

Holly's smile lit up. 'Dull place.'

'*Fashion weeks!*' yelled Aramint. Today, she was wearing a white boilersuit silk-screened with a huge face of
Pablo Picasso. She pointed to various whiteboards on which
were felt-tipped indecipherable hieroglyphics. 'The agency's
booking table. The War Room! Paris, Milan, New York. And
then there's London.' She sniffed dismissively. 'Though most
of my models are well out of the *local* price range.'

'I'm impressed,' said Holly.

'Don't be vacuous, darling,' barked de Lache. 'It's not
impressive, it's miraculous! One has to be a Master of the
Telephone! Split-second decisions. On the run. No safety
net! Fashion is a 3D chess game, requiring diplomacy,
intelligence and verve.'

Behind her Joel was making the sign for male self-abuse.

'I had no idea the fashion world was so unfrivolous,'
Holly deadpanned.

'Understand this,' said Aramint solemnly. 'It is my duty
to ensure the calibre of the booker. Monsters out there!
Besides, the whole game has changed beyond recognition.
It's no longer just a case of looking beautiful, having the
perfect proportions and not one scintilla of body-fat. You've
got to sing, act, dance as well as catwalk the world's most
beautiful clothes. Models are taking over the entire enter-
tainments industry – and that means far more scum for us to
filter out.'

Holly was beginning to feel claustrophobic. 'I really do
just need two minutes of Joel's time.'

Aramint pirouetted with a fresh-lit cigar and said, 'No,
stay. I want you to feel the pulse.' Holly reckoned Aramint's

was speeding like the clappers. 'You see, girls today don't just want the "in" to the celeb scene. They want totality of Opportunity. Modelling's just the means to infinity and one has to be mentor, best friend, shoulder to cry on and springboard. And yet, darling, one is also dear old nanny with a cup of sweet, hot tea and biscuits at the end of a cold, cold day.' She concluded with a billow of blue smoke.

'Bravo,' said Holly. This woman was good. Good at giving away nothing at full throttle.

'Sweet,' Aramint acknowledged with a little bow, adding, 'You just have to pray God is on your side.' With that she entered her inner sanctum, shutting the door dismissively.

Holly stood there feeling her temper rising. The woman just plain got up her nose.

'Ignore the bitch!' called Joel, cupping a phone. 'I'll be finished in half a mo.' A few minutes later, he threw up his hands, grabbed a coat and a black portfolio. 'Don't know about you, but I can't take this place one second longer. Shall we gonzo?'

Holly agreed with alacrity. At Widow Applebaum's just down the street, they found a space and sat with coffee and Danish pastry.

Joel said, 'As you requested, I put that stuff together for you myself. Included all of it, old and new.'

Holly perused Elfa Eriksson's portfolio with mixed emotions. Bonny babe. Pre-Raphaelite nymphet. Adolescent Edmund Dulac illustration come to life. Beanpole woman of breathtaking beauty. It was like watching an exotic flower unfold, knowing it was going to die at nightfall.

There was other stuff in there Holly hadn't known about. *SuperTeen* magazine Girl of the Year. A recent record for the European techno-pop market. And at the adult end she saw herself with Elfa – one of the Highgate *dojo* set.

She quashed her momentary pride and asked Joel abruptly, 'Did Elfa deal drugs?'

The pulsing temple-vein gave him away. 'Not that I know of.'

'Who were her best friends in the business?'

'Oh, that's easy. Ivana Petrakov and She the Eritrean.'

'Are they doing the shows?'

He thought about it. 'Yes. Both are in Paris.'

'How can I reach them?' said Holly. 'And I mean today.'

'With great difficulty, dear,' he flapped his wrists. 'I suppose I might possibly be able to find a number. Take an awful lot of digging up, mind you.'

'Joel, cut the camp. You want to help or not?'

He looked hurt. 'Elfa and I were friends. There's no way she killed herself. You need someone like me on the inside. The fashion world is hermetically sealed from concepts like truth, trust and reality.'

'As in Aramint,' said Holly, placatingly.

'Don't underestimate the woman,' said Joel. 'She started the agency in the Sixties. In this business that's a very long time to stay at the top. With a lot of help, of course, from the dispensable likes of poor little insignificant me.'

Holly patted his hand. 'How long've you been there?' The boy was probably harmless, but just maybe he knew something.

'Ten teeth-grinding years, can you believe it? Mind you, all that guff she gave you about Granny's hot tea is just one side of the story. Believe me, I know the other side. The torn pair of yesterday's knickers under the priceless evening wear. The chain-smoking skeletons who daren't even drink mineral water on show days for fear of water retention.'

Holly said, 'So you want to be candid, Joel? You really want to help? I've been looking for possible motives as to why someone would want to hurt Elfa. Most murders, unless random acts of motiveless evil, are committed by someone close to the victim – a family member or friend. Motives usually stem from passion, envy, anger or greed.

60

Someone wants something of the victim's – love, perhaps, which if not freely given, results in violence, rape and eventual murder. Or perhaps someone just wants your money, or a particular object of value. Might be simple or complex: theft, robbery, fraud or blackmail. Here the killer doesn't necessarily start out with the intention, but murder is the eventual result when things go wrong. Consider this: we've all heard the allegations of sleaze in the modelling world. Agents getting teen models to sleep with them before putting them on the books. Then we get motives like blackmail, passion, jealousy. Does Aramint have any kind of track record?'

Joel shrugged. 'They all do, sweetie. As far as I know, Aramint's slept with every model who's ever been on our books, both male and female. But I think you'll be barking up the wrong tree there. It's simply no big deal. A fact of life. They all do it.'

And right down the drain goes six months of criminology research, thought Holly.

'What do you know about Paddy Fistral? Was he the official "boyfriend"?'

Joel thought about that for a moment before answering. 'Was trying to be for a while but I don't think that little fairy-tale was meant to be somehow.'

'When did she stop seeing him?'

'Oh sometime towards the end of last year, I think.'

'Did he use drugs?'

'Paddy? Rather. Bangs up regularly, I hear.'

'Bangs up?'

'*Uses*.'

'You mean he uses hard drugs?'

Joel looked at Holly-Jean as though she'd just stepped out of some Victorian-value time-capsule.

'I mean he *spikes* smack, darling. Draws it up into a syringe and sticks it into his veins. Aitch. The white. Scag.

61

The soppy poppy's refined offspring, that Don Juan of Drugs, the ultimate seducer. Heroin.'

Holly digested that piece of information.

'Is that why the two broke up?'

'They were hardly a twosome, dearie. But even if they were, I mean you could hardly expect a relationship like that to succeed. What with him touring the world with his band on the one hand, and the pro-surfing contests on the other, and her doing shows and shoots just about any time, anyplace. Doomed to failure, honeychild.'

Holly could only take a certain measure of camp and she was beginning to find Joel tiresome. 'How can I get hold of him?'

'Another that won't be easy. I know the name of his manager. Lee Cowley.'

Holly noted it down. She said, 'Was it you who telephoned me on Wednesday night?'

'No, it wasn't.' Joel toyed with his spoon. 'Perhaps your computer really was down for a few hours.'

'My computer wasn't down, Joel.'

He looked sheepish. 'Well, if you must know, darling, I got awfully heavily involved in doing something I really shouldn't have, and completely lost track of the time.'

Enough fey for one day. Holly stood up. 'You want to be a friend to Elfa? Just get me a number for Ivana and She by six tonight at the latest.'

Chapter 5

Holly cabbed over to Sloane Street while the sleet gave way to thundery showers. As the taxi lurched round Hyde Park Corner she felt mixed emotions. On the one hand her curiosity was piqued in anticipation of an encounter with the famed Sixties 'acid princess'. On the other, she was dreading confronting a grieving mother.

After the maid had announced her, Holly said, 'I hope you'll forgive me intruding at a time like this, but it's my job to ask some awkward questions.'

At first sight Ingrid Ericksson seemed the perfect anthropological example of what happens when you take a beautiful young Swedish girl, place her chronologically to reach the age of seventeen in 1965 and drop her on the King's Road, Chelsea. The legacy of all that *fun*: lattice-worked eye-sockets, the thousand microdot stare. The famous blonde hair hennaed to death. The bead and mirror embroidered kaftan sprinkled with fallen fag-ash. The glass of Tanqueray gin, the overflowing ashtray, the crumpled pack of Lucky Strikes – strong Turkish tobacco – anachronisms from the Age of Indulgence, none of which looked the slightest bit out of place in this joss-stick smoky Moroccan souk overlooking Sloane Street on a wintry late afternoon.

At first Ingrid's only response was to let those eyes, Nordic blue long leaked away, drift slowly over Holly, across the room and out of the stained-glass windows. Suddenly racked by a fit of coughing, she slurped gin, lit up a fresh Lucky. 'You'll have to excuse the drunken old slag,' she announced between coughs. 'The only way I know how to cope.'

Holly saw now that she'd been mistaken. This was no burned-out zombie. Those eyes were on fire with pain and she spoke gently. 'Elfa was your brilliant success. You created that shining star – which is why we must find out the truth.'

Ingrid seemed to try and gather her wits. She nodded. 'Right. The truth. But it's so bloody unfair to have taken her instead of me – Ingrid Ericksson, the great *survivor*!' She spat out the last word. Then added with a mirthless laugh, 'Like a Grimm's fairy tale without the happy ending. The beautiful young princess inherits the wicked witch's shitty old karma and becomes the last victim of the Sixties!' She lapsed into silence. Hailstones began to rattle the stained-glass windows. The wind cried Mary.

'Did you know of – can you imagine – any enemies?' said Holly.

Ingrid reached out and rang a hand-bell. The maid poked her head round the Marrakesh kilim-hung door. 'Sustenance, Minda,' she waggled the glass, only then adding as an afterthought, 'enemies? Of course not. Everyone loved Elfa. They all did. Too bloody much at times.'

While Minda fixed a drink from the carved sandalwood Tuareg chest that doubled as a dry bar, Holly wondered what that last remark signified and studied the nearby bookcase.

'Would ma'am care for one?'

Holly turned to Minda. 'A small glass of white wine?' Minda smiled and a few moments later returned with a chilled flûte of champagne.

Ingrid Ericksson had a fascinating collection of esoterica. In amongst the art, anthropology, philosophy and religions,

Holly noted one or two large volumes bearing Ingrid's name.

She said, 'May I?' and pulled one out. It was a beautiful collection of photographs of the body-painting Nubian tribes of Southern Sudan. She checked the publication date – 1975.

'Once upon a time, my travel pix were quite respected, believe it or not,' Ingrid called out, slopping her glass.

'Oh, I believe it. These are absolutely wonderful,' said Holly with sincerity. She replaced the volume. The images of the elongated naked ebony men prompted her to ask. 'Elfa's father, the real father, does he stay in touch?'

'Never knew him, at least not in the *un*Biblical sense,' said Ingrid breezily. The fresh gin had evidently worked. 'The event took place at a party at Keith Richards' house in Cheyne Walk. I only figured out which one it was when I saw the baby: so beautiful but definitely not quite white.'

'And her stepfather?' asked Holly.

'The "rich little shit"?' snorted Ingrid bitterly. 'Oh, far too busy insinuating his proboscis into the rear-end of the Tory bosses and amassing more millions. Haven't heard a word from him.'

'You no longer live together, then?' Holly had checked the MP's entry in *Who's Who* before leaving this morning. Though there'd been no mention of divorce, she could hardly imagine a Tory politician living in this place.

'Not on your life!' said Ingrid. 'Threw him out the day I caught him playing horsey-horsey with Elfa.'

'Surely she needed a surrogate father?'

Ingrid smiled humourlessly. 'She was twelve at the time, they were both naked and covered in baby oil.'

'Oh,' said Holly.

'Though I can't say I really blame him. She was extremely precocious as a young girl, y'know, in *that* department. I think she first realised the effect she had on

65

men about the time of her fifth birthday. An angel, the most gorgeous thing you ever saw.' Without warning Ingrid flung her glass to shatter on the polished wood floorboards and cried out, 'She's gone! My one achievement in one life gone!' She buried her head in the embroidered cushions and began to heave terrible, racking sobs.

Minda came in and cleaned up the mess. Holly whispered in her ear, 'I'll have to be going soon. Will she be all right?'

'Just wait a moment, would you, please, ma'am?' Minda whispered in reply. 'It's been a terrible blow for her. She gets very confused at times.' Holly nodded. 'You'd better give her this when she's ready.' Minda handed Holly a fresh Tanqueray gin and left the room.

'No need to whisper!' Ingrid spoke from within the cushions and a hand reached blindly out. Feeling guilty, Holly inserted the gin. It was ingested in one gulp and Ingrid staggered to her feet.

'Stay. We could eat later. Something spicy, oriental. Wouldn't that be fun?'

'I'd love to but I'm afraid not, though thanks ever so,' said Holly. 'There is one thing you can do before I go. I need permission to act on your behalf in my investigations. Could you sign this?' She handed Ingrid a pen and one of her own desk-top printed forms she carried for this purpose, and secured a shaky signature.

With an addled look, Ingrid said, 'Will it cost? Not that I care, and you must think me utterly beyond the pale, but the "rich little shit" has long since stopped paying the ante. We're in the process of litigation, cash is definitely short.'

Holly said, 'Don't worry. I've been retained by her agent.' Then she added, 'Besides, Elfa was a friend of mine. This one I'd do for free.'

Holly said goodbye and walked to the door. Wanting to add some smidgen of comfort, she said, 'If anyone was responsible for the death of your daughter, I'll find them.'

Ingrid stared grief-mad at Holly. In the dying light of the stained glass, the crimson-mascara that had coursed down her ghostly pale cheeks appeared as blood pouring from her eye-sockets. 'You think someone killed my darling, don't you? Find them for me, please!' Her voice became a harsh whisper. 'And when you find them, I'd like to be there for just a while. You'll see to that, won't you?'

Holly nodded bleakly. 'I'll do my best.' She closed the door.

Before Minda let Holly out she answered a few questions.

It was dark, blustery and freezing when Holly finally reached home at Camden Lock. One time, years ago, stuck in a particularly horrible temp job, she got a sick note from the doctor for 'lethargy and malaise'. That was how she felt tonight.

The rouée gin-breath of Ingrid Ericksson, the fluffy fantasists of fashion and the bad feeling about the connection between Elfa and Ed had driven her down. She wandered around the studio-flat with GiGi following. She'd better eat – hadn't had a proper meal since when? The Rijstaffel. *Rijstaffel*. With Ed gone, how would she ever be able to eat it again?

She took a quick shower with the cat watching from the toilet seat, put on her towelling robe and made them each a Maltese sandwich, which act improved her mood a little. Pitta envelopes brushed with a dab of tomato purée and lashings of extra-virgin olive oil, she stuffed with tomatoes, garlic, olives, anchovies, chopped fresh coriander, oregano, basil and chili pepper.

She gave GiGi his, then took her plate and a mug of ice-cubed Pinot D'Alsace and sat cross-legged in front of the box. CNN on cable. After the world bad news, transcripts from the latest trial of the century and international sports, some scumbag Brit gossip columnist came on and did a job on Elfa. Stroking GiGi, Holly forced herself to watch the bobbing blow-dried bouffant.

> *'Elfa Ericksson had a body to die for. And tragically, that's exactly what she did. The beyond-beautiful young woman had everything to live for, yet ironically, died of a fatal overdose of the increasingly widespread drug* de chiox *of those who make their living in the world of fashion: heroin.*
> *Yes, viewers, heroin – the* Très chic *way to lose those extra pounds. And keep them off.*
> *In this case, permanently.'*

Picture of Elfa looking extremely thin came onto the screen. The muppet-like talking head returned.

> *'Yet Elfa Ericksson, this beautiful young woman, was considered by many to have the perfect human frame. That is, for hanging clothes on. Certainly hot-shot Brit designer Mike Mancini thought so. He always booked Elfa for his shows.*
> *'Mike, is it true that Elfa was one of those handful of top international models who reputedly required a ten-thousand-pound shot in the arm to get up in the morning?'*
> *'You know, Brian, when I was creating my Spring Collection . . .'*

Blah, blah-dy-frocking-blah. Holly switched off the TV. She checked her answer-machine. As requested Joel Unmack had left a message. Holly called the Paris number and had a very interesting conversation. Following which she e-mailed the electronic booking service at BA, punched in her credit-card number and made reservations on a couple of flights.

68

Sitting doodling at her trestle-table workstation, something had just occurred to her. She pressed the playback on her answer-machine till she found the call from Wednesday night.

'Elfa Ericksson got herself killed. *Giri*.'

Whoever had made that call was familiar with the Chinese concept of unavoidable duty. *Giri*. A husky woman or possibly a young man, Mrs Howell-Pryce had said. Holly knew different.

That voice was the legacy of years of Luckies and Tanqueray, and it belonged to the owner of a bookcase rich in world culture. To invoke *Giri* had been to place a debt of honour in Holly's account. A job that could not be turned down. Which proved nothing but a big So What – and left two questions begging.

Why had Ingrid Ericksson feigned ignorance when Holly had visited her this afternoon?

And why make such an impersonal, odd announcement of her daughter's death? Unless, of course, Holly thought grimly, the answers to both questions involved the excessive consumption of alcohol. Ingrid had been unable to cope, and in the drowning gin storm had made the strange call, the remote plea that carried an awful burden of duty. *Giri*.

Holly made the call she'd been putting off.

'I was expecting you to call couple of days ago. I wasn't sure if you were still out of town,' said Marika, after they'd exchanged mutual expressions of grief and sorrow at the loss of a friend, and mutual speculation as to the likely effects of the return of Ho Ma-ma to Camden Lock.

'Marika, did you recommend me to Ingrid Ericksson?' asked Holly.

'Poor Ingrid is utterly devastated; Elfa was all she had left. Yes, I did say if she needed help, you were the one to turn to. Was I wrong?' Her voice rose defensively.

'No, no, of course you weren't wrong,' said Holly. 'Oh, I
don't know ... it's all so close to home, somehow. I hate jobs
like this. When it involves people you actually know.
Especially after last year...' She let the words dangle.

Marika spoke harshly. 'Holly, for heffen's sake, pull
yourself together. Stop acting like a child and think of poor
Elfa!'

She was right, of course. Holly appreciated the slap of
coldly practical Swedish. Self-pity she didn't need. (The
one luxury you can't afford, as her dad put it.) 'For what it's
worth, I'll do my best,' she said.

'It's worth an awful lot, darlink,' replied Marika, soften-
ing. 'And, Holly-Jean, you know, your best is the very best
there is.'

Before she rang off, Holly elicited a list of phone numbers
of Elfa's friends. Another chilled bottle of Pinot D'Alsace
got Holly through a lot of tedious phoning. Bereft, people
resorted to cliché. Elfa was 'special, magic, a one-off, they
broke the mould.' No one could imagine the slightest
possible reason for her death. Everyone had loved her.

If Holly heard one more 'she had this amazing kind of
aura, y'know?' she'd scream. By ten-thirty she'd got
enough hot air to float a Zeppelin and none of it worth a
Hakka curse.

Deciding it would be rude to call people any later at night,
she grabbed a bag and rode her Yamaha Fuzzy up to the *dojo*
at Highgate.

She'd inherited both the martial arts gymnasium and his
senior place on the England Taekwondo Team selection
committee from *Lao-shr* Chen – 'Beloved Master Tommy
Chen' to his followers – following his death last year. Holly-
Jean had been shaken, given the extraordinary circumstances of his passing, to find herself the sole beneficiary of
his will. Which in essence amounted to the *dojo* and its

70

debts. Since she had neither the time nor desire to run a martial arts school, finding a suitable manager had been a big headache. Luckily, the few part-time assistant teachers stayed on. Just before Christmas she'd managed to persuade one of them, a veteran bronze medallist at the World Championships, to take over running the place. They'd agreed twelve months was long enough to see whether the place was going to lose her more money than she could afford. If it did, she'd let it go to the highest bidder.

By chance – her money karma was a riot these days – the gym sat on the only highly desirable corner of Highgate to survive the property bubble-burst and with planning permission for redevelopment already approved, the land was extremely valuable.

But then so was the memory of Teacher Chen.

The *dojo* was deserted when she let herself in and switched on the lights over the *tatamis*. She sniffed the sweet scent of the rice-stalk mats and felt her *chi* rising. She went to the dressing room, changed into her kit and began her work.

First, gradual stretching, arching and bowing, urging suppleness into her tight muscles. When primed, she began multiple repetitions of set pieces, starting simply and progressing to complex routines lasting more than five minutes. Finally to end in flying mortal ballet.

She was finished, showered and ready to leave before two a.m.

Backing the Yamaha out of the hallway and onto the pavement, she heard running steps. Reluctant to drop her precious bike, she pulled it onto its stand. The hesitation proved her undoing and she turned too late to mount any defence. An iron bar smashed into her kidneys and she went down. Three men, steel-toe-capped boots crunching her flesh, stamping. Nothing to do but protect her head with her arms and curl into the foetal position as the bar repeatedly

71

thrashed her lower back, the boots kicking remorseless, efficient. The beating was methodical, conducted in silence except for grunts of effort and the thud of the blows connecting.

Flooded with serotonin, endorphin and adrenaline, the body's natural painkillers, and the years of martial arts and *chi kung* conditioning, meant Holly felt little actual pain as the beating took place but rather experienced the exact awareness of damage being done.

'You've made your point!' she finally cried out. 'Better stop, unless you want to kill me!'

With one last swing of the bar, they ran off into the night.

She lay for a long time without moving. When her breathing had steadied she fractionally tested her reflexes. Thankfully her limbs seemed to respond. Nothing major was broken. She tried to rise, and pain released at Mach I burst through her body like a supersonic bang. Tracing the agony she reckoned maybe a rib or two was cracked. Lying back, for the time being immobile, she drifted in and out of consciousness.

A couple in the middle of a drunken spat passed her at three o'clock. Gasping with effort, she got their attention and asked them to fetch her cellphone from the bike box. She had to endure another five minutes of inebriated debate over whether the man should steal the phone, the Yamaha or both.

Luckily, the woman prevailed. 'You all right, dearie? 'Ere, I'll call the ambulance.'

The woman got through to the emergency service. An ambulance arrived shortly after that and Holly was expertly lifted onto a stretcher and into the back of the van.

'What do you want us to do with the bike?' asked one of the ambulancemen kindly. Holly wondered if he wouldn't mind locking the Yamaha back inside the *dojo*. The keys should still be in the bike. The man wouldn't mind at all.

Holly sank gratefully back as the ambulance rushed her to the crowded Casualty department at the Royal Free in Hampstead. It wasn't the closest hospital, but Holly managed to grunt out that since she was carrying five-star private medical insurance the ambulancemen could put in a claim. 'You wouldn't fancy a private room at the Sunningdale Sanitarium!' kidded the driver as he wheelspun away.

Once a nurse had run her plastic over a charge slip, Holly was taken by stretcher to a private examination room and immediately seen by a doctor. He confirmed hairline fractures in two ribs and she was strapped with a heavy-duty spandex bandage, given a shot of morphine in the lower back, a bottle of distalgesic capsules containing heavy doses of codeine from the dispensary, and a urine-sample bottle to check for kidney damage to be filled and returned at her convenience. She was also told a police officer would duly arrive and interview her, so when the last nurse had moved on, and sufficiently numbed by the morphine, Holly wound herself onto her feet, grabbed her bag, shuffled her way through the mobbed waiting room and out of the front door where she flagged down one of the waiting cowboy mini-cabs to take her to Heathrow.

Chapter 6

Saturday pre-dawn: Heathrow, Terminal 5.

Holly hobbling painfully, face scraped and suppurating and with her left eye blackened and swollen, bumps into Hua Shen-shen, Mr frocking Plum Blossom himself, in the arrivals hall, also waiting at the barrier for the Taipei–London redeye.

Synchronicity? Holly thinks it highly unlikely, and fears the worst. She doesn't need any arcane Oriental intrigue shit this early in the morning. Not with two cracked ribs and a face like Arafat with eczema.

But it turned out Mr Plum Blossom was there to meet the point man for the *Ju-lyang bang* – the Bamboo Union, the most powerful of the Secret Societies of the Chinese diaspora also known as Triads, coming in advance of the February Conference delegations.

Mr Hua asked after her health, too polite to mention the fresh wounds.

'A slight difference of opinion with some drunks, nothing out of the ordinary.' Still she thought to mention Ed's demise again. 'That anything to do with me?' she said casually. 'You know – bombs and things?'

'As far as I know, it was not.'

'It'd be nice to set the mind at rest,' said Holly.

'Yes.'

They stood in silence. Too damn early for chit-chat.

75

Hua cleared his throat. 'Actually, certain information concerning your friend has come to our attention.'

Holly straightened up. Forgot about the ribs. Ouch! Doubled over and clutching the barrier she grunted, 'Really?'

'Yes,' said Mr Plum Blossom. 'Following your request, we did look into the matter. We were, of course, very concerned initially that the Dutch authorities might be led to take an interest in the upcoming Convention.'

'Forget that – not a chance they know a thing!' gasped Holly, in too much pain to be glib. 'So what did you discover about the explosion in Volkspark?'

Mr Hua said, 'You're a senior selector for the English Taekwondo team, correct?'

'I am,' said Holly impatiently. 'What of it? What about Ed?'

Mr Hua looked put out. Such directness was ill mannered.

'Little Sister Ho, we do value your work on our behalf,' he spoke smoothly. 'We trust you are ready to assist in a little further business.'

With Ma returning, the Conference looming, and *mei-you* progress on Elfa, Holly needed 'further business' from him and his ilk like she needed a boil on the end of her nose, but she understood the conversation was now a negotiation.

'Very busy the next couple of weeks,' she informed him.

'Your selection committee, does it have any influence with the AIA?'

'The Association of International Athletes? Hardly.' What was he up to?

'But wasn't Master Chen a member?' Mr Hua persisted.

'He was, but it's not something that gets handed down on a plate. Very exclusive little club, that. Self-appointed, unaccountable. A major twentieth-century scandal.' Holly

76

added with a sneer, 'Bunch of corrupt greedheads.'

'You soon might be facing the test of such greed yourself,' Mr Hua insinuated.

'Too damn early for word games, Mr Hua,' said Holly, her patience exhausted. 'I'm here to meet my mother. Don't spoil the moment.'

Hua said solemnly, 'Ho Ma-ma's return has been noted. Taiwan's loss will be Camden's gain.'

Holly said, 'All right, all right. You tell me why Ed died, and I'll listen to your proposal. Mind you, I make no promises.' Which remark was about as pointless as a Manila taxi meter. What the Societies want, you damn well make sure they get.

'Little Sister Ho, you do oblige me,' said Mr Hua, smiling thinly. 'Your friend Edward was killed by Dutch professionals on contract to a Lebanese organisation.'

'Drug deal gone wrong, I suppose.' Holly sighed. Eddie, you *fool!*

'Something of that nature.'

'Was Elfa Ericksson also part of the contract?'

Mr Hua looked puzzled.

Holly prompted, 'The supermodel who recently died, on all the front pages?'

Mr Hua sniffed. 'I have no idea.'

'If you could find out I'd be very grateful.' Holly tried to emphasise the very personal nature of the gratitude, but for once Mr Hua wasn't biting. Holly figured either too many knock-backs in the past or too much facial seepage too early in the morning. '*Please?*'

'Yes, yes, very well.' Mr Hua waved his hand dismissively. 'Now as to our concerns: the Secret Societies of the Han diaspora are angry over Mainland China's refusal to allow the Republic of China on Taiwan to participate in international sporting events under her own name or flag. The ridiculous emblem of the Association and the words

"Chinese Taipei" are seen as a humiliation, an unforgivable loss-of-face, and we are no longer prepared to tolerate it.'

He paused. The doors to Customs were opening. 'As you know,' he murmured, 'the AIA is extremely susceptible to financial incentives.'

'Bribery and corruption are the terms, I think,' said Holly.

'If you say so,' shrugged Hua. 'Little Sister Ho, it is being arranged through these methods for you to take up the vacant seat left by Master Chen.'

Holly watched the first exhausted travellers bearing TPE/HTR stickers stumble into the arena, thinking: This I don't believe.

'The next meeting of the Association is to be held in March. You are to work within the organisation to extend Taiwan's influence among the members. Failing that, we shall be taking other more decisive measures.'

'Tell me you're kidding.' But she knew he wasn't.

Knowing Taiwan's huge slush fund: the highest foreign reserves in the world after Japan. Knowing the osmotic relationship between the Bamboo Union and other Triads and the ruling Nationalist Party, the Kuo-ming Tang (KMT). And knowing the Chinese evaluation of 'face' above all else.

The deduction was logical. Mr Plum Blossom was deadly serious.

But then Holly caught sight of little Ho Ma-ma bustling along behind a piled pushcart, and her heart leapt. She began to wave furiously.

'What do you mean by "more decisive measures"?' she asked out of the corner of her mouth.

Hua held up a small flag with the Chinese ideogram for Dragon painted red on a blue background, and said, 'Many think it's time for a change of leadership.'

'But Francisco Frank Goya, the President of the AIA, has the job for life!'

'Precisely.'

Then Ma was there, and that awkward, lovable bundle of energy blotted out all else.

If you've ever suffered a cracked rib, you'll know what Holly was going through. Breathing was pure pain, a sneeze was diabolical agony. She dropped another painkiller; how many did that make so far today? Couldn't rightly recall, m'lud. Nine o'clock. Ma in the shower. She made another espresso and filched a fresh-cream chocolate eclair from the fridge.

On the way back from Heathrow with Ma, she'd had the cabbie wait while she'd stocked up at the new bakery on Chalk Farm Road. Six a.m. and the two Irishwomen who owned the place had been up baking for hours. Sweating, cheerful and ready for the onslaught of the Saturday market at Camden Lock. An anxious glance at Holly's wounds, 'Hope yez beat the bejasus outta him!' had resulted in a couple of free jam doughnuts.

At ten past nine, with Ma still in the shower, Holly licked the last of the eclair from her lips and called Coulson at ALCO to ask if he had any pals in Special Branch.

'Like whom?' said Mick.

'Repellent prick name of Beezer.'

Coulson laughed. '"Soreballs"! I was at Hendon Police College with him back in the early Seventies. Prick is right.'

'Good,' said Holly. 'Give Soreballs a message. Edward van Schrempft was a contract hit: locals on behalf of Lebanese traders. Unimpeachable sources from Chinatown. He'll understand.'

'Uh-oh,' said Coulson unhappily. 'Why do I get the

79

feeling I'm about to land in wonton noodle soup with my dim sum missing? Can't you tell him yourself?'

Holly wondered if Mick ever got his chimney swept. 'You've met the guy,' she pointed out. 'Besides, like all law-abiding citizens, I have a healthy paranoia when it comes to Special Branch.'

'So have I,' complained Coulson.

'This is a hot one, Mick,' Holly urged. 'Earn yourself some brownie points.'

He hesitated, then with a sigh of exasperation, said, 'What was the name again?'

'Edward van Schrempft,' enunciated Holly.

'Better be for real,' muttered Coulson.

'Of course it's bloody real!' Holly snapped. The lousy bastard. *Wan-ba Dan!* 'You've got a nerve – after all the stuff I've given you. You still owe me, Coulson.' She didn't need to say it. He owed her his career success.

'All right, all right, don't snag your panty-liner,' he carried on breezily. 'By the way, Holly, you're probably right not to mess with Soreballs. At Hendon he got Tie of the Year in self-defence.'

'I'm all a-quiver,' she said drily. Adding, 'Why "Sore-balls"? Not that I care, just curious.'

Coulson reverted to laddish youth. 'In twelve months of North Circular Road disco-ing, despite the combined, heroic efforts of Brut, Clearasil and a red Triumph Spitfire, Soreballs never scored once. Not even close.'

'Scored?'

'Chicks, man, the Seventies, four nights a week,' said Coulson ebulliently. 'But not poor old Soreballs. By the end of the course he was desperate, cunt-struck.'

Marvelling at the man's subtlety, Holly said, 'Meanwhile you, Coulson, were fighting the girls, or should I say "chicks", off on every side, of course.'

Coulson's reply was full of sweet reminiscence. 'I tell

you, Holly, back then it was dolly-birds-a-go-go, the pill, the Bee Gees and no HIV.'

'"Bliss was it in that dawn to be alive",' quoted Holly. And Coulson amazed her by completing Wordsworth, 'But to be young was very heaven!'

The cab to Holland Park went via the back doubles of St John's Wood, Little Venice and North Kensington. It was a clear, ice crisp winter's day, the sky bluer than blue, the low sun sowing diamonds on reflective surfaces. Holly sucked in the clean-ish weekend air with relish. She felt perversely optimistic though she couldn't tell you why. (Maybe it was the codeine. Maybe it was early indications of Saturday Night fever.)

Passing Trellick Towers and turning down the north end of Ladbroke Grove brought sweet flashbacks of hot young summers around the Portobello Road. The diaphragm-punching bass from the Reggae sound systems, the August carnival, smells of weed, joss and patchouli.

She chuckled to see a waif totter by on oyster-green platform boots and scarlet flares; a new generation adopting the styles and poses of those days of sartorial idiocy. At the traffic lights, music came blaring from a stall, and she thumped the seat. 'In your hippy hat! And It's Hi-Ho Silver Lining! Ba-Boom!'

The mood inside Apartment No. 117, Pusey House was sombre by contrast. Epifania Pangalina was in mourning.

Her jowly face was laden with make-up under the dark embroidered veil. Long black moustache hairs were accentuated by the white powder distempering her copper Visayan skin. Layers of creaking black satin covered her cushiony frame. Holly felt stifled just looking at her. The building's central-heating system was on full crank, the radiators blasting out throat-drying heat.

In the tight confines of the kitchen, Epifania's perfume was overpowering. Holly guessed it was something brought over from Manila – an extra-rich whiff of her distant tropical home. Molasses, frangipani and overripe bananas. They were drinking bad coffee and eating gluey lemon-curd tarts from a large bamboo tray placed in the middle of the narrow table.

Epifania reached for her black lace embroidered handkerchief and blew her nose noisily. '*Aw, ai-nakaw, malungkot talaga!!*' she sighed. 'My heart drowns in sorrow.'

Tears welled up in her dark brown cow-eyes and Holly thought: Even her cleaning lady. Seemed as though everyone fell under Elfa's magical spell. On the other hand, getting anything remotely more real than tears and sighs of woe from Epifania was proving difficult.

Every time Holly mentioned her former employer by name, Epifania's fingers clacked her plastic rosary beads and she crossed herself, muttering in Tagalog. Holly was beginning to feel this might be a wasted trip, but she had no choice. And anyway, one of her Tiger bile-duct itchings was growing insistent . . .

Nobody could be this perfect.

Either Elfa was a saint or an Apache squaw at covering her tracks.

'Did Elf— she have any close male friends, perhaps who would stay the night?'

'Stayovers?' gasped Epifania, horror-struck. 'Why, certainly not! Not at least while I was working there.' She looked thoughtful, then added, 'Well, of course, I don't suppose Madam was a cherry girl but—'

'Cherry girl?' asked Holly, perplexed.

'*Cherry* girl – cherry, you know: birgin.'

'Birgin?' Holly repeated, totally bewildered.

Epifania looked at Holly as though she were a halfwit.

82

'Birgin girl like The Birgin Mary.' She crossed herself and mumbled in prayer. Holly noticed the rosary held not the usual plain cross, but a pink plastic baby nailed to a tiny white crucifix.

'Oh, I see.' Holly's grin stayed fixed.

'Ah, but don't mistake me. Madam was no butterfly, either. No way.'

'Butterfly?' Holly could only guess.

Epifania explained patiently, 'Butterfly here, butterfly there, everywhere a handsome boy, you know: *prom-isc-u-ous*. Not Madam.'

'No, of course not,' agreed Holly, with what she hoped was a knowing look.

'Did you ever hear Madame mention the name Paddy Fistral?'

Epifania slapped her meaty palm on the table. 'I won't hear a single bad word about Mr Patrick! A lovely boy, a real gentleman, and so handsome! *Ai-yo bayan!*'

'So he used to be a regular visitor here, then?' said Holly.

'Of course he was, for nearly a year he was courting Madame. It was a tragedy last Autumn when he stopped coming to see her. I knew she was heartbroken, but she never showed it. Sometimes Madame was just too proud, though I won't speak ill of the dead, especially not my dear sweet Madame.'

'But you just said no stopovers...' Holly's voice trailed off. Logic and epistemology were apparently not Epifania's strong points. 'Why did he stop coming, do you know?'

Epifania thought for a moment. 'Jealousy,' she said finally. 'Both as bad as each other. They were always fighting about his picture in the newspaper with some pretty girl. And hers in another newspaper with a handsome boy.'

'Did it end angrily?'

83

'You mean did he leave with a slammeen door?'
She sighed and nodded.
'It was only a few weeks ago.'
Holly sat up. 'Really? I thought you said—'
'He'd come back to try and have – a what do the papers call it – a recon-cil-iation, but it didn't work out. She'd changed. There was lot of shouting and when I saw him out, that handsome boy's eyes were filled with tears – *akaw-lalang!*' The telephone rang. Epifania picked it up, listened and said, 'You just wait there. I'll be right down.' She said to Holly, 'There's a delivery at the tradesmen's entrance. Will you excuse me for a few minutes?'

'Of course,' said Holly. Epifania left the kitchen. When Holly heard the apartment door close, she slipped out of the kitchen into the corridor. There were only three other doors. One proved to be the guest bathroom and toilet, immaculate in pink and silver Deco. It yielded nothing of interest. Holly entered the door to her left. This diagonal-shaped space was the drawing room. Holly'd been in these old luxury blocks before. When built, the place was grandly adorned with spacious apartments and servants' quarters. As usual, sometime since then the whole place had been carved up, and haphazard partitioning had created lots of little odd-shaped flats.

The drawing-room wallpaper was pastel striped, pink, yellow and peach and the Repro furniture and fittings retained the Deco theme of the building. There was a tiled fireplace with a chrome grate holding false logs from which danced gas flames. The multi-paned windows were of polished brass and overlooked the back of Holland Park. The curtains were heavy full-length velvet patterned in Burgundy and grey, and tasselled. A giant mirror with an etched Thirties' motif of cloche-hatted ladies in long-flowing cocktail dresses occupied one entire wall, and faced a massive sofa with armchairs at either end in the same

Burgundy and grey pattern as the curtains, doubling the size of the room.

A low glass table in the middle was loaded with fashion magazines. No TV or music system was visible. Three tall lamps stood sentinel at carefully thought-out junctures. Framed pictures of Elfa adorned the empty wall spaces.

Holly spotted a teak escritoire in the farthest corner and nipped across the pastel carpet to riffle through the cubbyholes and drawers. Bills, letters, receipts, postcards, an envelope full of negatives – she stuffed that in her pocket – a carved dragon-headed wooden letter-opener, a penknife, sundry pencils, Waterman fountain pen, crayons, a bottle of emerald Quink, a couple of broken watches. No diary, no telephone or address book, no snuff boxes full of white powder. No such luck.

Back in the corridor, the remaining door led into the bedroom. Here the silk bedspread was the same silvery-grey as the patterned wallpaper. Two bedside table drawers yielded nothing but aspirin, Vick's vapor-rub, baby oil, a novel by Manuel Vasquez Montalban, and under piles of brand-new underwear, a packet of condoms and a vibrator. The mirrored walk-in closet was heaven but Holly had no time to enjoy the designer wonders therein. The private bathroom next to the walk-in was in the same immaculate condition as the rest of the place. Unfortunately, Epifania had done her work diligently. Elfa's bathroom cupboard contained nothing out of the ordinary, except in terms of cost. Complete sets of Sisley skin products, a single item of which Holly sometimes splashed out on, were racked in profusion. But there was no diary, and no junkie's works.

Holly heard keys turning the front door dead-bolt. Shit! She skipped out of the room and re-entered the corridor just as Epifania was backing in, struggling to manoeuvre a huge box of groceries.

'Can I help?' asked Holly.

Epifania shook her head as she bustled into the kitchen, sighing, 'I forgot to cancel the weekly delivery order. *Aiyo-bayang!* So much to remember, and now I suppose I'll have to look for a new job and in wintertime too, *akaw, la-lang!*'

Holly suggested she took the edibles home with her, rather than letting them go to waste. Epifania brightened considerably at this.

'You think I could? See this Chinese herbal tea? For slimming – that was Madam's favourite. I drink it myself. Doesn't do me much good, does it?' She slapped her ample thigh and roared with laughter. Stopping suddenly to remake her face in sad contemplation.

'Take it all home, Epifania. If anyone asks, say I told you to.'

Holly was about ready to bail, but she decided to give it one last shot. She'd exploit the Philippine addiction to gossip. She lowered her voice. 'Is there anything, anything at all, Epifania, that you think I should know about Madam's *secret* habits?' She paused dramatically and leant forward. 'Did you, for example, ever come across such a thing as a syringe, a pipe, packets of white powder?'

'Tchaw!' Epifania clucked angrily and slammed her palm on the kitchen table, making the bamboo tray jump a few inches and reveal, peeking out from underneath, what looked to Holly-Jean very much like the corner of a black leather notebook. 'I know they sayin' it was the drogs. But as I told the police, that's all lies. Lies!'

She looked from side to side, moved closer till their noses were an inch apart and clutched Holly's arm. 'I know different.'

'You know different?' pressed Holly, smiling through the cloying emanations, her fingers inching towards the little black book. 'Go on, Epifania. You can tell me.'

86

Epifania fingered the rosary intently, her big brown cow eyes on Holly. 'Yes, I think I can trust you, but you must promise not to tell anyone what I am going to tell you now.'

Holly nodded vigorously. 'I promise,' she lied.

Epifania crossed herself, closed her eyes and began a long prayer in Tagalog. Holly reached out, lifted the tray an inch and deftly pocketed the little black book. Then she had to wait in excruciating anticipation till Epifania finished her supplication. At last the Filipina opened her eyes. She clutched Holly's hands and began to speak in a hoarse whisper.

'*Aiyo-bayang!* Don't be scared by what I am going to tell you, but this is what really happened. As you know, there were no marks of violence on Madam's body. The doors were locked when I came to work as usual. Madam was lying there peaceful as a sleeping babe in front of the fireplace. But when I felt her pulse was gone, that was when I knew.' She hesitated, once more peering bovinely at Holly.

'Tell me, Epifania,' Holly urged desperately. 'Please, I can help.'

Epifania sighed long and aromatically. Crossing herself with an extraordinary elaboration Holly assumed was a deluxe version used for warding off a particularly nasty variety of imminent evil, Epifania glanced heavenward and whispered, 'It was the vampires.'

Holly's heart flipped. 'Vampires?' she echoed weakly.

'They live in Holland Park,' Epifania confided. 'You can see them every day. In the daylight they inhabit the bodies of the pink flamingoes. But at night, they fly into the sky and feed on the living. Madam always left her bathroom window open an inch or two to let out the condensation – the central-heating radiator in that bathroom is faulty. That's where they got in. *Vampires!*' Epifania sat back in triumph.

87

Holly saw herself out as quickly and politely as she could.

Back at Camden Lock, Holly paid off the cab, gingerly negotiated the crowds flocking the market, and entered her studio as quietly as a church-mouse. She looked across the darkened room, and saw by the steady rise and fall of the futon, that Ma was blessedly still sleeping off jet-lag with GiGi curled up on top of her.

Holly opened a chilled bottle of Hugel Gewurztraminer, poured herself a large glass, popped a painkiller and wondered for 0.003 of a second if she was drinking too much these days. At the kitchen table she continued the examination of the little black leather prize begun on the cab-ride home. She'd already checked Elfa's diary-appointments-address book for evidence of trips to Holland. Found them conspicuous by their absence. Concealing the fact?

She flipped through the pages of a clotted life. Practically every time-slot had some kind of scribbled date, shoot, show, city – Milan, Berlin, Barcelona, Dublin, Paris, NYC, London/home.

Holly had fun playing with the names, initials, indecipherable squiggles, spotting the fabulous ones. Ellen V.U., Jean-Paul, Hervé, Wayne H., Thierry, Betty, Gianfranco, Klensch.

Taking her time with a more methodical perusal, Holly found two puzzles: first, a preponderance of the letter K was sprinkled throughout the book (she really hoped it wasn't K for kilo), and second, that NYC was dotted about almost as liberally as London. Always short trips, two days at the most. Why?

She read on. In between the chaotic schedule of individual dates were the big seasonal shows, the Fashion Weeks in Paris, Milan, New York, London and Tokyo. Entire pages blocked-out with bookings. End of January and

February were Fashion Weeks for the Autumn/Fall/Winter shows. In September and October came the Spring/Summer Collections.

Here and there were other biggies. The second week of February was meant to have been Barbados – swimwear for *Sports Illustrated*, followed by four days in Rio for Carnival. A week in Sydney was scheduled in March. April she was due in Ootacamund, of all places, for *Vogue* with Oliver Meisel. *Ai-yo!* The girl got around! *Used to* . . .

Holly was fascinated. This kind of life. Got to have Mercury in your veins. Got to love that perpetual motion. *Keep on keeping on. Yeh!* Nodding, lips pursed, Holly thought: I could handle it. For a while. Flipping through again, a Tuesday in early January caught her eye.

5.45. Milan early call. Taxi! *6.15.* Mario D.'s studio. Outdoor shoot dawn Abbiategrasso. M. lift to airport! Alitalia 11.00 dep. Paris arr. 1.15. **Pre-book* Premier Drive – half-day – request Yann, hunky Croat! Arr. Karl's studio, asap. Fitting for 3.00 HRH D. private show. 5.00. at George V mezzanine tea-room. Interview Mag. Front cover/story Albertine Sonnenberg, pics by Kriega (!) Phone Concorde pre-check-in. CDG. 6.45 for Dep. 7.15 p.m. (+ K?) arr. NYC 5.15 p.m. Duty-free 2 bottles Belle Epoque! 12.00. Tribeca Rest Ivana/She.

Holly noted the Kriega reference. Did that explain all the Ks in the diary? Epifania had copped the German fashion photographer as a regular male visitor to Holland Walk, yet at the Highgate *dojo* shoot in December, Elfa'd appeared just as repelled by the weird black-leather and chains fetish-freak as Holly, and apparently just as anxious to dump him in favour of a drink at Marika's Wine Bar.

Kriega and Elfa? About as unlikely as Ed and Elfa. Holly scratched her spiky black hair. It just didn't make sense. Or did it?

Deceptive appearances were a model's craft. They had to have the chameleon's ability to adopt protective colouring. What else was catwalking but disguise, camouflage? They made their living *dressing-up*, for frock's sake! And not to forget Elfa had kept her friendship with Ed a secret. Maybe the girl had a lot of secrets.

Lost in thought, staring at the diary entry, Holly was momentarily puzzled at the apparent speed of Concorde before she remembered the Transatlantic time difference. The three-and-a-half-hour supersonic flight arrived two hours before you left. Holly wondered how Elfa had filled the four whole hours of freetime before her midnight date at the Tribeca restaurant.

She continued to read through the rest of the diary. It contained no gems. Holly noted that the whole month of November had lines drawn through it and the single word 'Angeles'. Presumably that was a holiday.

Holly checked and found Ed van Schrempft's name and number in the address section. Next to the entry were the letters J.U. with a question mark. She'd tackle Joel later.

Nothing under K for Kriega.

Holly closed the little black book and tiptoed over to the Chinese carpet. Lifted it up and then prised up the loose cork tile in the middle. She dialled the combination of the floor-safe set into the concrete, stashed the book inside and reversed the procedure. Next she stepped over to the trestle workstation. There had been something bothering her. She checked her sticky notes, slapped on the wall above her PC; found the one she was looking for. *0.07 mm low-density polyethylene stretch-film.*

She looked it up in her reference books.

Polyethylene: a tough light translucent thermoplastic

90

polymer of ethylene. Polymer: a compound whose molecule is formed from a large number of repeated units of one or more compounds of low molecular weight – monomers. Ethylene: hydro-carbon of Olefin series – C2H4.

Thank you, she already knew that: a fossil-fuel derivative. Plastic bags from primordial trees.

The question remained, what were traces of it doing on the pierced earring and false eyelashes of the much-beloved and lovely, late Elfa Ericksson? What was the common use of such material? How easily could it be bought? Since no answers to these questions appeared willing to materialise in the middle distance, Holly did what she always did at times like this: she turned to her brainiest pal. Unfortunately, Professor Janet Rae-Smith at SOAS, the School of Oriental and African Studies at London University, was not in for work.

Holly'd forgotten it was Saturday. Using her cellphone from behind the closed bathroom door in the dual interests of not waking Ma and delaying for a few moments longer the cessation of any semblance of peace in the studio, she reached Janet at home in her flat in Old Street.

'Janet? Got any ideas?' she asked, *sotto voce*, after she'd explained the Ma situation and the problem of the polywhatsit.

'Sounds like saran wrap. Why do you want to know?' Holly told her about the traces found on Elfa. Janet said, 'Ever heard of Professor Hegarty at Sheffield For-Path?'

'Sheffield University's Department of Forensic Pathology?' Holly said, referring to the UK's foremost academic institution devoted to the scientific study of criminal forensics, evidence-analysis and criminal psychology.

'Right, Doc Hegarty. Professor Emeritus. Behavioural Forensics and the Psychopathology of the Criminal Mind. A pal of mine. Tell him what you just told me about the traces.

I've got a feeling he'll be interested. And tell him it's time he came down to the Smoke for dinner on me. On second thoughts, strike that: he wouldn't enjoy it now I'm TT. God, Holls, how I do sorely miss the plonk.' Janet was a reformed alcoholic. In the old days they'd have sunk a gallon of Alsace at one lunchtime sitting.

Holly said, 'One day, kiddo, we'll look back on all this and laff!'

A few moments later she reached Sheffield University. The faculty switchboard was extremely reluctant to give out home phone numbers.

'I know it's a Saturday,' inveigled Holly, 'but I'm working on the investigation of a death, possibly murder, of a young woman. I'm absolutely positive Professor Hegarty would be only too happy to have me reach him without delay, and I promise I'll tell him I badgered you rotten.'

The woman on the other end laughed and gave out the number. Sleet and snow were reported to be falling all over the country south of the line from the Humber to the Mersey, so Holly felt pretty confident of catching the Prof at home.

'Doc Hegarty?'

'Yes?' The voice was frail and ancient.

'Janet Rae-Smith said I should call you – my name's Holly-Jean Ho. I've been retained by both the agency and the mother of Elfa Ericksson.'

The Prof had never heard of the dead supermodel. Holly filled him in.

'And Janet? How is the dear girl?'

'She's fine – really well, in fact.' There was an awkward pause. Mutual friends at one remove, not knowing the exact nature of the information access ratio.

'Still ... hitting the old nectar?' asked Doc Hegarty.

'No, no. Totally reformed. AA regular and all that.' Holly

went on to tell Hegarty about Janet's comment concerning the lack of wine at any future dinner the Professor might like to join. She added, liking the old mucker instinctively, 'Since you're obviously of like mind when it comes to the bounty of the old disputed borderland, I'd be only too happy myself to introduce some interesting Alsace varietals and maybe share a mountain of *choucroute* next time you're in town.'

'Can you guarantee Hugel?'

'I'm drinking one right now, so I'll have a bottle on ice for you. If, that is,' she said, 'you can tell me what exactly is 0.07 mm low-density polyethylene stretch-film?'

'Kitchen-strength clingfilm,' came the immediate answer. The old boy's mental faculties were evidently still intact.

'Now why on earth do you think traces of cling film would be found on the dead girl's earring and false eyelashes?' mused Holly innocently.

There was a long silence. Finally, Holly said, 'Doc, you still there?'

'When's the inquest?' asked the Professor.

'Tuesday morning,' replied Holly.

'I must be there,' muttered the old boy. 'There's a very early train gets into King's Cross at eight-twenty Tuesday morning. Could you meet me?'

Doc Hegarty was going to keep the case alive!

'Certainly will! Do you want to tell me why the sudden interest?'

He hesitated for a moment, then said, 'You know, I like the sound of your voice, Miss Holly-Jean. It's a very trusting voice and therefore trustable. If you must know, I have been working for some time now, more than two years, on a series of murders where the victim has been completely embalmed in many layers of clingfilm before being subjected to the most horrific sexual assaults. Death seems to have been prolonged for a considerable time – a plastic tube is inserted

93

through the clingfilm into one nostril to allow the victim to breathe. Despatch appears finally to come as the result of a systematic beating with a padded object which crushes the vital organs.'

Holly held her breath and counted silently.

'So far there have been three similar cases. All the victims have been beautiful young professional females working in Central London. Two from the City, one from the chorus line of a successful musical.'

'Why the clingfilm?' exhaled Holly-Jean, in a hoarse whisper.

'My theory so far posits that the killer is so full of fear of the female body in general and of sexual congress in particular, that he must first completely preclude any physical contact with his victim – thus the protective barrier of clingfilm, before he finally allows his rage free expression.'

Holly said, 'Don't miss that train, Doc. The inquest is scheduled to begin at eleven o'clock at the Middlesex Coroner's Court, which is somewhere in Hammersmith.'

'You'll know me by the hat,' said the Professor, enigmatically.

'You'll know me by the black eye and freshly scraped face.'

'Oh dear,' said Doc Hegarty.

The office phone began trilling in the other room. Ma! She flew across the studio and grabbed the thing just as Ma started stirring.

'Miss ... ah ... Ho?' a Sloaney lady asked.

Holly snarled, 'Do you mean, Miss Holly-Jean Ho, Minister of State for Infinite Possibilities?' Doc Hegarty's story had put her in *that* kind of mood.

'Yaah ... right, um, excuse me one second, won't you?' The phone was covered at the other end, and Holly heard the murmur of conversation before the voice came back on. 'Is that the Miss Ho who is a *Private Investigator*?' She enunciated the last words with the repugnance of one discovering a maggot in her mango.

'I'll see if she's available,' said Holly and put the phone on the trestle worktop, reached down, yanked the jack from the wall, carried the phone to the kitchen end of the studio and rejacked, stretching the coiled lead with her into the bathroom.

'Holly-Jean Ho here, may I help?'

'Yah, super, I'm Catriona Pyles, personal secretary for Adrian Morehouse. Can we set up a meet? Know it's awfully previous, but tomorrowish?'

The stepfather who overstepped with the baby oil. Next on her list to call. Still in that kind of mood, Holly-Jean feigned ignorance and said rudely, 'A Morehouse being whom or what?'

'Yah, right, super, um … Adrian's the Tory MP for Irkdale South. Ring any bells?'

'No bells. Might I ask in what connection this meet?'

'Yah, absolutely, um … it's about his stepdaughter, the model who died recently – Elfa Ericksson, you know?'

'*That* Morehouse. Of course I know. I am currently acting on behalf of the mother in respect of her untimely end.'

'Yah, it was rather thought you were. Late supper a remote possibility?'

'Not too remote. Where?'

'Adrian's staying in town for the weekend, so it was thought perhaps a quiet little drink at Champers Wine Bar, Kingly Street. Nine-thirty or thereabouts?'

'Super, yah,' said Holly and rang off. One good thing at least: Champers was a favourite wine bar and belonged to her old friend Simon Pearson.

The bathroom door was rattled vigorously. 'You in there, Shao-Lan?'

Ma was awake. The plates of Life shifted. Holly's freeway buckled.

'Did you sleep well?' she enquired.

But Ma was already in and out of the bathroom, now hustling around the kitchen, opening the fridge door, pulling out food items and rejecting them. Holly offered to make some simple noodles for breakfast. Ma okayed that, and began to interrogate her daughter.

'So, Little Orchid, any regular boyfriends or are you still being as choosy as the Grand Eunuch on his birthday? And how about an approximation of the truth about that black eye, those wounds!'

But Holly was prepared. 'Sure, sure, we'll talk about that later, Ma. Right now I've got to ask your advice, I'm in a terrible pickle.'

Ma shut her mouth and listened as Holly talked about the agency's current busy workload, exaggerating wildly. She pointed out that Mrs Howell-Pryce was only part-time – the two widows hadn't met yet, but Holly felt there was a good chance of like meeting like and liking – that she really needed someone else to help, was thinking of hiring an office girl to work the computer...

'I've got this sticky job on, tracking these *wan-ba dan* bastards selling child pornography on the Internet. Trouble is, I'm full-time tied up working on the Elfa Ericksson case. I need you to help me interview prospects and then choose an office assistant.'

Ma's eyes had narrowed. 'Tell me about the Internet.'

'The Internet? Oh, that's the way we did the e-mail. It's like the telephone only quicker and cheaper.'

Ma reacted crossly. 'I said *tell* me, don't *luo-shuor* me as though I were some brainless turtle-egg. Of course I've heard of the Internet, but if I'm going to be working for you tracking these *da-bien tou* shitheads, then I need to know exactly what I'm dealing with.'

Holly smiled happily. That was her Ma.

'The Internet is a worldwide system of computer networks that use a common communications protocol – language,' she explained.

'Who owns it?' demanded Ho Ma-ma.

'Nobody. It was started in the late Sixties by the Advanced Research Admin. Division of the US Defense Department so that the boffins in the universities could talk directly to the high-tech defence contractors.'

'It was started to help build better bombs for Vietnam?' said Ma.

'Right,' said Holly, 'but the Net soon spread a thousandfold into what it is today – an anarchic global communication forum accessed on a regular basis by upwards of fifty million people and the numbers are growing by the nanosecond. Unfortunately, the idealistic period of the early years is now mere roadkill on the greed-jammed superhighway.'

'So it's grown too big to control.'

'Exactly. And since electronic communication is global, no one government or agency can start to think about policing it. Some people even fear the Internet might be used by organised crime or extremist groups to bring the global infrastructure to its knees.'

'Ah so,' said Ma. 'They created a benign monster.'

'I think they'd call it a problem child of psychotic tendencies fast approaching psychopathic adulthood. Anyway, by its very nature nobody can subdue it. Oh, they can pass laws, enactable in their various home countries, but there's no global enforcement.'

Ma nodded. 'An unfettered world was something we always dreamed of.'

'Wherein lies the rub, Mum,' said Holly-Jean, using her childhood name for Ho Ma-ma. 'The very freedom inherent in the global communicative forum offered by the Internet allows in everything and anything. Good, bad, and ugly. And some of it is very, very ugly.'

'Got the picture,' said Ma, rubbing her hands. 'So, show me how to get started.'

'First, eat your noodles, you'll need sustenance for the job ahead,' said Holly, placing in front of her mother a bowl of steaming wheatflour noodles in beef stock brimming with chopped scallions, tiny desiccated shrimp, fermented tofu and hacked chunks from the wind-dried Chinese sausage.

Ma picked up her chopsticks, tasted with a loud slurp and immediately complained, 'Where's the *la-ja*, Daughter? I need to pack some heat if I'm going to be "surfing the World Wide Web on the Internet!" Ha!'

Holly looked at the twinkle in Ho Ma-ma's eye and knew she'd been had. Never ever underestimate Ma, Holly reminded herself as she swiftly chopped raw red chili peppers, garlic and a big bunch of fresh coriander leaves, dumped them in a dipping bowl and covered them with Soy Sauce and a little Taiwan-strength sesame oil.

Ma demolished the lot.

They spent Saturday afternoon together at the work-trestle, visiting sites on the WWW. Ho Ma-ma immediately proved even more adept than Holly's wildest speculation. So Holly left her at it while she made calls of her own and caught up with Agency workload. Glancing over at her mother from time to time and watching the little woman's confident handling, Holly chided herself for ever doubting her mother's ability.

Ma liked to come the old Chinky peasant, but that was just her front – a mask she had first put on to deal with the prejudices against mixed marriage in late Fifties' England. She'd explained it to Holly once. 'They think I'm a coolie, I'll act like one.'

Holly called Rita in Rotterdam.

'Pardon the pun, but did you get any dope on whether Elfa had been dealing drugs for Ed van Schrempft?'

Holly still didn't know whether the perfect girl had just a smudge or a real blemish. Suspicion, conjecture, gut-feeling ... she'd loads. Hard truth – *mei-you*!

Unfortunately, Rita couldn't supply. 'Sorry, kid, your friend Ed's spectacular finale has caused a major clenching of sphincters and other orifices. Couldn't even get a nod let alone a wink.'

Holly said, 'Thanks for trying anyway, Rit'.'

'Don't mention it. By the way, Kripo did pay me a visit, and I confirmed your story.'

'Ta, Rit', I miss you.' Remembering Tuesday dawn in Rotterdam after a night of dancing and Tequila slammers, the two of them holding hands as the light came up over the Maas River, watching the giant barges with their lace curtains and window-boxes full of crocuses plying their way up from the Rhine and every corner of the continent to the biggest harbour in the world.

'I miss you too, Holly. You'll be back over soon for your Conference at Den Haag?'

'Yep, end of February. I'll be getting a room at the hotel, and on my feet twenty-three hours a day dealing with that gang of monkeys, but I'm sure I'll find a free moment afterwards. About the twenty-fourth?'

'Great if we can connect.'

The phone rang as she put it down. It was the call she'd been waiting for. Joel Unmack gushed breathlessly over the line, 'You lucky so-and-sod, Aramint's just this minute come through for you. She's got you an invite to the Les Bains-Douches bash!'

'Les Bains-Douches bash?' Holly pretended not to understand.

'The seedy-ritzy public baths in Paris,' explained Joel excitedly. 'They always have the après-shows party there.

Just for the biz people, the designers and the models themselves. They give prizes, it's like a kind of private Oscars – best catwalker, best fun person, best keeper of secrets. I mean it's just the most fab-u-lous-est fashion party of the year – and *the* most exclusive invite in town. I could scratch your eyes out for that ticket!' He paused. 'Only one snag, though.'

'What's that?' asked Holly innocently.

'The party's tonight. Starts around eight. Think you can make it?'

'Think I'd miss it?' said Holly. She'd booked her seat yesterday. Her packed bag was by the door.

Joel said, 'The despatch rider's just left. Should be with you in twenty minutes. Have a divine time, you lucky bitch!'

Holly looked at her watch, three o'clock. Just time to get Ma really started. 'You ready, Ma?'

Ma had obviously been having fun browsing the Web. 'Listen to where all I've been!' she cackled, reading out the homepage sites scribbled on a pad beside the PC. 'The Binders of Splodgeness, Tolkienmaniacs, NASA's Astro-2, Lavamind, Pigs in Cyberspace, Lonely Planet's Virtual Tourist, Random Band Names, Sir Winston's Bogie!' Ma stood up. 'Ai-yai-yai-yai-yai! What lunatics inhabit your so-called cyberspace, *Shao-lan*!'

Holly took over Ma's seat and said, 'Anarchy's fine if the intent is benign, but some of the whacko stuff out there is evil. Maybe the information superhighway is just a highway to hell.' She looked at Ma and said, 'Wouldn't it be ironic if this Tower of Babel we call cyberspace was really the Devil's sublime seduction.'

Ma looked serious. 'Daughter, you mustn't fear the new. The Internet is just another of those rickety rope-bridges of evolution. Halfway across, it starts to sway, you look down into the giddying drop and you get wet knickers. But you can't stand still, you've got to walk on to reach the other

100

side. Remember, we Chinese have always said, "Knowledge is civilisation. Mindlessness is darkness".'

'But that's exactly it,' said Holly. 'By exploiting our urge to learn more and more, Old Nick subliminally feeds our brains through the mangle of gobbledygook.'

'Undoing Socrates, Shakespeare and Siddhartha in a nano-second,' said Ma.

'Right! Or as Doc Hunter used to say, "Kill the head and the body will die".' Holly hugged her mother and said, 'I love you, Mum. You ready to save the world?'

'Daughter, I'm ready. Take me to these toad-lice!'

Holly clicked onto the homepage of the so-called Prawn Club with its red on jet-black graphics and the sinister red prawn logo with the words:

An international network for those men who appre-ciate the unique aspects of life in Asia.
The Prawn Club.
Revealing Asia and the Dawn of Life.

'"Dawn of Life"!' spat Ma fiercely. 'I'm going to take down those *Tser-lan* Coloured Wolf sex-monsters! Don't forget I still remember the days of bound feet. Child-brides sold off at the age of six. The cages where they kept the eight-year-old girls, faces painted over with adult make-up, tiny feet perched inside adult high-heel shoes.'

Holly-Jean knew Ma's anger was real. She'd lived as a child under Japanese occupation, Chinese warlordships, the war: she'd seen it all. Holly was quietly elated. This was the perfect way to drain Ma's boundless energies. At the same time, she'd be able to give COMSEM a dynamic and righteous point-person. Or at least, let Ma as spokesperson for the Agency confuse them with her Hakka razor-brain and motor-mouth.

101

Chapter 7

Holly and Ma got togged up for a Saturday night out.

When the cab arrived it was dusk outside and the weather had stayed clear and frosty. Stepping out, Holly had put on heavy make-up to lessen the unsightliness of her facial scabs. Dressed in a clinging black mixed-silk-nylon fabric smock – a Betty Jackson knock-off that didn't show the rib-bandages – black high-heels, a full-length black raincoat from Harrods' January sale and black shades to hide the shiner, she elicited a cheery leer of appreciation from the cabbie.

Ho Ma-ma looked snug as a bug in a navy wool outfit from M&S, a charcoal Taipei-style padded jacket and a big red and white striped cashmere scarf that covered her head and went round her neck a few times.

Holly dropped Ma off downtown at her favourite old *mien-tang* haunt in Gerrard Street and left her in the company of her old gang. Judging by the crowds of other well-wishers thronging the noodle shop, the return of Ho Ma-ma from Taiwan was hot and happy news on the Street.

'Heathrow,' she told the cabbie.

Her flight touched down at CDG at 6.25. As promised by Ivana and She, a uniformed driver holding her name on a large card was there to meet her. He introduced himself with, '*Yann, à votre service, madame.*' The hunky Croat from Elfa's diary.

103

Yann steered the extended black Cadillac deftly through the insane traffic with little unnecessary conversation, apart from checking the air-conditioning was warm enough, telling Holly to help herself from the bar, and a quick demo on how to use the remote to make a choice from the music menu and operate the CD-player.

Listening to Dinah Washington Live at the Colony Club December 1948, and drinking frozen-syrupy Lemon Stolichnaya Vodka from a Baccarat crystal double-shooter with painkiller popper, Holly felt not entirely glum. Indeed, she experienced a tinge of regret as the limo reached the Left Bank and swished to a halt on the narrow cobbles of Rue Mazarine outside a dimly lit bistro called La Cafetière, with its huge black tin coffeepot hanging over the door. She checked the piece of paper in her hand. This was it; their rendezvous.

She was about to haul herself across the expanse of grey carpet to the door, when Yann's voice came over the intercom. 'I just called Ivana and she says since we're running late already you're please to wait in the car. They'll be out in a minute.'

'Okay, fine,' said Holly, addressing the black glass partition. No problem. Roll on Dinah, roll on Stoly, roll on painkiller.

Actually it was more like ten minutes later when Yann finally opened the back door and helped in the two giggling, tottering, stunningly beautiful women.

'You must be Holly-Jean Ho!' shrieked the white one. 'I'm Ivy, this here's She!'

The tall Eritrean girl collapsed beside Holly on the back seat, waving a fan in front of her face. 'Holly-Jean!' she kissed both Holly's cheeks. 'Sorry we're so out of it! The owner of that place M'sieur Diet's our good pal.'

'Maître Di-et' – Ivana pronounced it in phonic English – 'was definitely named wrong when it comes to champagne

104

cocktails!' She knocked on the partition and shouted, 'Yann! Pedal to the metal fast as you can! We don't want to miss the awards!'

'Pleased to meet you both,' said Holly happily.

Les Bains-Douches après-season party was already in full swing. The dark mosaic-tiled walls lit by flaming torches fanned phantasmagoric shadows to flicker and fade into the gloom of the dark vaulted ceiling. Extravagant floral displays real and unreal hung down on chains. The flights of fantasy prevailed at ground level too. Everywhere she looked, Holly-Jean saw knee-weakeningly beautiful people.

She was sitting at a small candle-lit table halfway back from the stage with the Eritrean model She and Ivana the Russian, but the whole place was so tightly packed that tables merged with each other and chairs shifted with the ebb and flow of partying friends. It was obvious to Holly that everybody knew everybody else intimately.

'So this is divine unreality. I'd always wondered,' joked Holly as she stood up to make her way to the loo.

The ladies' comfort room was full of thoroughbreds doing their faces and powdering their noses, figuratively and literally. Holly smiled wrily at the scene. School's out for summer, she thought, noting one doesn't normally come across talcum powder that blue, crystalline and sparkly, neither does one ingest it up the nostrils with a rolled-up 100 dollar bill, nor for that matter, rub it in one's gums. One girl staggered into a cubicle and threw up noisily.

'You all right, Riza?' last month's *Vogue* cover enquired from the floor where she was propped against the marble wall.

'Nah problem, touch of the wobblies, s'all,' came the reply from the cubicle.

Holly helped the *Vogue* girl up to her feet, and made her

105

way back to her table, her eyes scanning the pulsating room for the German photographer, Kriega. No sign. She'd ask Ivy and She to introduce her later.

The prizes – laurel wreaths – were being awarded.

The MC was a very rotund designer famed for his brilliance but not presumably for the subtlety of his humour. His jokes were so blue, so scatophagic and so politically incorrect as to offend every possible permutation of humanity and thus cancel themselves out.

As the laurel wreaths were perched on those gorgeous heads, hysterical giggling speeches were delivered and there was much kissing of cheeks, air and lips. She won a laurel wreath for most beautiful neck. Hardly surprising, since the jet-black girl was a Handandouin and that tribe of wandering desert nomads were genetically blessed with legs to heaven, proud faces with sharp noses, delicate lips with the perfect pout and elongated swan's necks that defied gravity.

Ivana was given one for being 'party girl nonpareil'.

Since it had been agreed in the Cadillac on the way to the party that they would leave any serious talk till the morning and (this was insisted) that Holly would share their huge suite at Le Bristol, Holly sat back and relaxed, observing all through a film of Belle Epoque pink champagne and painkiller.

The beauties were offguard. They'd dropped their fronts, letting their hair, and in some case, knickers, down to their ankles. People were dancing now, and there was even a 'moshing pit' for wilder slam-dancing at the front of a stage full of hunky male models and some intrepid, or more likely, over-intoxicated girls. Ivana nodded towards a nearby table where an ageing turkey-necked Hollywood goddess was spoonfeeding Beluga caviare to her green-dyed miniature horse, while a few feet behind, a relative of the Queen, eyes firmly shut, glass in hand, fan in other, slid ever so slowly down the wall to rest perfectly supine on the floor without spilling a drop.

Suddenly, loud chords of real live music started clanging; it sounded excellent. Holly, craning her neck to see, was left slackjawed. There were Hutchence, Hucknall and Bono with sundry members of their bands. Holly couldn't believe it. She yelled above the din at Ivana, 'I'm pixycated!'

'So am I, darling!'

'No, I mean that!' She pointed at the stage. 'Music aristocracy become barrelhouse monkeys for their super-model lovers. Desperate stuff, eh?'

But Ivana pricked Holly's bubble of self-righteousnous. 'Darling, everyone knows fashion and pop have become one. Jean-Paul hosts the MTV awards, models cut singles. Anyway, shut up and enjoy the music, you old crab!'

Holly laughed. 'Right, what the frock am I complaining about!' Besides, she wasn't about to miss a chance to see Mick Hucknall, the great contemporary songwriter, live.

Later on, when the band were taking a breather, Ms de Lache stopped by to greet the table, but when the models burst into song, 'Ara-mint! Ara-mint! The too butch to marry-mint!' she stayed only long enough to remark on Holly's wounds, 'You utterly poor thing! Trust you earned those on our *per diem*, darling!'

Watching her retreat, it occurred to Holly that they were all forgetting something. And when an angelic boy at their crowded table sent back his bottle of Belle Epoque because the bubbles didn't make his eyes water, Holly waited till the fresh dark-green bottle with glazed Art Nouveau flowers arrived, and said to the waiter, 'May I?'

The waiter wiped the drips of ice from the bottle on his thigh-length white apron, said, 'As you wish, madame,' handed it to Holly, looked for a free space on the cluttered table, found none, put the ice bucket on the floor at Holly's feet and hurried off. Holding the cork and turning the bottle,

107

Holly eased the champagne free with a skilled hiss and a wisp of smoky gas. When their glasses were replenished, Holly whispered something in Ivana's ear.

The Russian girl jumped to her feet and shouted, 'Stop! We've all forgotten something!' She pushed her way through to the tiny stage. Grabbing the microphone, she screamed for the assembled company to fall silent. It took a while but she eventually succeeded in claiming the attention of the entire throng. Then she dramatically raised her glass and bellowed into the sound system, 'Elfa! Wherever you may be: shine on, you crazy diamond! *Nazhdrovneya!*'

It was a chaotic toast. A maddened *momento mori* but finally those who could, stood, while the rest, in various altered states of adjustment, raised their glasses to honour their departed friend.

What happened next made Holly shiver. For a suspended moment the harsh, glittering façade dulled and a short-circuit of mass-something: love, *amour*, karma – whatever – sparked like lightning round the room. All motion ceased. The place became silent enough to hear a diamanté pin drop. As though holding a communal breath.

Words came unbidden into Holly's mind. Flesh retired, saints were dumb, and through the earthquake, wind and fire, a still small voice of calm. *Love*. And then the Salon Des Bains-Douches erupted to a deafening chant of, 'Elfa! Elfa!' and following Ivana's Russian example, glasses were flung against the flickering torch-lit walls, the sound of breaking crystal a gentle tinkling against the background cacophony as the drummer hit the snares one-two-three and the band belted out the Beatles' 'Back in the USSR'.

Holly turned to She and said, 'You know Kriega the German photographer? Is he here?'

'Creepy Kriega? Yeuch!' was She's response.

Ivy leant across and said, 'I think I saw him arrive just now. This about Elfa?'

Holly nodded. 'I'd like to talk to him.'

Ivana shook her head. 'If you knew what I knew, you'd steer a mile away from that man – but we'll talk about that tomorrow.'

'I want to meet him now, Ivy,' insisted Holly.

The Russian stood up. 'If you must, then all right, let's go and find him. But just remember one thing: the man's strictly bad news. And I mean bad.'

They eventually found Kriega at the buffet, with a fat King Edward cigar clenched between his teeth, talking to the rotund designer and laughing at something said. His head had been shaved not too recently and a fuzz of blond stubble covered his cranium and his beardline. His tall muscle-pumped frame was so tightly encased in some new synthetic black fabric, that it seemed spray-painted. Closer in, Holly saw by the nipple rings that it really was.

Apart from a tiny thong covering his genitals, Kriega was buck-naked, the black body-paint had been so skilfully applied that the *trompe-l'oeuil* was perfectly executed.

Holly and Ivana stood and watched as Kriega spooned a huge mound of Beluga onto a large slice of gravadlax which he had first rolled into a cone and crammed with slices of white and black truffles, fashioning it to resemble a weird ice-cream cornet which he then topped off with a thick dollop of fresh dill sour cream and a sprinkling of capers.

Stubbing the cigar into the eye of the fast-melting ice-sculptured elephant, he carefully inserted the whole cone into his mouth and with two chews swallowed the lot.

The rotund designer bounced on his feet and clapped his pudgy hands.

'That was about two hundred quid a chew,' muttered Ivana, approaching. 'Hey, Kriega, you ugly Kraut! Think you met my friend before. Holly-Jean Ho.'

Kriega ignored Ivana and gave Holly a cool slow

appraisal. Dropped his head to one side as if another angle would help the recall. His eyes widened. 'I really like those wounds. Are they real or accessories?'

'They're real,' said Holly drily. 'You took pictures of Elfa Ericksson with me at my *dojo* in Highgate.'

Kriega snapped his finger. 'The Queen of Kung-Fu. How could I ever forget?' He turned to the designer and said, 'This tiny creature is a very dangerous breed. She's got black belts in just about everything, am I right?'

Holly shrugged.

The designer reached out and kissed her hand, '*Enchanté, ma petite femme fatale.*' Holly blushed. Couldn't help it. She'd always loved the fat-boy's clothes.

'*Fatale* is right, so be warned!' snarled Ivana as she took the designer off by the elbow, leaving Holly for the moment alone with Kriega.

He picked up a black leather satchel from the floor and lit a fresh cigar, first offering the pack to Holly who declined with a shake of her head. But she was curious. She'd never seen that brand of wooden cigar box.

'They're not King Edwards, then?'

Kriega blew out a thick cloud of delicious-smelling smoke. 'I only smoke Philippine tobacco,' he announced. 'These are handmade for me personally in Manila. Do you mind?'

'Actually, I'm enjoying it,' said Holly. 'I know I shouldn't – the evils of second-hand smoke and all that – but a good cigar does smell really enticing when first lit. Reminds me of Christmases with my dad when I was a child.'

Kriega studied her, savouring the cigar. 'Your father is dead?'

Holly looked him in the eye. Discerned the question wasn't merely to shock. There was intent. Something darker. She nodded.

'Miss him?'

'You miss Elfa?'

His eyes narrowed and locked into hers, challenging. Holly immediately perceived that Kriega was an adept of some kind and quite advanced. As to which particular esoteric discipline she was as yet unclear. Crystal-clear, however, was the fact that her own debilitated awareness left her extremely vulnerable. She would therefore lure not repel and so, for once, she didn't summon her *chi* to penetrate and intimidate. Instead she softened her focus to drift alluringly so that his eyes met an unpierceable, unknowable sheen which mesmerised like the sea in that moment of suspended time when the sun dips below the distant purple horizon.

Kriega blinked first. Smiled and bowed his head. Whether sincere or teasing Holly couldn't tell; she did note however that the ash on his cigar had grown two inches.

Steady hands on this dangerous monkey.

'We must get together again,' said Kriega suavely. 'I want you in another shoot – just you this time. I must think carefully. The place. The style. The energy. All must be perfect. That is absolutely vital.' He reached a card from his satchel. 'I have studios in New York, here in Paris, in Flensburg, northern Germany, Denmark, and in the Philippines. I will facilitate. Money, tickets, all. Do you have a card?'

Holly fished one out.

Kriega read it and slapped his forehead, exclaiming, '*Ach so! Alles klar!* I forget everything. You are the private dick!'

'Private clit, is the preferred terminology,' said Holly.

Ivana and the designer returned just in time to hear this last exchange and burst into roars of laughter. Holly and Kriega then moved off into different orbits of the riotous party, though from time to time their stares would meet with uncanny synchronicity across the crowded room.

At three in the morning, Yann appeared and with a little difficulty managed to persuade She, Ivana and Holly into the Cadillac and delivered them safely to Le Bristol.

Arms linked, with Holly hugged in the middle, they sallied across the carpet to the concierge with only four changes of tack. Collected the electronic key-card with straight faces and veered at a pronounced list over to the nearest elevator, where inside their inane expressions staring back from the mirror broke the dam of giggles. They staggered hysterically as the doors opened on the sixth floor and tried to do the silly walk of over-lapping left feet, right feet all the way down the corridor to their suite. After much fumbling with the key-card, they finally achieved entry to the room. In drunken-belaboured stages, accompanied by the choruses of old pop songs they finally managed to strip, shower and collapse onto the suite's king-size bed. Staring up at the ornate embellished ceiling and the giant chandelier on low dim, they talked of many things; of stories old and dreams anew, of imaginings, of secrets, of wants. As the night deepened they drew closer and closer until the talk faded away and another kind of energy embraced them.

Mindful of Holly's cracked ribs they softy slid and slipped, gently rocked and rode, a sweet shared entanglement of skin, fur, limbs. Of touch, lick and succour. Of scents, gasps and sighs of release, as all imbibed that most secret liquor.

At nine in the morning, Holly woke and padded to the bathroom in an out-of-body experience which grindingly morphed as she peed into a hangover so horrendous that it had apparently completely severed the connection between mind and body. Despite which she dutifully called home to check on Ma.

'You're not going to believe this, *Shao-lan*!' yelled her mother. 'I've been up all night on the computer. You know the Prawn Club always carries a Celebrity Special?'

112

Holly's mouth emitted a croaked affirmative.

'You'll never guess the *wan-ba-dan*'s latest offering.'

Holly re-croaked.

'Pictures of your friend Elfa at about the age of eleven. Very serious stuff, I'm sorry to tell you. I can't bear to look at them. You'll see them when you get home.'

Holly managed goodbye. Then she sat looking out at Paris chewing painkillers while her brain tried to assimilate Ma's information.

She was still sitting in the same position when Ivana and She woke at eleven and ordered breakfast from room service. Holly took her turn under the shower. No one did much talking, other than to remark upon the exceptional quality of the hangover.

Then the waiters arrived with fresh flowers, baskets of tropical fruit and silver pots of steaming fresh coffee, including a small jug of espresso for Holly. The gloom lifted considerably thereafter as the smell of coffee mingled with the scents of flowers, fruit, freshly baked baguette, croissants, brioches and Disques Bleues cigarettes.

The girls had both ordered steak tartare and Ricard pastis. Holly was wondering about the state of their taste-buds when she realised that since waking they'd both smoked Disques Bleues like chimneys. Which explained it.

Looking around at the borderline-gross luxury, Holly said, 'On the whole, fashion people don't let reality inconvenience them, do they?'

'Better believe it,' said Ivana, tearing a croissant.

Holly said, 'Time to talk, do you mind? Elfa's death. I take it you agree it wasn't suicide or a mistake of some kind, an over-indulgence.'

She said, 'You get all these twenty-year-olds, give them huge amounts of money, fame and power, you'd better expect a few tragedies.'

Holly was shocked at the apparent callousness. But then

Ivana said, 'Take no notice of her, she doesn't mean it. She loved Elfa so much, she just can't handle her being gone. Isn't that right, you lonesome desert nomad?'

She responded by stubbing out a cigarette and forking a mouthful of raw spiced beef into her mouth. 'Mmm. Just like home.'

'Whaddayamean?' said Ivana.

'Don't you know? Raw beef is the national dish of Ethiopia.'

'Thought you were Eritrean.'

'Nah: we Handandouin don't care for borders, names and flags.'

Holly got serious. 'When I called you the other night and explained who I was and what I was trying to do – namely, discover the truth about Elfa Ericksson's death – you both seemed really supportive. Somehow, amazingly, you got de Lache at the very last minute to produce an invite to the Les Bains-Douches party. You made me so very welcome and I'll never forget last night.' Three pairs of eyes met and shared a tender acknowledgement. Holly continued, 'For all of which I really want to say a big, big thanks.' She hesitated. 'But now you seem to be avoiding the subject. Ivana, She, I desperately need your help. I want the truth.'

Ivana yawned and said, 'It's probably just the hangover. Ask away.'

Holly said, 'Okay. Was she dealing?'

She choked on her Pastis. 'Don't mince words, do you?'

'Elfa sold a bit of Bob Hope now and then, nothing serious,' said Ivana casually.

'Just Ganja,' agreed She. 'Nothing *hard*. The heroin story is a load of utter rot! I knew Elfa like my own sister and I never saw her so much as sniff anything hard.'

'So how did the heroin get into her system?'

114

'I straight out don't believe there *was* any heroin,' said She.

When Holly told her she'd read the Medical Examiner's report confirming the heroin, She just shrugged and looked away, shaking her head.

'All right then, who was she selling the grass to – the other models or people outside the business?' asked Holly.

'Look, don't get the wrong idea,' said Ivana. 'Elfa wasn't a big connection or anything like that. Just occasionally someone'd ask, she'd get a bit of draw for them. She never distributed herself.'

'Joel Unmack?'

Ivana shrugged.

'Well, did he sell it outside the business?' asked Holly. She was hoping to narrow the area of her search to the confines of fashion. Some confines.

'No, I think it was all fashion people; staff mostly. Designers' assistants, pattern-cutters, seamstresses, photographers' gophers.'

'Not the other models?'

'The models can't handle the munchies you get from dope,' giggled She.

'Too right,' said Ivana.

A waiter came in to clear the table, and Holly ordered glasses of Marc de Calvados all round. To thaw tongues.

'Where was she getting her supply, do you know?'

'Where everybody gets it,' said Ivana.

'Holland?'

Ivana pursed her lips but didn't disagree.

'Ever hear her mention a guy called Ed?'

Both shook their heads.

Holly persisted: 'Well then, will someone please explain to me why Elfa was dealing dope in the first place? It simply doesn't add up. She didn't need the money, so why take the risk? Endure all the hassle?'

115

Ivana answered. 'I've thought about it a lot, tried to make sense of it too. I came up with this – for what it's worth. Elfa wasn't just a model, right? You know she was also a competitive athlete when she had the time. She was always pushing the limits. She liked to – no, *needed* to – live on the edge. Isn't it true athletes get addicted to the adrenaline, the endorphins? I think selling dope, taking that kind of risk, the intrigue, y'know, was just another way to keep the adrenaline at full throttle.'

Holly digested that. 'Did Elfa have a lover?'

The girls exchanged glances.

'She may have had, we've both been speculating,' said Ivana. 'In recent months, Elfa became a bit weird, secretive. Really worried us.'

'Yeh, we'd always been tight as that,' said She, crossing her index and third fingers. 'The three of us used to hang together even when we weren't working.'

'We *partied*, you understand?' said Ivana, giving Holly a meaningful glance.

Holly got the message: the three friends' relationship was intensely close. Physically and emotionally.

'But then in the last few months,' said Ivana, 'Elfa kept suddenly disappearing for days at a time. Could never find her. Really worried us at times.'

'Yeah,' agreed She. 'Like that time she just turned up at a show in New York, walked in off the street fresh as a daisy, remember?'

'Whereas we were all jet-lagged from Concorde,' said Ivana.

'So you thought—'

'So we thought maybe she had someone "special" in New York.'

'Like who?' asked Holly.

'That's just it – we don't know. She wouldn't tell us.'

'So you speculated,' said Holly. 'And came up with?'

116

'Speculation isn't going to do you much good, is it?'

'When you've got nothing else, speculation'll do very nicely, thanks. Though I guess you're referring to Paddy Fistral.'

Ivana cocked her head to one side.

'The gorgeous one? Possibly. There's no doubt he's a wild boy. Typical soul-buddy for Elfa, always way out there riding the big waves or playing the big stadiums. Always on the furthest-out edge.'

'Don't worry,' said Holly-Jean. 'He's top of my list. It's just been extremely difficult tracking him down to earth. His manager doesn't even seem to know how to get hold of him.'

'Like, we said, he's a wild one.'

Holly looked at the hungover angels. She sensed something wasn't quite right. They were holding something back. She noted the troubled look in the Handandouin girl's amber-petalled eyes.

'Something's still bothering you, isn't it, She? Was there ... someone else?'

She hesitated looking at Ivana for help. 'Only a maybe...'

Holly reached out and clutched the girl's hands. 'Who?' she urged. 'Tell me.'

It came to Holly with the slick motor-drive of a Leica on high-speed exposure. She spoke softly. 'It was Kriega wasn't it? You've been speculating that Elfa was seeing Kriega?'

She shrugged no denial.

'Well,' said Holly, quaffing some mineral water, 'I think you're definitely wrong about that. She told me she thought him "peculiar".' Holly went on to tell them about Elfa's cold-shouldering of the German photographer after the Highgate shoot. When she'd finished, Holly noted they didn't seem particularly convinced. Ivana lit up yet another

117

Disque Bleue and abruptly changed the subject. 'Did you see what John G. was wearing? He looked like a cross between a pale rastafarian plumber and a Bosnian militia man.'

'I know. I can hardly believe he showed up looking like that. Yet his designs are just so gorgeous.'

'Divinest!'

They talked idle fashion-world gossip for a while. Fascinating stuff, maybe, but Holly sensed she hadn't got the true story yet and she asked, 'Why did you feel there was something wrong about Elfa the last few months? Tell me more about it.'

Ivana looked bored but eventually spoke first. 'Look, if you knew Elfa well, you could never imagine her, well ... scared is the way I saw it.'

She said, 'Elfa always used to be so full of positive vibes. Nothing could bring her down; she was our gang's boss. But starting round about last autumn she began to change. Lost her happy-go-lucky fizz. Seemed unsure of herself.'

'Something or someone put a dimmer on her lights,' said Ivana.

Holly thought, If this were true at the Highgate shoot before Christmas, Elfa was hiding her torments well. All Holly could remember was the dazzling energy.

'And now she's dead with a discernible amount of heroin in her system,' she observed. She didn't mention Elfa's new starring role on the Internet. It would only bring more heartache. Besides, Holly was damned if she was going to help in the inevitable breaking news of that evil violation. The Prawn Club might be a secretive organisation, but once on the Net, word of Elfa's pictures would eventually seep out and somebody would call the tabloids for a few pieces of silver – if the professional muck-rakers hadn't already down-loaded themselves.

* * *

Long after breakfast was cleared and the Parisian afternoon had all but drifted lazily away, Holly said goodbye. The three girls exchanged reachable numbers and made a promise to get together as soon as they could.

Holly arrived back in London at eight in the evening. By the time she'd cleared customs and queued for a cab it was nearly nine, so she called Ma from the cab and went directly to Champers Wine Bar, that epicurean delight discreetly tucked away behind Liberty's.

'Nothing dreary dietarily, I trust. Half the folk one meets nowadays are veggies or lacto-halal-vegan-cudchewers. You're not? Splendid. Then oysters and shampoo do you? I know oysters can be a problem with some chaps.' The Right Honourable Adrian James Morehouse MP, dressed in cavalry twill, dark green Harris tweed hacking jacket, blue striped open-neck shirt and purple paisley silk cravat, might have already had a few.

'No problem at all. Oysters will be fine – may I choose the wine?' Holly smiled disingenuously.

'Certainly may!' replied the MP. 'Ah, that is, within the bounds of reason, pricewise.'

'Got you.' Holly chose well – as long as he was picking up the tab. The place was quiet. Weekends, the TV and Ad agency crowd that worked around here were at their country cottages and they had the front window to themselves.

The superb food came, served by Holly's old friend the congenial host, Simon Pearson himself. Hauled by the basket fresh from the pristine ice-cold sea-loch water and onto the overnight train, the Loch Fyne oysters on ice were accompanied by an exquisite and uncommon bottle of Cramant Cremant by Mumm.

Holly squeezed lemon and a single drip of Tabasco on hers.

'Tuck in,' said Morehouse. ''Fraid I've got to catch a late meeting. Bit of a rush.'

'Don't worry on that score,' said Holly, vestiges of hangover still lingering as she turned up her mouth to let one of the edible bivalve molluscs slide down her throat, followed by a wash of Cramant.

Simon had waited to see if the wine was in condition. Morehouse sipped, pursed his lips and tasted. He nodded in appreciation and with an expectant glance at Simon Pearson, as though to say, 'Watch the silly bint handle this: it'll be good value', he asked, all oleaginate good humour, 'I'm fascinated by your choice of fizz. Not one I'm altogether familiar with. Since you're obviously a wine buffo, why don't you describe it for us?'

Without putting down her glass, Holly said *sans* hesitation, 'Creamy but citrus-zesty, punchy with grape yet beneath the vanilla silk you quickly become aware of one arid mother of a dry boner breaking through, you patronising pillock.'

Simon clapped his hands and said charmingly, 'Absolutely right. On both counts.'

Morehouse pouted for a minute, till Holly clinked his glass, said, 'Howzat?' and he shrugged in reply, 'Clean bowled, I should say.'

They laughed in somewhat strained fashion and Simon went off to his other customers. After an awkward silence, Morehouse asked about Holly's wounds. 'Were they received in the course of what I imagine is rather a fascinating line of work?'

'You tell me,' she said, deadpanning. It was worth a try. But the MP's face gave nothing away. As for her line of work, she said, it was in turn fun, boring, safe, dangerous. She asked him about politics.

'You could probably say the same,' he drawled.

The oysters and wine passed on in less than ten minutes.

120

He cut to the point. 'I'm very concerned to protect the reputation of my stepdaughter. I would hope very much to be able to persuade you to drop any further investigation and let the dead rest in peace. Surely no good can come of any further digging and delving? The only certain result will be the sullying of my dear stepdaughter's name.'

The dead? Dear stepdaughter? The name was Elfa. This chap was displaying major signs of avoidance.

'And perhaps your own?' observed Holly.

'I wouldn't pretend,' he smiled deeply, suavely, know-ingly, attempting a hint of seduction as he fondled the stem of his champagne flûte, 'that as a politician it would not be in my interests to have anything of a personal, private family nature kept less than a million miles out of the gutter tabloids. However, in respect of Elfa, I have absolutely nothing to hide.'

Holly looked at him frankly. 'You're positive about that? You know I've talked with your estranged wife.' Not to mention certain photos.

Morehouse seemed unperturbed. 'You may take anything *she* says with at least gallon of gin.'

Sipping her wine, Holly remarked casually, 'Have you ever been interested in photography? Darkroom, that sort of thing?' From behind her glass she studied his face carefully.

Apparently genuinely puzzled, Morehouse replied, 'Not inordinately, why?'

Holly said, 'Hobby of mine, actually. Anyway, back to Elfa. The complete absence of track-marks on her body belies she had been an intravenous user. She might have been a sometime smoker, a *Chaser of Dragons*, but without an autopsy the relatively tiny amount of heroin found in the bloodstream of what was a perfectly fit young woman suggests otherwise. The obvious unlikelihood of suicide in one so successful and apparently universally loved makes that theory seem hogwash. Also: I've yet to find even the slightest hint of animosity towards your stepdaughter, let alone anyone remotely resembling such a thing as an enemy. Face it: the common consensus is your stepdaughter was an angel. But then *why* did she die? I'm determined to find out the truth, and I'd have thought you'd be only too happy to help me.'

Morehouse used his finger to adjust his cravat. 'Of course I want the truth, but can't you see, she's *dead*, for God's sake! Nothing can bring her back. And all this muddying of the water is just going to leave her memory dirty and marred.'

Is it, thought Holly. How come he's so sure?

'Which is precisely why we can't let her go to her grave the "victim of accidental death",' she said. 'It leaves too many unanswered questions: too much room for innuendo, conjecture and fiction. That's why, out of respect and love for her, we go for the absolute truth.'

She didn't mention the clingfilm killer or Professor Hegarty. Nor did she confront him with the news that photos taken at the time of his stepdaughter's adolescence, a time when he was still living with her, were currently fanning across the globe. She knew it was only a matter of time before the word got out, at which point Morehouse would have to face both the press and probably the police.

If he were responsible for the photos, she didn't want him forewarned.

If he weren't responsible – after all, Elfa's modelling career was already well advanced at that time, plenty of photographers had the young girl in their lenses – then she didn't want to add to his heartbreak.

Or was she just being plain chicken?

Dog-tired and hungover is what she really was, so frock all this introspection.

'Besides, it's out of my hands,' she said finally. 'The inquest takes place on Tuesday and from what I understand, information from other sources, not myself, will be presented and a stay on the release of body will probably be granted.'

Morehouse became clearly agitated; his fingers gripped the stem of the champagne flûte with white-knuckled intensity. When it came, his voice was strangled.

'They're going to defile her, aren't they?' he said.

Holly felt pity. 'Yes, they probably will.'

'They're going to cut her up into pieces for scientific experiment!' he looked away. 'My God, can't you let her be! Desecrating my sweet angel, *and for what end*?'

Holly felt the emotion was genuine enough. But was it inspired by love of his stepdaughter, or fear of what might be revealed?

Morehouse fell silent then and after a few more awkward minutes, called for the bill and settled. He nodded and left, unable it seemed even to speak.

Holly shivered.

No human with a heart that beat could be anything but cowed by the thought of a body, any body, let alone one that you have known and loved, going under the pathologist's knife.

Chapter 8

Monday was spent licking wounds, mulling over ideas and doing chores around the studio. First thing in the morning, Holly had the messenger service deliver a bottle of very pink urine (whether blood from damaged kidneys or the stain of too much Belle Epoque remained to be seen) over to the Royal Free.

Next she endured the ordeal of a careful examination with magnifying glass of the pictures Ma had down-loaded of Elfa. It was her unavoidable duty to look for clues.

Like the fact that on first observation, the eight pictures had all been taken at the same time by the same camera in the same room. Colour, good quality.

Like the signet ring and the dark hairs on the middle finger next to the inserted index. The distinctive scar suggestive of shrapnel entry on the male adult thigh near Elfa's chin. The Lady Penelope doll's riding-to-hounds outfit. The titles on the spines of the books piled in two columns on which were placed Elfa's bare feet as she squatted above a glass with ice and slice of lemon. The background William Morris repro wallpaper against which Elfa did a split-headstand...

Holly-Jean studied Elfa's eyes for any tell-tale dilation which might indicate drugging, but couldn't say for sure. The young girl's expression in most of the photos was blank, if not even a bit relaxed. Disconcertingly, there appeared to be no sign of fear, hatred, or compulsion. Or maybe that *was* evidence of doping. No good: Holly-Jean needed a far closer look.

She called the photo lab she always dealt with when analyses of print-jobs were needed in her I.P. Copyright Infringement cases. She spoke to the boss, Beth Lawton, herself. Explained the extremely sensitive nature of the material and thus the reason she requested electron-enhancement of all eight photos to the highest degree that Beth's equipment could produce. Before she allowed Beth to down-load she secured her solemn promise that she and she alone would handle the photos.

In the afternoon, when Ma was off visiting her pals for mah-jong, gossip and Oolong *cha* at the Temple of the Merciful Goddess, Kuang-Yin in deepest Chinatown, Holly had a heavy telephone conversation with Joel Unmack. She was in no mood for fey games and she threatened him with exposure to de Lache if he didn't tell her the whole truth as to the extent of Elfa's drug-dealing. Since de Lache turned out to be an occasional customer, that threat didn't work. Holly-Jean really lost it then: she called Joel a miserable spineless coward, who was possibly responsible for Elfa's death, which if indeed turned out to be the case, she would personally rearrange his sexual apparatus prior to approaching her 'friends in the police' to ensure evidential inevitability of a prison term in Brixton and the subsequent auctioning of his body among the black gang bosses.

Joel broke down at that and tearfully swore that the dealing with Elfa was just as Ivana and She had described. Small-time, fashion business only. Nobody outside a very small group. Not very big quantities.

'How not big?'

'Half a weight at the most.'

Eight ounces. Plenty enough to send her to gaol. What had Elfa been thinking of! Holly-Jean spent the rest of Monday waiting for Tuesday.

* * *

Tuesday morning she drove early over to King's Cross
station, leaving Ma alone at the studio, having first
prepared her for the arrival of Mrs Howell-Pryce to do her
part-time shift. She had also taken the sensible precaution
of calling Mrs H-P at home on Monday evening to fill her
in on the sudden change of environment at the Camden
Lock studio. Fingers crossed, the two widows would get
along.

Doc Hegarty presented no surprises. Turned out to be as
sprightly an old boy as their brief telephone conversation
had suggested. Wire-rimmed specs, white moustache and
long wispy side locks, the rest of his head covered by an
Oakland Raiders cap.

They reached the Middlesex Magistrate's Court in good
time and found the inquest was being held on the fourth
floor. It was over in fifteen minutes. The presence of
Professor Hegarty, one of the country's leading forensic
pathologists, caused a rumpus among the assembled press,
police and court officials, not to mention the Coroner
herself.

Coroners come from all walks of life, and this one had
clearly come from local politics. As soon as it was quietly
explained to her by the police officer representing the Met,
after he'd got over his own shock at seeing Doc Hegarty
arrive, that 'new information, not yet to be released to the
public, in the interests of our ongoing investigations', had
been discovered and that the 'renowned, and most eminent'
Professor Hegarty would be helping in the enquiry, she
pronounced an immediate stay of release of the body.

After a quiet confab at the Bench with the Doc and the
police officer, she set a date for the Coroner's Court three
weeks hence and adjourned the inquest. As they were
leaving, Holly was unpleasantly disconcerted when Beezer
the Special Branch officer, lurking in his Barbour jacket just

inside the door, pushed through the mêleé and wished Holly and the Doc a hearty good morning.

'Un 'onour, Professor, a real 'onour, loik. Be seeing you, Miss Ho,' he grinned like a shit-eating monkey.

Doc Hegarty wanted to be dropped off at St Mary's to start without further delay his post-mortem work on the body of Elfa Ericksson.

'Where're you going to stay?' asked Holly as they drove up through Shepherd's Bush. 'I'd offer you my sofa-bed, but it's occupied. Man, is it *occupied*.'

'No need, I've booked at the Bonnington on Southampton Row. Changed a lot in recent years, and not for the better, I might add. Full of tourists yammering away nowadays, but where isn't?'

Holly clucked sympathetically.

Hegarty mused, 'Used to be marvellous after the war. Serena, my wife – the dear lady has passed on, I'm sad to say – used to come down when I was still at Cambridge getting my Ph.D. We always stayed at the Bonnington, went to the Opera – standing up in the gods, of course – and afterwards ate cheap Italian in Soho. I'll never forget the Bonnington's wafer-thin toast and homemade marmalade at breakfast.'

'Here we are,' said Holly, stopping outside the hospital. 'Our Alsace dinner has to be tonight, I'm afraid, because I'm probably going to be in and out of the country these next few weeks.'

'Tonight will be fine. Shall we say seven at the hotel lobby?'

'Seven it is,' said Holly, passing his overnight bag out through the door.

'Just remember it's got to be a Hugel Gewurztraminer.'

'No worries, Doc, it will be. Have a nice one!' Cutting up bodies.

Dinner with Doc Hegarty at Les Amis du Vin was a

mixture of highs and lows. The wine was indeed Hugel Gewurztraminer and in excellent condition, but the *choucroute* was a mountain of sauerkraut and meats far too high for the two of them, though delicious all the same. GiGi would be eating like a King for a week.

The autopsy, discussed in the flickering candle-light after the meal was over in deference to taste, and with a third bottle already half-empty, proved a similarly mixed affair.

'Well, lass, following a day's worth of wet work,' said Doc Hegarty heartily, 'I'm afraid I have both good and bad news as far as your investigation's concerned. Your search for the truth about Elfa Ericksson's death appeared at first to progress no further. That's the bad. The good news is the fact that your friend's last moments of life seemed not to have been at the hands of a maniac. At least not at the hands of my maniac.'

He went on, 'I had an assistant from the Yard's Pathology Unit – Sheila Benson. We've worked many times together before. She's excellent.'

Holly nodded.

Warming to his story, the Doc carried on, 'We undertook an extensive and complete examination of the body. No external damage at all. No indication of restraints on wrists or ankles. We completed a full dissection of the entire area from larynx to trachea, a so-called peeling of the throat, and there wasn't the slightest evidence of ligature.

'We were looking for signs of the trauma associated with the other victims of our madman. Thankfully, we found none. The internal organs were all in good condition. The heart was that of an athlete. No bones were broken, muscle fibre in perfect shape. There had been none of the systematic beatings to produce the meat-pounding effect found in the other cases.' He took a drink, and smacked his lips in pleasure. 'Aah, such lovely stuff, "the tears of the

129

Rhinemaiden", they call it. Only wish Janet Rae-Smith could have joined us, but you were probably right not to ask her. It would be inhumanly cruel to drink this in front of her. I'll pop over and see her in the office tomorrow before I go back home. Here's to you, Jan!' They clinked and gulped some more. 'Anyway, we opened up the lungs and examined for evidence of opiates or other drugs in the mucus membrane of the lung-walls. Only nicotine tar was present. Nothing else.'

'No *Dragon-chaser*, she,' murmured Holly-Jean.

'The contents of stomach and the entire intestinal tract were analysed. Your friend hadn't eaten for over eight hours at the time of death, and her last meal consisted of at least one full packet of chocolate digestive biscuits and a large mug of Ovaltine made with full-cream milk.'

'Some diet for a model,' commented Holly.

'Do you think we ought to ah, should we, um?' said Doc Hegarty, emptying his glass.

'Why not?' said Holly, signalling the waiter.

'Talking of wine,' continued the Professor, 'the toxicology report showed that apart from the heroin and a residue of diazepam – probably a Valium taken before bed, there was only alcohol toxicity – the presence of extracted juniper berry, ginger, nutmeg and quinine, strongly suggesting the drink was gin and tonic.

'We took scrapings from the congested nasal membrane, and the presence of heroin in fine powdered form was detected in the thick mucus indicative of a nasty head-cold. We therefore concluded the drug was ingested by nasal inhalation. A line or two of heroin at most.'

Holly nodded as Doc poured the new wine.

'Examination of the vagina revealed the presence of a spermicide commonly found coating a condom, and a high degree of both natural and artificial lubrication – baby oil, the latter. As for the former, glandular secretion was evident in such quantity as to suggest that your friend had been in a highly pleasurable state of sexual arousal some time before she died.'

'How much time before she died?' asked Holly.

'Impossible to pinpoint,' replied Professor Hegarty. 'We can only say it occurred after the time of her last internal cleansing. As she was found in her nightgown and underpants, and since her body was in a clean condition, an intelligent guess would be sexual activity took place some time after her bedtime shower.'

'Meaning the lover came and went in the night. Must have had a key of his own. No sperm, so no DNA. Shit.'

Doc looked at Holly's disappointed expression and said, 'Be very thankful, my dear girl, that this is all we found and not what we were looking for. Far better your friend should die in the afterglow of love-making than to endure the evil expression of a madman's rage and self-loathing.'

'But then what did Elfa die of, Doc?' asked Holly. 'And what about the clingfilm and the false eyelashes?'

'Ah well, that was the puzzling part,' he said, picking up a piece of ripe Camembert and masticating slowly between sips of wine. 'By gum, that tastes good! When we opened up the cranium and cut into the brain, we found no haemorrhaging, or any sign of rupture of the blood vessels which might cause sudden death. No sign of haematoma; brain tumour. No haemostasis: no stoppage of bloodflow. Nor any rigidity of the neck tendons or other marks of trauma on any of the blood vessels to the brain precluding catalepsy or loss of consciousness caused by seizure or fit.

'In fact, we were getting rather bloody-well mystified until we noticed the rupture of some veins around both eyes, as sometimes occurs when a diver goes too deep, too fast and the change of pressure results in bursting capillaries. Or,' he paused to drink, 'as when sudden asphyxia occurs. The defective aeration of blood. Suffocation through lack of oxygen.' Holly must have looked puzzled in the candle-light. 'Like a blocked windpipe, for instance. You've heard of people choking to death on a piece of bubble-gum or even a ham sandwich. But then we'd already examined the entire throat from larynx to trachea and found nothing there. I was just beginning to wonder whether it might be time to chuck in the old rubber gloves and call it a day once and for all, when Doctor Benson thought to check the police bag containing the victim's clothes and possessions at time of death.'

Holly wondered what was coming.

'A pink rubber baby's pacifier – a dummy – was labelled as having been found a few feet away from the body. We analysed the rubber for any coating and found it was completely covered with your friend's saliva.'

'Meaning what?' Holly couldn't think. A baby's dummy?

Doc Hegarty held his glass to the candle in the middle of the table and studied the colour of the wine. 'Sheila Benson theorised that your friend must have fallen asleep with the dummy in her mouth. Assuming the heroin and gin, the Valium, the love-making and the head-cold had all contributed to a state of brain-numbingly deep sleep – this is all pure conjecture, mind you – but then, say your friend, as described by the maid, was lying flat on her back by the cosy fireside, remember that her nasal passages were blocked with thick mucus so she would be breathing through her mouth, and say, perhaps, that in her deep sleep she suddenly yawned or just involuntarily opened her mouth wide in a dream – that dummy, being fit for a baby and far smaller than the aperture of her mouth when wide open, would have dropped inside to neatly block the windpipe. I doubt she even woke from deep sleep at all. The dummy was probably expelled by a reflexive expulsion of trapped air from the lungs after consciousness had already been lost for ever.'

Holly stared at the old man. 'Doc, with all humble respect due you and your esteemed colleague Dr Benson, you don't seriously expect me to believe that poppycock, do you? I mean, choking on a baby's dummy? It's just . . . ridiculous!'

Professor Hegarty finished his wine with a smile. 'I've seen far stranger things and I've never been to sea.'

'The clingfilm and the false eyelashes!' exclaimed Holly. 'You still haven't accounted for them.'

Hegarty massaged his temples with two thumbs before speaking.

Chapter 9

That Friday it was blisteringly cold on the M4, heading west
before first light with wind-factor below freezing. Which
was why Holly-Jean chortled along as snug as a bug with the
heat on full-blast at the wheel of her brand new Land Rover
Discovery, newly leased from a new leasing company – the
old one had not been amused by the condition of their
Peugeot when they finally fished it out of the NCP car-park
at Manor House. By contrast this motor was a gleaming
black tank that rode like fresh cream with 4WD, computerised braking system with anti-lock, airbags all round,
tinted windows, crumple-free safety-frame and solid-steel
crash-bar fitted as an optional extra – Holly was frocked if
she was going to let any other dickhead sideswipe her again
in a hurry!

The CD player was stacked and at the moment it was
relaying with ear-bleeding intensity, Mark E. Smith's 'The
Fall', and the adrenaline-surging black wall of sound the
man called The Chiseller.

Turning left at Bristol onto the M5 she crossed the Tamar
into Cornwall just after noon. With only one stop for gas and
a pee, she made Sennen Cove near Land's End as the
afternoon finally succumbed to the nagging dusk: anxious,
it seemed, to bring on the night, turn off the light and move
to warmer climes. Holly parked in the car-park above the
beach and stepped out on stiff legs and numb toes. She
breathed deeply and did some *Chi-Kung* inner stretches.

Ahead of her was the fading pink-grey of the far Atlantic horizon and a dark-slate sea upon which the big waves curled luminous pale. A wet wind teased her skin and the air was pure cherry-wine. A giant smile spread over her face as she walked across the sand to the ocean. The surfers were out, sitting astride their boards waiting for the big sets to roll in. Dotting the waves in their multi-coloured wet-suits like the scattered blooms of sea-burial wreathes.

Holly joined a group of watchers, some with giant lenses on tripod cameras, others with binoculars. She spoke to a girl in a duffle coat nearby. 'What's the occasion?'

'No special occasion,' said the girl. 'Just sunset at Sennen in the season of the biggest waves.'

Holly moved on down to the edge of the tide, letting the wind blow the stale car air from her lungs. Stood on a slab of black slate rock and watched the drama unfold. A slow drama. Seemed to Holly-Jean that the surfers spent a lot of time motionless, perched on their boards facing the ocean in silent contemplation like penitents at prayer before an altar.

The body-boarders, on the other hand, a lesser breed she'd read somewhere, were having far more fun, kicking off with their flippered feet and recklessly sliding up and down and around and around the smaller waves.

But then, as though with a silent drum-roll, a vast shuddering of the sea signalled a sudden burst of activity. This was it. The big one. Rolling in from some far-off Atlantic swell. Instantly the surfers threw themselves down, spun their boards around and began paddling madly as the ocean lifted them up into the sky. Three or four managed to catch the wave's momentum and took off down the same precipitous shoulder of sea.

Holly held her breath and watched as, in a slow-motion split-second, one of the surfers, a flash of purple and orange, seemed to carve his own path down the thundering wall of water. With a casual palm he flipped one usurper out of his way and off his board to tumble head-over-heels down the vertical drop, ankle-tied board gyroscoping out of control to disappear beneath the crashing white water, only to shoot up again a second later. No sign of the surfer. The others seemed to have got the message and veered back over the crest of the dark-water shoulder to the haven of the ocean behind leaving the purple and orange rider to ply with marauding grace the still growing surge of unbroken curl, always just a few inches ahead of the gaping mouth of the wave's tunnel, as the towering edifice raced towards its own demolition.

Without warning the behemoth changed momentum and with a deafening explosion of white water broke directly over the lone surfer and he disappeared beneath the wave.

Watching from the sand, Holly waited for what seemed for ever. Began to think the man must be dead. Smashed to pieces by the impact of megatons of ocean.

Suddenly the purple and orange flashed out the other end of the pipeline, arms raised in exultation somehow still standing on his rocketing board, to the cheers of the assembled watchers, the yells of his fellow surfers and the shrieking of the seagulls.

Of course it had to be.

The pretty lad himself. Paddy Fistral.

Holly followed him up the beach to the car-park and waited till he had propped his board up against a Wrangler Jeep and unzipped the heavy-duty winter wet-suit.

'I'm Holly-Jean Ho.' She held out a hand. 'Your manager, Lee Crowley, told me you'd be expecting me.'

He smiled that famous boyish grin, perfect set of gnashers, ridiculous eye-lashes and piercing ocean-blue eyes.

'Holly-Jean Ho . . .' he cocked his head to one side. 'Nice name. But sorry, babe. No interviews. Wrong time, wrong place.' He gestured around at the gathering dark.

'But I've just driven down from London.'

'First I've heard of it. You know Lee: dumb fuck.'

The man's arrogance took her breath away. She said, 'Look, I'm not a reporter for some teeny-bop magazine. I'm a private investigator looking into the death of Elfa Ericksson.'

She watched his face. He didn't blink an eye as he rubbed a towel through his hair, wet-suit half-peeled down.

'Your last meeting with Elfa Ericksson following an attempted reconciliation ended with a row and a slamming door. You might like to know that in certain quarters you're considered a prime suspect for murder.'

That got his attention. He threw his towel into the back of the Jeep, muttering darkly, 'Fucken women: women, women, what did I do to deserve them?'

With a pained sigh, he turned to Holly. 'Look, love, I know you've got a job to do and all that guff but right now you're just what I don't need. An hysterical female come all this way to spoil a good day's surfing.'

'How about I stay and spoil your night and tomorrow morning, maybe even lunch, too.'

He pulled on a bundle of t-shirts then casually unpeeled the lower half of the wet-suit revealing his private parts with a grin.

'Want some?'

Holly stood her ground. 'Just a few answers to a few questions would be more than adequate, thank you.'

He swiftly dried his legs, pulled on baggy ski-pants, slipped his feet into canvas boots and humped the board onto the roof-rack. 'Jump in.'

'No. I'll follow. That's my car over there.'

A few miles inland was a caravan site. Rows and rows of identical white boxes planted on a sloping field above the ocean. The last of the light was fading as Fistral pulled up next to the last caravan in the furthest corner of the field. Holly's headlights spotted the satellite dish clinging to the caravan's rear-end jutting out into mid-air over yellow gorse bushes and steep bracken cliffs.

Inside was a mess of clothes lines draped with damp clothes steaming in front of a five-band electric fire, an expensive sound system, TV and microwave. Holly looked around while Paddy Fistral put on a kettle. The inane jauntiness of Britpop filled the clammy air. Fist-holes dotted the plaster-board wall-lining. Spent splodges of multi-coloured candlewax adorned every flat surface.

He handed her a mug of Earl Grey tea, a stack of hand-written ink letters and pointed to the TV with a remote control, 'Drink that. Watch this. Read them. When you've finished the lot you can piss off.'

With that he sat down at a small table and opened a small carved wooden box. With care he pulled out a syringe, a spoon, a small suction-pump dripper and a poly bag of white powder.

The tea was good. The video was of the recent pro-surf World Championship round 3, held in Durban, South Africa, January 18th–25th. Paddy Fistral had managed to make it through all the prelims right through to the final day. His final placing was a pretty good seventh place, which placed him tenth in the overall championship standings. The letters were from Elfa to Paddy. Love letters: tender, intimate and, in the one dated January 10th, a promise that 'whatever happens, I know we will one day be together, for ever, because, my darling Patrick, us two were meant to be.'

She left him nodding out, with the uncharitable words, 'Britpop's for wankers!'

139

* * *

Holly decided the Discovery would be a lot more fun than an inadequately central-heated local B&B, and the prospect of soggy fried bread for breakfast. Besides she loved to drive and think. You could get a really heavy grey-matter work-out during a long solitary night-time drive, reckoned Holly, as she reached the Penzance to Plymouth link.

Pondering the pretty boy's literally water-tight alibi to the accompaniment of the magical Chinese harmonies of Dadawa's Sister Drum, she knew now where this strange trip was inexorably homing.

She stopped at Taunton Deane services at about ten p.m., toted a cup of lousy coffee back to the Discovery where she checked her notebook PC for Melanie Wand's phone number.

The fashion editor at *The Face* was at home.

'Melanie? This is Holly-Jean Ho.'

'Holly! Hi. Been a long time. How are you?'

'Great thanks. Look, Mel, I really wanted to thank you for putting my name up for the Elfa Ericksson thing.'

'Oh, Elfa. What can you say? A really tragic loss. You know she had a certain aura. Magical girl.'

'I totally agree,' said Holly. 'An absolute waste, which is why I am determined to uncover the true story of why she died. Here's where you can help me – I hope you don't mind?'

'No of course,' said Melanie. 'But what can I do? Nothing dangerous. I trust.'

'No, no, nothing dangerous. Just fill in some gaps for me. Okay?'

'Talking I can do. You remember my nick-name at Camden?'

'Parrot-mouth!'

'Right!' laughed Melanie 'So ask away.'

'Thanks, Mel, you're a real sport,' said Holly. 'You see, in the course of the job a name keeps cropping up, and I think you might know a bit about him. Kriega, the German fashion photographer.'

There was a long pause at the other end. When Melanie spoke again there was a tremble in her voice.

'L-l-look, I find if very difficult to talk about that man. Suffice to say I once had a very nasty encounter with him.'

Holly waited, said nothing. Let Melanie decide if she wanted to talk. She began to speak in a neutral tone, as if reading from a prepared script.

'As you may or may not know, Kriega is infamous for his black and white fetishist work. Robert Mapplethorpe rip-offs, if you want my opinion. But anyway, his approach, his angle, is always ... sex. Kinky sex. Never straight stuff. Never a hint of romance. He equates sex with violence. Believe me, I know...' Her voice quivered and failed.

Holly waited, wondering, as she always did at times like these, why she continued this kind of work. Then she remembered Elfa's eleven-year old, tranquillised face staring out at her from the Internet.

Melanie was speaking again. 'With Kriega it's always got to be whips, S and M, Bondage, water sports. All the sick shit. You want to know the worst? There are even rumours he's into child pornography. Keeps a house in the Philippines.'

Holly's skin erupted in *chi-pi*, and she felt the tingling of revelation on her scalp. She asked a few more questions then said goodbye. 'I'm truly sorry to drag all this up for you, Melanie, but I want you to know you've been an invaluable help. Thank you so much.'

She rang off with a giddy feeling compounded of elation and guilt.

When she was back on the motorway, she punched in the

141

number Ivana had left her. By some miracle she reached the supermodel. They exchanged pleasantries. Ivana sounded a little bit too merry. Holly cut to the point. 'Remember at breakfast in your hotel you thought that Kriega the photographer might have had some kind of clandestine relationship with Elfa? At the time, I reckoned not. Well, something's come up to suggest you two might have been right. Tell me everything you know or can guess at, about the two of them.'

Ivana hesitated. 'Nothing concrete, as we said before. Just speculation, right? The thing is, whenever he was around, she acted so strangely. Scared, maybe ... And like the – what you call – "bad penny" – he just kept turning up. Towards the end of last year he always seemed to be hanging around our shoots or shows. One time, and I never told She this, I thought I actually saw them together at the Bowery Bar, watching Lou Reed read poetry. But as I was off my head, I couldn't swear to it.'

With one hand Holly steered the Discovery down the empty late-night motorway. 'Say, for the sake of argument, that Kriega did have some kind of secret hold over Elfa, and please don't think for one minute I'm desecrating the memory of your good friend. But, knowing the man as you do, would you guess such a hold involved drugs or may be far-out sex, or what? Don't forget, they found a discernible amount of heroin in her system.'

Ivana replied, 'Like I said, it would be just guesswork, but all I know is that an utterly fearless girl, who loved to test the ultimate levels of endurance, suddenly seemed to act like a frightened child whenever Kriega showed his ugly great shaven skull. We all know about his brand of "extreme" lifestyle, so I just put two and two together and my guess is Elfa found the lure of danger about him irresistible.'

Holly added. 'And maybe discovered to her ultimate cost,

that he went one step beyond the bounds. Whatever they may be.'

Ivana said. 'If you're going after him, Holly-Jean, take very, very great care.'

Chapter 10

The second Wednesday in February, the same day that the inquest into the death of Elfa Ericksson concluded with a verdict of accidental death and the Coroner signed an order for release of the body, most of the tabloids led with the news that pornographic pictures of Elfa at eleven years old were available on the World Wide Web.

It was a bitterly cold day with an overnight frost making yesterday's record snowfall harden into Christmas cake-icing sculpture and turning the roads of Britain into treacherous skid-pans. It was all the fault of a week-long massive low over Scandinavia whose glowering breath had frozen the entire landmass of Western Europe.

Snowflakes were even to be found floating in the gin and tonics of the Algarve, according to the giggling meteorological glam-girl on Breakfast TV.

At the Black Swan on the river at Hammersmith afterwards, Holly left Marika and Ingrid for a minute and used the phone by the ladies' loo to ask Mick Coulson why there'd been no mention at the inquest of the lover, nor why her tip on Kriega as a candidate for that role hadn't been acted upon. Coulson's reply was typically full of tact and masculine charm. 'A, because there has yet to be a law enacted against polishing the pork polaris, and B, because his alibi was as tight as a Boy Scout's bum. He was at an all-night party at a rock star's castle in Cornwall.' What's the big deal about Cornwall all of a sudden? thought Holly.

'That poison on the Internet,' she protested angrily, 'why wasn't that brought up? Doesn't the word blackmail mean anything to the brilliant minds of the law?'

Coulson said, 'Holly, it's over. Face it. You gave it your best shot. Even got Professor Hegarty involved, fuck-knows-how, and he couldn't find anything wrong. She died in her sleep. Let her rest in peace.'

When Holly got back to their seats, the others were just finishing their drinks and Marika said it was time to take Ingrid home.

As Holly drove the Discovery out of the Swan's car park a chaotic scramble of cars hurtled in the pub gates, skidding and sliding on the snowy gravel. Someone must have recognised the three women in the pub and called the paparazzi who should by now have been halfway to Reading on the M4, led on a wild goose-chase by three masquerading employees of Marika's Wine Bar driving Ingrid's red Saab. 'Duck!' yelled Holly as she gunned out onto the main road, and up onto Hammersmith flyover.

They decided against Sloane Street, knowing the press would already be encamped there, and headed on to the wine bar in Islington. On the way Holly asked if there was anything more she could do to help. She meant in terms of taking care of the necessary arrangements following a death. As far as her investigation into the death of Elfa Ericksson was concerned, she had not the slightest intention of unclamping her jaws from the tearing metallic tang of the bit.

Ingrid reached out her hand from the back seat and clutched Holly's shoulder in a silent gesture of gratitude. The woman had been battered to within the last threads of sanity by the storm of publicity breaking about the pictures of Elfa, coming on the same day as the inquest and the reading in court of Professor Hegarty's autopsy findings.

Marika had taken complete charge of her old friend, and she said no, Holly'd already done so much for which they were both deeply grateful.

'You've done wonders, Holly, we can't thank you sufficiently. Anyway, I know you well enough to understand that you'll continue to dig for the truth whatever anyone may say, right?'

Holly mumbled an affirmative, and Marika continued in her brisk Scandinavian efficiency mode: 'And as for the mundane stuff, I'm handling everything. Happy to say the undertakers have already been prepared in advance for the release order. Now Elfa will finally be able to rest.'

As they were saying goodbye at Islington, she told Holly that the funeral was to be at the West London Crematorium in Kensal Rise at nine-fifteen on Friday morning and then afterwards at Marika's Wine Bar.

Holly made it back to Camden Lock at dusk, as fresh snow was falling under a low full moon. It was a beautiful sight to behold. Dirty old London transformed by the glittering brushwork of the Snow Painter.

Only GiGi's tri-paw prints broke the pristine blue-white coating of the iron staircase to the studio. Two paws on one step, one on the other. Inside, Ma had left a scribbled note to say she'd taken Mrs Howell-Pryce to Chinatown to play mah-jong, and that they were going on to a concert at the Albert Hall afterwards so she wouldn't be back till late.

Holly happily interpreted this as confirmation that the two widows had got over their initial wariness and were really hitting it off. Good news. The agency would be in capable hands full-time; meaning worry-free travel for Holly. All she ever did these days. In and out of planes, taxis, countries. Always in a rush. Always feeling she must be

147

forgetting something. Some detail that would unlock the truth. Perpetual motion. *Keep on keeping on!* Hah! Holly-Jean knew she wasn't really going anywhere.

The doorbell rang. A despatch rider dripping melting snow handed over an envelope in return for Holly's signature. She tipped him and shut the door against the icy wind. The envelope was marked *House of Commons*. She tore it open. Desk-top print job.

The Right Honourable Adrian J. Morehouse, Member of Parliament, requests the pleasure of Ms Holly-Jean Ho's presence at his Private Office in the Houses of Parliament at seven this evening, informal dress only. Enclosed is a security pass valid for this single visit. No need to RSVP.

There was a scribbled signature and an added PS. *Must come, something vital! Don't be late!*

Holly hadn't seen Morehouse at the inquest. Not surprising, with today's breaking tabloid frenzy at child Elfa on the Net. Holly already knew that would be the subject of vital import.

Among other revelations, Beth Lawton's enhancements had shown the letters A.J.M. on the signet ring. Moreover, a week back, Holly had called Ingrid Ericksson for confirmation on two items of information. First, that Elfa had owned and cherished her Lady Penelope doll, especially loved to dress her in the riding to the hunt outfit. Second, that Elfa's stepfather's study was wall-papered with a William Morris repro floral motif.

The policewoman checked Holly's pass carefully, searched her bag, asked her to turn out her pockets and patted her down before she was allowed inside the public entrance to Westminster. She followed the signs for females and joined a queue of visitors where she was finally seen by another woman officer, her bag sent through an X-ray machine and she was marched through a metal detector. An enquiries

148

desk employee in suit and tie showed her on a lay-out map of the Houses of Parliament how to reach Member's Private Room 897.

It took a fifteen-minute walk and three other requests for directions before she reached the end of the gloomy corridor and knocked on the dark-varnished door at just after seven p.m. as requested.

No reply. She knocked again. Still no response.

Holly thought, Frock this, I'm not coming all this way for nothing, and she grabbed the door-handle and shoved.

The door opened easily into darkness. She stepped inside. Was met by a foul odour of shit and piss. Very recent. She swallowed hard. Slid her hand up the wall. Found a light-switch and then was staring eye-to-lace-eye with the dangling brown brogues and still-dripping contents of the late MP for Irkdale South.

Kicked the door shut behind her. Clamped a hand over her mouth, ducked by the brogues and the puddle beneath, ran across the tiny room, tore aside the curtains and tugged the window open to let in an icy blast from Old Father Thames whose rank breath had never been more welcome as it set the grisly mobile into gentle swaying motion.

Keeping her hand over her mouth, Holly quickly glanced around the room. Bookcases lined the walls. *Hansard* and *The Times* on a leather chair by the door. Coats and hats hanging from a stand. Pictures of college sport teams on the walls. A rowing eight holding high the stiletto hull.

Everything seemed tidy and normal.

Apart from the kinetic art.

Propped against a pewter pen-and-inkstand on the mahogany desk was a white envelope. She picked it up and read her name written in red ink. Sinking into the ship-captain's chair, Holly opened the envelope and unfolded the single sheet and the enclosed cheque. The handwriting was neat and orderly.

Thank you for coming, Ms Ho.

By now I'm gone for good, but even so I still need your help.

Yes, it was I who took the photographs of my dear darling Elfa, may God forgive me!

Until today I had thought them completely destroyed, just as completely as I was destroyed by the remorse, the self-disgust, the black despair that has never stopped punishing me from that day since.

It seems I was mistaken; somehow some of the negatives must have been mislaid or removed beforehand. Please, I beg you, Ms Ho, do your utmost to find out who is responsible. For Elfa's sake, if not for mine.

For your information: the photos were taken in October nine years ago and destroyed three weeks later. During that time they never left my study-room at the Sloane Street flat. I enclose a signed blank cheque for your services. Thank you.

I have already tested the light-fixture and belt. They can carry my weight. I am a coward. I cannot face the shame. I shall now jump from the desk with a noose around my neck.

The letter was unsigned.

Holly thought for a few moments. Better for Elfa, better all round, to preserve what vestiges of honour remained for the memory of Adrian Morehouse if the contents of the suicide note remained a secret.

Trouble was, there was neither time nor place hereabouts to safe-destruct the note. She unzipped her jeans and slid the note, cheque and envelope inside her knickers. She picked up the phone, asked the internal operator for assistance.

During the drilling of routine questions, the senior detective opened his electronic hand-book and punched in a few lines as Holly answered. She reckoned her words were being relayed directly to one of the giant Crays at Cheltenham. Apparently Big Bro was not unduly alarmed. No sirens went off, Holly wasn't suddenly pinned to the ground, nor was a standard-issue Colt All American chambered with a 9 mm Parabellum cartridge inserted in her left ear.

However, the corduroy-jacketed detective did turn his back to make a verbal communication on the same hand-held device. After speaking for a minute or so, he closed the notebook and dropped it in his baggy jacket pocket. He turned back again and asked to see Holly's visitor's pass. She handed it over.

'Let's get this straight. You discovered the body, but you say there was no note, no last thoughts, musings or whatever?'

'Nothing that I could see.'

'Why was it you, Miss Ho, he chose to be his final witness, I wonder?' asked the detective.

Holly shrugged and looked thoughtful. 'I really couldn't say, but it might have been because I was being professionally retained to investigate the death of his stepdaughter by both her employers and the mother.'

'Yes, so I understand,' nodded the detective, signalling to a woman constable for a cup of tea with two sugars. 'You must know a lot about that unfortunate affair, then. At the inquest today, were you?'

Holly said nothing. Wasn't she going to get offered a cuppa?

'The wife, the girl's mother – she and the deceased were separated, that is correct?'

'As far as I know. Look here, Officer,' she said, 'I really hope you can arrange for news about this to reach Ingrid Ericsson officially asap, before the press gets there. They've already made her life a misery, and now with two

151

new scandals breaking on the same day as the inquest, they'll be completely rabid!'

'It's already been taken care of, don't worry.' The detective sipped his hot tea. 'You say "two new scandals" – I take it you're referring to this filthy stuff in the papers about pornographic photos of the daughter at a young age on the Internet. Why don't you tell me what you know about that?'

'It came as a very unpleasant surprise to me and to everyone else, I should imagine.'

'He couldn't handle the guilt, I suppose.' The detective's eyes never left Holly's as he thumbed over his shoulder at the body now being laid out on a stretcher.

'Don't know what guilt you're implying. A broken heart, *I'd've* thought,' replied Holly, staring neutrally back at the policeman. 'You have children of your own?'

The detective shrugged. 'She was a stepchild in my understanding.'

Holly said, '*Diao niah bei tsai, go-dr da-bien tou!*' A combined Mandarin Hakka ventilation. Dog-shit-head-mother-fucker!

'Clever cunt, aren't you,' said the detective mildly. 'But we like to speak English here in England, particularly when standing in the Mother of Parliaments. Another of our great gifts to the world.' With that he walked off and began to confer with another plain-clothes man.

A woman officer took Holly by the arm, politely. 'Right then, Miss Ho. Would you mind waiting a while over there.' She pointed to a row of seats lining the corridor, which had been cordoned off by two burly constables. 'An officer will shortly come and take down some details.'

Holly nodded and went over to join the others waiting to be interviewed. A cleaning lady, a porter, a couple of menials from the Conservative Whips' office and the late MP's personal staff: his private secretary, a middle-aged woman in a raincoat, quietly snuffling into her handkerchief, two nice-looking county-type/Sloane 'research assistants' conversing in whispers and looking wan with shock, and two Young Tory fatboy spin-interns who were scribbling notes, making calls on their Nokias and as far as Holly could overhear, frantically attempting damage control. After another wait, comforting cups of tea arrived by trolley and were passed across the yellow police tape by the constables.

In turn each was led aside for questioning by the police team.

They were finally done with Holly-Jean at about ten-thirty that night and she was told she could go. Passing by, she glanced at the naked corpse as the Medical Officer finished up his preliminary examination. Noted the unusual scar as of shrapnel on the thigh.

The same woman officer, escorting her back along the winding corridors and stairs of Westminster to the public exit, commented, ''Course, he had no choice but to do himself in. After all, he was sponsoring some Bill against pornography on the Internet.'

Chapter 11

Thursday morning at ten a.m. Holly-Jean had her bandages removed at the Royal Free and her prescription for codeine distalgesic cut down to one a day for another two weeks only. She celebrated by walking back to Camden Lock across Hampstead Heath, stopping at the top of Parliament Hill as she had done every day of her childhood to take in the view of London.

A sudden jerk of the choke-lead of nostalgia turned her feet to the east and she walked back past the old family home in Woodsome Road. A professor from North London University (used to be the Poly in her day) with writer wife and two teenage kids had bought the place. Done a nice job on the tiny front garden. Daffodils and snowdrops were beginning to show.

If home is, as they say, where the heart is, for the girl whose heart had been tanned to old leather after its first tentative stepping-out last year, having been kept under split-race, split-sexuality lock and key from schooldays, this winter day's wandering was a fabric softener.

She had a glass of draught Guinness in the Pineapple in Kentish Town, and there, in the women's loo, she flushed the ashes of the Rt. Hon. Adrian J. Morehouse's last communication into oblivion or at least the *cloaca maxima* of NW5.

The mood of nostalgia prevailed. Cutting through Prince of Wales Road, Holly-Jean had no choice but to walk back

to Camden Lock via Harmood Street, the row of gentrified
Victorian brick houses where she'd once squatted in the
Seventies and where one Summer day some scuzz-sucking
hippy bastards nicked her entire collection of vinyl LPs and
broke her heart in the process.

Irreplaceable stuff like Paul Butterfield Blues Band, early
Stones, Robert Johnson ... 'Course, some of it was already
or would eventually be re-issued on CD, but not all of it.
Besides, it just wasn't the same. And she wasn't only talking
about the blandness of digital re-recording, the missing
crackle of stylus on groove. She was talking about the
memories of cataclysmic *temps perdu* and all the amazing
stuff of youth that was transubstantiated by those cardboard
album covers. As when coming across a dog-eared copy of
'Disraeli's Gears' or 'Hunky Dory' at a friend's house or in
a market stall, the very act of touch could beam her back in a
flash to those wild days just before the dying of the freak
light.

Lost in reverie under the ivy-stunted holly tree at No. 85,
Holly-Jean's face was suddenly lit by a smile at the memory
of the beautiful crazy 'head' who lived in the squat next
door. What was her name? *Charas.*

Charas regularly used to knock on Holly's front door, say
she'd lost her key, trot sharpish through to the back and nip
over the garden wall to her place. It was only later Holly
learned that Charas was dealing a lot of dope and she
realised that 'losing her key' meant the girl was holding
weight and, in case she was being tailed, wanted Holly's to
be the first door kicked in by the Drug Squad.

At the end of Harmood she turned left into Chalk Farm
Road, dropped by the Irish bakery, exchanged a happy chat
with the two women and bought fresh baked soda-bread and
Cornish pasties for tea. Humming Carlos Jobim she crossed
the cobbles to the studio at the back of the Lock. Called out
'GiGi!' and saw that the wall of the old warehouse at the

156

back of Camden Lock had been freshly spray-painted. Swastikas and *Fuck off home, Chink!* among other such epithets. Luckily, Ma was out and about somewhere.

Holly-Jean quickly disposed of the paper-bag of dog excrement that had been shoved through the letter-box, dumping it in the big steel Borough of Camden rubbish skip across the cobbled yard.

Using her key she opened up Minty's studio, found a wire brush and a gallon tin of white spirit and, with GiGi watching, spent the rest of daylight scrubbing the bricks clean, wondering if it were random local hate. Or was it part of something orchestrated whose Overture had been the RV sideswipe in Volkspark with North Sea telephone threat theme, and First Movement, the Highgate Hill kicking.

Elfa's funeral on the Friday was packed with mourners, and the service at the flower-bedecked West London Crem. went very well. Holly-Jean was moved to tears by the outpouring of love as the hymn 'Dear Lord and Father of Mankind', an echo of her premonition at Les Bains-Douches, followed by 'Crimond', were sung at enough volume to raise the roof of the chapel and send a message all the way to Heaven. When a world-famous designer in his square-framed spectacles gave the oration in halting French-accented English, Holly realised that Elfa Ericksson really had been someone very extraordinary.

The designer ended by saying, 'Today ze rainbow 'as lost one of 'is light-bulbs, and 'e will nevairr shine zo bright again.'

A collection was taken for the charity Children with AIDS, and it was announced that the flowers were going to the children's cancer ward at St Mary's.

Outside the Crematorium there was another massacre of privacy by the frothing sewage press. As there was

157

afterwards, at the gathering of friends and fellow-mourners at Marika's Wine Bar across town in Islington. Out of sheer malice, Holly delivered a lightning strike at one prominent Adam's apple as she fought her way to the door. Marika had hired a bevy of heavies from the Greek mini-cab office across the road to handle security and Holly had to show I.D. and point to her name on the long guest list.

As the wake progressed into the afternoon and the numbers of visitors swelled, the flash-bulbs kept popping. Elfa had a lot of famous friends. Everyone wore black, although a cornucopia of new man-made fabrics ensured no one looked the same.

There was only one choice of drink, served in identical shot glasses to all, like it or not. Aquavit, from bottles set in frozen blocks of ice wielded by the staff. There was only one choice of food. Ten wooden boats of whole gravadlax salmon soaking in their marinade, and large crystal bowls of fresh dill mustard.

Holly-Jean moved about, chatting with old friends and new. In the glassed-in garden area out back of the old Islington townhouse she spotted Ivana and She. Holly needed to talk to the two models, but just as she took a step in their direction, her path was blocked.

Aramint de Lache marched her away to the other side of the planthouse dining area, and in what passed for *sotto voce*, told her that with the inquest verdict in, the funeral marked a formal closing, and thus Holly was to discontinue her investigation on behalf of the Princess of Sheba Agency.

Aramint didn't say thanks.

She did say, 'Understand you were responsible for the eminent Professor's involvement – so don't worry you'll still get your bonus.'

Holly's response was that she could stick her bonus where the sun doesn't shine.

'Oh well, if that's the way you feel, suit yourself.'

'I always try to.'

Holly had to get away from the woman, but Aramint grabbed hold of her sleeve with a grim smile. 'Those ghastly pictures on the Internet have anything to do with Elfa's death? But then they can't have, can they? The verdict was accidental. But all the same it's very odd, wouldn't you say? Utterly, utterly odd.'

Holly-Jean looked at Aramint's hand clutching her sleeve. Glanced up at the woman's eyes with just a flicker of *chi*. The hand recoiled as though stung by a scorpion.

Holly joined the others with a smile.

'You didn't meet up with us in Milano. We were expecting you. When you didn't call, we were very upset,' said Ivana, looking sad. Wistful feelings permeated the wake, so Holly couldn't tell if she was being serious.

'Ivy, I tried to, but there was no time for partying. I was working. *It's what I do.*'

'We understand,' said She hugging her. 'Another time?'

'Definitely.'

Aramint and Joel Unmack came up then and all present said how they thought the service and wake the perfect way to honour the passing of Elfa Ericksson. Meanwhile, Holly wondered just how much each knew and wasn't telling.

'None of you would have the slightest idea how those pictures got onto the Internet, would you?'

They all made suitably shocked remarks about the horrible story and Joel said, 'The stepfather's suicide does rather point the finger, doesn't it?'

Ivana whispered in Holly-Jean's ear.

Out of earshot of the others Holly murmured in reply, 'He won't show up here, will he?' Not needing to invoke the name.

'I doubt it,' said Ivana. 'Fashion Week in New York

begins Monday, but the circus already hit town: previews, publicity, interviews.'

She joined them. 'Manhattan's one big catwalk this weekend, and as the saying goes, "You wanna work, you gotta strut the strut".' She added, 'We shouldn't even be here really but for our sweetheart, our sister Elfa.' A passing waiter handed over three shots. They slammed them back. 'To Elfa.'

'Fact, the driver will be here any minute – our plane leaves at seven-fifteen,' said Ivy, looking at her watch. Holly could tell she was the organiser of the two.

'Concorde?' Holly couldn't resist asking.

'Natch.'

'You're absolutely *positive* that Kriega will be in New York for the whole of next week?'

Ivana's eyes clouded with worry and what Holly glimpsed as genuine fear. 'I dunno what you're up to, but you damn well take very, very great care, Holly-Jean Ho. Remember, I wasn't kidding what I told you about him.'

'Don't worry,' said Holly. 'Even though the lines are blurred and this new Dark Age marks the End of Morality, I think I already got the picture: he's *bad*.'

'A wicked, evil man,' muttered Ivana.

'Bad ju-ju,' whispered She, grabbing another frozen Aquavit.

Holly hitched a lift in their limo and got down at Hyde Park Corner. She had a seven o'clock dinner appointment at the Connaught Hotel.

Who, you might be wondering, would choose to invite humble Holly-Jean Ho for dinner at probably the most expensive and certainly one of the very finest eating establishments in London, if not the world?

Clues: someone whose expense account was as deep as

160

the Mariana trench, as wide as the Taklamakan Desert (in Chinese 'the desert you go into but don't come out of') and as open to public scrutiny as the Pope's underwear. You got it; Francisco Frank Goya, President-for-Life of the AIA.

'Mr Goya's table,' Holly-Jean announced to the Reservations Desk manned by three liveried assistants to the Maître D'.

The old man who rose to his feet to greet her was short in stature but larger than leonine life with his thick white-maned skull, huge Roman nose and the sheen of daily facials.

Sadly, the hoped-for effect of total refinement was marred by the beady little eyes that flickered over her body like an electron scan of lust and the startlingly long, narrow purple tongue which kept darting out as though to monitor the air for secret scents.

Old Frankie was about as enticing a prospect as a Komodo dragon. And apparently, just as endangered. Which Holly-Jean thought most unfair, since through no fault of her own she'd been cast in the role of conservationist.

The meal as befits the Connaught was magnificent. But unfortunately for Holly-Jean, the timing was all wrong.

This day of Elfa's laying to rest truly was a Black Friday, and Holly's one chance to eat at the Connaught was ruined by a lack of appetite and a recurrence of her old complaint, 'lethargy and malaise'. Suffice to say they weren't served faggots, peas and chips. Nor was the food accompanied by pints of lager.

They retired to a drawing room where a Baccarat decanter of Taylor's 1908 vintage port was passed. Over which complex nougatine nectar, Holly agreed formally to accept the proffered invitation to membership of the Association.

'The acceptance vote will be a formality, my dear, though

you must join the next gathering in order to be nominated,'
said the old man, his voice an adenoidal baritone. 'I trust you
will do me the honour of attending as my personal guest. It
has always been one of my follies to champion the advance
of female members.'

'Where and when?' asked Holly. Her dance-list was
getting a mite crowded these days, and she was wondering
what 'advances' old Frankie-boy might have in mind.

In response, President-for-Life Goya handed her a
Burgundy leatherette-bound folder full of beautifully
printed cards, booklets and notes of great significance like
'Ladies Blow-Pipe Competition'. She found the lead item
clipped to a first-class air-ticket on Philippine Airlines. *AIA
gathering March 5th–10th, Shangri-La Hotel, Cebu, R.P.*

Which naturally made it a whole different kettle of squid.

'I'd simply love to,' said Holly-Jean, smiling to sprain
her dimples, eyes glinting as she scooped up the folder and
rolled her tight little Chinese bum all the way across the
drawing-room carpet which had once graced the Peacock
Throne Room.

That'd give the old boy's laser-beam plenty to lust on.

After she finally got rid of the runs Saturday morning, (the
raw sliced goose *foie gras* probably did it), Holly-Jean
drove Ma to Oxford and treated her to a night at the
Randolph Hotel.

It was the first chance they'd had to mark Ma's
homecoming. A celebration. In the morning they walked
around the Mile at Christ Church with snowflakes falling,
had lunch at the Trout Inn and heard Evensong in the
cathedral, Thomas Tallis responses, Stanford in C, and 'O
thou the Central Orb', C. Wood's sublime anthem echoing in
their ears as they drove back to town on the jammed M40.

Chapter 12

Monday was the last before the Friends of Chinese Opera Convention weekend, and Holly-Jean had already decided to arrive at the Surabaya Hotel in Den Haag, Holland, a day or two early just to make sure every last detail of the convention schedule was perfectly in order. With clients like hers, she was naturally a wee bit nervous.

Which meant she still had a couple of days free to make another trip in the general vicinity of north-western Europe.

It was mid-afternoon when Ma returned and reported that her luncheon meeting with the COMSEM representatives had gone very well. Slapping a cheque for a very large amount on the kitchen table, she announced that the public outcry following the 'tragedy' of the Right Honourable Adrian Morehouse's suicide, along with the mountain of evidence provided by H-J. H. & Associates, had resulted in an emergency debate tabled for the Commons tonight followed by a free vote with all the parties' whips suspended.

It was widely expected that an amendment to the Computer Misuse Act to include extremely harsh penalties for both intent to distribute or simple possession of down-loaded underage pornography would be voted through with only the smallest opposition from a handful of MPs concerned at censorship and invasion of privacy.

Ma cackled triumphantly, 'A job well done, Little Orchid. Do I get to spend half?'

Holly had smiled. 'You bet. As for the job, it's only half-finished. We have yet to nail those *da-bien tou* shitheads who call themselves the Prawn Club.'

Ma looked grim. 'Don't think I've forgotten those *Tsr-lan* Coloured-Wolves. I'm still dug in. Getting closer every day.'

'Great stuff, Ma. *Jai-yo!* Keep at it. As for me, I'm afraid I'm off on my travels again tonight.'

She hadn't told Ma about the hate-message sprayed on the studio's brick wall, nor any of the other possibly linked attacks. She hadn't wanted to spoil Ma's return home nor have her unduly worried. On the other hand, if the threats were linked, then Ma might also be in danger, so she ordered her mother to take extra care with locking up at night, opening the door to strangers, and just to be on the general look-out for people behaving suspiciously.

'Goes with the job, Ma. You never know who you might have pissed off.' She added, 'I'll call you every day at breakfast, so make sure you're home.'

'Where to this time?'

'Oh, y'know, Europe.' She flapped her hand vaguely. Big-time jet-setter.

'Got enough warm clothes?' Ma looked worried. 'Snowing everywhere.' Ma watched as Holly packed her carry-on bag and just as Holly was zipping up, she stuffed in an extra sweater and woollen leggings.

Ready to leave with her black coat, scarf and beret already on, Holly-Jean sat at the kitchen table staring at the Chinese carpet with that now-familiar nagging feeling. Just what was it she kept on overlooking? Actually, her mind was a complete blank, apart from: *nice old design on that carpet*.

Then it came to her.

In a flash she kicked aside the carpet, lifted the cork tile and dialled the combination of the floor-safe. Lying undisturbed inside was Elfa's little black book, and inside that was the folded envelope of negatives she'd lifted from the escritoire at Holland Walk and which since that day she'd forgotten all about!

She was just about to reach down when she stopped herself in time. Dashed over to the kitchen area and extracted a new poly freezer-bag from the packet. Precluding further contamination of any latent or blatant fingerprints, she used the poly-bag as a glove to extract the envelope from the little black book.

There were eight frames in the single strip and though she already knew, she still had to hold them up to the light, to confirm the sad selection.

Holly carefully inverted the poly-bag so that the envelope and negatives were protected inside and sealed it with a knot. She placed the bag back in the safe, slammed the door shut, spun the combination, kicked the cork tile in place and dragged the carpet back. Stuffing the little black book in her pocket, she grabbed her bag and kissed Ma on both cheeks, hugging the awkward bundle. 'Bye, Ma!'

'Take care, *Shao-lan*, my Little Orchid. Take care!'

She drove the new Discovery onto the Harwich–Hamburg ferry in time for the six p.m. night-crossing, docking the following morning at twelve-thirty a.m. It was a long night, but worth it for the deep sleep in the private cabin, with ear-plugs, last of the painkillers and a bottle of clear Genever.

She spent the morning on deck, face to the wind, thinking.

This job wasn't just about Elfa any more. There was a far deeper stench pervading it all. The corrupt stench of some primordial bog, where angels get stuck like pigs and turned on a spit.

165

Holly-Jean looked out at the cold waves. Sure, she was still utterly determined to uncover the truth about the beautiful young girl's death. But Elfa was dead and buried. And so was Eddy van Schrempft.

De Lache might be immoral, but these days who wasn't?

Joel Unmack played awfully dumb, but as far as this case was concerned he was an *idiot savant* by Holly's reckoning, and yet so what?

It wasn't just about drugs either, nor mere fashionworld sleaze. Nor did it concern Holly-Jean ultimately that persons unknown were out to get her for reasons equally unknown. She'd face them down any time.

No, there was a deeper stench still emanating. And Holly was going to excise the source. Because this affair was now about taking down an evil one, a Grade A shithead, a man who for profit and gain, and maybe for some deeper, darker motivation too, plied the brave new global village paths touting his stinking wares that shattered the lives of children.

For Holly felt instinctively that Kriega was the key to it all.

Her priority was still investigating and solving Elfa's death, but there was more to it now. Far more. And as she gulped the North Sea wind, she saw clearly that this was all about taking a stand.

Drawing a line amid the chaos.

Dark or no Dark Age, Holly-Jean was going to wreck those who wrecked children.

Following signs for Denmark and the North, Holly drove the Discovery out of the car-ferry dock onto the E22 Autobahn and few miles further onto the E45 Autobahn, windscreen wipers gouging a hole in the white wall of snow as the needle tipped 190 kph/120 mph. Holly-Jean loved to

166

drive. Especially this creamy tank. Favourite music blasting all the way up Schleswig-Holstein. She reached the port of Flensburg at dusk and found the Hotel Prem on a quiet cobbled lane called Papenhuderstrasse just off the north side of the fiord.

The owner, whom Holly-Jean had spoken with when she'd made the booking Monday morning (after consulting the *Lonely Planet Virtual Traveller Guide* on the WWW), was waiting for her.

'Herr Fiedler?'

'Sea-Captain Fiedler,' he bowed. 'Welcome to Flensburg, dear mystery lady Ho, arriving in the middle of a winter's blizzard.' He took her bag and ushered her inside the carved wooden doors of the tiny Jugendstil building.

The houses on either side were old, half-timbered Baltic Sea dwellings. Holly stopped and remarked on their beauty. 'The Allied bombers missed this place, then?'

Fiedler smiled. 'You're observant. Flensburg was mostly lucky or rebuilt exactly as before. We're a conservative bunch, us Flensburgers; don't take to change. But let's get inside, this wind's got a bite like a Polar Bear.'

Kapitan Fiedler really looked the part; jaunty sailor's cap on his red Brillo pad skull, eyes sparkling merrily just above the first hairs of a huge carrot-coloured beard that hung down onto his bull's chest, complete with protruding pipe of sweetly-pungent tobacco.

'Borkum Riff?' sniffed Holly. Fiedler gave her a thumbs-up.

After showing her to her room, he insisted she come straight back downstairs as soon as she was ready, to the tiny bar of the Hotel Prem where the lone waitress presented her with a steaming bowl of seafood stew, dark rye bread and Hansen's Black Rum toddy.

'My daughter Lutzi,' said Fiedler. Holly shook her hand and Lutzi blushed furiously, bobbed a curtsey and rushed off. 'Fourteen years old,' explained her father.

A languid hour or so later, after swapping stories with Fiedler beside the blazing fire, interrupted only by the occasional needs of the few other customers coming in out of the dark, Holly-Jean, replete and refreshed, threw down her serviette and said, 'That was just the job. Now, how about a constitutional? I can smell the sea. Which is the quickest way to the harbour?'

She had wrapped up well, and as Sea-Captain Fiedler took the keys to the Discovery so he could drive it off to the Hotel Prem's distant parking space, he pointed with his curved pipe down the lane. 'Turn left at the bottom and follow the sound of breaking glass! The Finnish Navy's in town and a bunch of Danes have come over for the festivities. The border with Denmark's just two miles up the road.' He looked at his watch. 'Things'll be warming up about now. You'll find plenty of fun. Just don't go into the bar with the red "W" sign called Werner's. It's Flensburg's biker bar. Otherwise you should be all right.'

He added, eyes a-twinkle, 'I've been at sea most of my life, travelled all around the world and reckon I'm a pretty good judge of character. You, Madame Ho, give me an instinct you're a real gutsy lady and can handle yourself in just about any situation.'

Holly-Jean just winked and wrapped the scarf round her fâce as she headed into the snow flurries of the Nordic night. Watchful, she kept to the shadows, strolling atop the wide round-stone harbour wall, just across the road from the bright lights of the row of bars lining the North shore of the fiord.

If Fiedler reckoned this was fun, his definition of the word was rather broad, Holly decided. Her own word would be mayhem. Vomiting, brawling, bleeding and plain lost in a pitching sea of booze, a motley meld of seamen, fishermen,

sailors, naval ratings, truckers, spitting whores and meandering groups of civilian locals of all agegroups zig-zagged
in and out of the bars along the harbour road, casually
babysat by baton-wielding Finnish shore patrol MPs and
bored-looking local cops. And this was *Tuesday*?

Under a lamp she checked the name card and the address: *7,
Havenweg*. Found it, right next to the last bar of the row,
where the town ended in countryside and the fiord widened
on its way out to the Baltic Sea.

The bar with all the hogs parked out front.

The bar with the red neon 'W' called Werner's.

Holly turned back towards town and was strolling along
when a blond giant detached himself from a gaggle of
friends passing by and marched directly up to her. He
seemed not to notice her until the very last moment and just
avoided collision as with a great roar he threw up over the
harbour wall. He said something in Danish which Holly
didn't understand.

'A tourist!' he yelled. 'Komm! We have big party!'

Holly-Jean figured how better to recce Flensburg so she
joined the blond giant, whose name was Gunnar, and his
equally gigantic, equally blond pals of both sexes, as they
bar-crawled.

Sea-Captain Fiedler came and brought her home as the
fishing boats were leaving on the early tide. When he found
her, Holly-Jean was in a packed bar called 'Tick's',
alternating table-diving with martial arts slam-dancing to
twenty-minute acid-trance-hip-hop-ambient-house-dance-
remix of 'Zombie', completely delirious on Hansen's black
rum.

The next morning, Fiedler served extra-strength espresso
with a shot of Underberg and a bacon-egg-potato rösti. She
forewent the rösti and set off for 7, Havenweg.

It was an excessively bright sunny morning. Fortunately, Holly had brought her shades. The reflective surfaces really pierced the brain, as did the seagulls' jeering *yike-yike-yike*.

At 7, Havenweg she rang the bell of the pink half-timbered Baltic seashore building. No one answered. Holly looked around. An old woman was smoking fish over a brazier about fifty metres back along the harbour wall towards town. The bar called Werner's was shuttered and deserted. She rang again.

She'd misplaced her watch sometime during the night before, but a clock on the harbour-light said it was nine-thirty.

Wednesday morning, right? There wasn't a soul to be seen. So the fleet had already sailed on the early tide and schoolkids would be in school. In the distance, back towards town, there seemed to be a bit of bustle, but what about the harbour folk of Flensburg?

Hansenised to the world, guessed Holly as she inserted two pick-locks and waggled the lock open. Quick glance about, nip inside and in a flash she'd shut the door silently behind her.

Holly took off her shades and found herself facing an enclosed door-width staircase leading steeply up to the first floor and another door. Stepping carefully she made it to the top with a deafening creak on every step. Praying that any inhabitant of the building had also partaken of Hansendelics the previous night, she pushed open the door and entered a huge open space which reached up the remaining three floors to the interior eaves of the building's roof. The old sea-front structure had been completely gutted inside, and the whole place had been painted in white, apart from the chrome-steel open gallery ringing the top-floor level.

The main space was a fully equipped photographer's

studio, crammed with lamps, spots, mirrors, and curtained-off darkrooms. Holly found a computerised mixing desk-cum-console that looked like the deck of the *Enterprise*, and began flicking switches just for the sheer Hansenity-hell of it. Lights came on, colours changed, backdrops of different coloured paper unrolled in descent, re-rolled in ascent. Fans began to blow golden leaves. Snowflakes fell or whirled about. Music boomed out: one switch, Beethoven, another, reggae, yet another, Balinese gamelan. Lenses were piled high, film canisters stashed, a brace of Bolex 16 mm film movie-cameras here, a long row of varied video-camcorders there. And all about were diverse still cameras. The latest and best of every kind of equipment, as befitted the residence of a world-renowned lensman.

Holly spent the next thirty minutes on a thorough search. Hoping to turn up exactly she knew quite not what. A big red decal with the sign *Prawn Club* would have helped. No such luck.

Holly climbed up the steep circular stairs to the gallery.

Four unpartitioned spaces: living room and bedroom at front and back, with windows overlooking the harbour and fiord hillside. Bathroom and kitchen/dining space on either side. Another fruitless search. But what did she expect? The guy was obviously very smart. He'd hardly be leaving incriminating evidence lying about the place. Disconsolate, Holly sat down on the bed, fell back and let her Hansengover have a breather.

It was only when she opened her eyes some minutes later that she noticed the tiny red beam in the darkness of the roof eaves. She'd probably activated the cameras as soon as she opened the studio doors. She shrugged and gave the hidden lens the middle finger.

Maybe she'd slept a bit, or maybe she'd lost track of time,

but when she reached the bottom of the steep staircase and stepped outside onto Havenweg, it seemed the daylight was already fading. The space in front of Werner's Bar was already lined with customised motorbikes, the owners of which, now that her eyes had adjusted to the gloom, appeared to be standing in a menacing semi-circle around her.

A semi-circle of exceptional ugliness.

North German outlaw bikers are known neither for their subtly scented breath nor their charm, good looks and attention to etiquette, and this lot were no exception. Holly folded away her shades and adopted a defensive posture as they moved in closer.

An oily boot, steel toecap visible through broken leather, swung lazily towards her left rear; she reached out and caught it. Jerked up to the vertical and dumped the attached bearded brute upon his arse.

With an angry roar the bikers charged at her.

Holly struck out as accurately and effectively as she could and was holding her own for a time before sheer strength of numbers, the protective effect of the outlaws' leather-denim 'colours' and the unremitting rain of blows, began to slowly overwhelm her. She was down on one knee, kicking out behind her and twisting the testicles within one rank-odorous crotch while elbowing another's beer-gut, when suddenly a new bout of yelling began from behind the mêlée and her attackers turned to face some kind of rearguard threat.

Holly discerned quickly that the new party was raising apparent objection to cavalier treatment of a woman. She recognised some faces in the bloody strife. It was Gunnar and his pals!

While the Danes and the bikers mixed it up, Gunnar waded in with a weird discipline Holly had never seen before. A rhythmic lolloping crouch with catherine-wheel

limbs which despatched opponents with the ease of a
baseball bat. He soon reached Holly, prised loose her vise-
hold from the crotch of the now-gibbering prone outlaw and
yelled, 'Let's go!'

Holly nodded and followed him at a run down Havenweg.

At the Hotel Prem, Holly-Jean said thanks to Gunnar, shook
his ham of a hand, and went up to her room to wash, change
and have a little nap. Strangely, that evening when she came
down for dinner, she found Gunnar being served at the bar.
Only this time he was wearing a dark jacket, shirt and tie, his
blond hair had turned black and neat and he said, 'Good
evening, Holly-Jean Ho,' in an American accent. Midwest –
Iowa, Holly guessed.

'Flensburg's full of surprises. Must be the air.' She leant
on the bar and greeted their host. 'Good evening, Kapitan
Fiedler.'

'Madame Holly,' said Fiedler with a little bow, waiting
for her order.

'I'll have a bottle of anything Alsace, whatever my friend
here wants and one for yourself.'

'Same again,' said Gunnar. He was drinking Dortmunder
Union Beer straight from the bottle.

Fiedler had a pepper schnapps. They all raised drinks.
'Skol!'

'You'll be eating dinner with your friend?' asked Fiedler,
indicating the dinner menu chalked on a board. 'The special
is smoked pig's knuckle. Not bad. Or maybe try the
smorgasbord. Besser, I sink.'

With a nod of respect to her host, Holly said, 'And I *sink*,
Mr So-called Gunnar, that you and I had better have a quiet
chat first.' Holly-Jean took her bottle and glass and led
Gunnar over to a small table by the fire. The Prem was half-
full, mostly with couples eating a quiet dinner.

'First things first,' said Holly. 'What was that martial art you used back there? Kind of a crouching rhythmic lope, almost a dance. But brilliantly free-form and by the looks, lethally effective.'

'Capoeira,' said the American. 'You described it perfectly. Comes out of the Brazilian African-Latin mix of Bahia. Escaping slaves' self-defence. About ninety years old, give or take five hundred years of tribal Africa. Training is done to chanting and drumming. It's the complete antithesis of the rigid Asian disciplines that you're an adept of. With Capoeira you become a private and unknowable tune of death.'

Holly-Jean, ever the split-end, liked the sound of that. 'Brazil, you say?'

'Yep. Master Carlos in Rio is about the best right now.'

Holly sipped her wine. 'So. Your name's not Gunnar. Nor are you some wandering Dane one-toke over the borderline for a bit of Deutschland nightlife. Allow me to guess. DEA Nark? US Drug Enforcement Administration agent following up the Volkspark bombing?'

'Close but no cigar.' He held out his massive hand. 'Daniel Z. Mikaluk, Ukrainian out of New Orleans. My friends call me Danny the Mouth.' Holly shook the big hand. 'I do on occasion work with the DEA,' he went on, 'but, Fraulein Ho, you'd better believe The Mouth's no nark. Much heavier brand. I'm HUMINT.'

'Glad to hear that,' said Holly.

Mikaluk smiled. 'Not referring to the genus. It's an acronym stands for—'

'The Defense Human Intelligence Service, the DHS,' said Holly. 'Part of the Defense Intelligence Agency, the DIA, not to be confused with the CIA, the FBI, or the IUD.' She looked at his hand now holding the beer bottle. 'Should've noticed those black hairs didn't gel with the gel. Sloppy work, Ho.'

She leant her head back and studied his face across the

candle-light. 'Danny the Mouth? Seems to tinkle a distant bell. You ever been in Taipei?'

'Veritable shit-hole,' he nodded, his gaze never leaving her. Trying to size her up. 'Since you're knowledgeable of HUMINT, you'll have guessed why I'm here and, I trust, understood the implications.'

Oh, Holly understood all right. Unfortunately, the purport of that understanding was not just endlessly fascinating but quite likely fatal. She decided to back-pedal.

'Since it's not any Lebanese drug-cartel connection with my late friend Edward van Schrempft, then I can't imagine. Sorry to disappoint.'

Mikaluk upended the beer down his throat, put down the empty bottle and said, 'Since I don't believe for one second that you aren't fully cognisant of the potentialities we're talking about here, you don't disappoint me one bit, Miss Holly-Jean. After all, you didn't seriously think we'd let your little pow-wow at the weekend go untended, did you?' He cocked his head. 'Half the Triad section heads of East Asia applying for Dutch visas and flying first-class or private into Schiphol this coming Friday.'

'Oh, *that*.'

'That,' concurred Danny the Mouth. He looked amused. 'Friends of Chinese Opera. You stole it from *Some Like It Hot*, right? Tony Curtis, Jack Lemmon and Marilyn Monroe. One of the funniest movies ever made.'

Holly said, 'Homage to Billy Wilder.'

Mikaluk opened his hands in a friendly gesture. 'I want to level with you, Holly-Jean. Since I first became acquainted of the fact you were the Convention organiser, I've been doing some extensive research.'

He signalled for fresh beer. 'And I've discovered, very felicitously, if I may say so, that you have just about the finest *guanchi* with the Secret Societies of the North European Chinese diaspora that I've ever come across. And

I'm going to come right out now and put my cards on the table. That all right with you?'

'Be my guest,' said Holly in Mandarin.

The Mouth beamed. 'I'd very much like to employ you, Holly-Jean Ho, or should I address you as *Ho Shao-Lan shao-jye*. British citizen and passport-holder. Unmarried. No children. Only close relative: natural mother, with whom you're currently residing at Flat 8B, Camden Lock, North London.'

'Don't make it sound like a crime,' complained Holly.

'Believe you me, that's the furthest thing from my mind, Holly-Jean.' He leant forward, towering over the table, his fervour that of a travelling tent-preacher. 'Holly-Jean, as I'm sure you know, organised crime is the biggest threat to world peace today. The crooks've become too powerful for single governments to contain. The whole goddam infrastructure's on the point of crumbling, the global economy's awash with dirty money, and it seems only the US of A stands between the Rule of Law and total anarchy.'

The beads of evangelical sweat glistened on his brow in the candle-light. 'I think I know you well, Holly-Jean. You want to make some difference in this world. Well, so do I. And with just a bit of mutual good fortune, together we're going to rise our stars.' He sat back and nodded rhythmically.

Now she knew why they called him The Mouth. Holly swilled her wine around her tongue, savouring the developing flavours.

'What if I were to say to you that I didn't want my star interfered with, and what's more, that if ever I should decide it needed any rising, that I was perfectly capable of self-propulsion?'

'Let's not kid about,' said Daniel Mikaluk, his face deadly serious. 'I didn't come all the way up here for the beer. I know you, Holly-Jean Ho. Know all about you, who you are, what you want. I know what's brought you to this place and I know *why* you're all fired up. Here's the deal: you work your *guanchi* clandestine-wise for me, and I'll get you Kriega.'

Holly's hand jerked spasmodically and knocked over her wine-glass. The wind howled down the chimney sending a milky-thick tongue of woodsmoke to lick the bar of the Hotel Prem.

Kapitan Fiedler marched over and adjusted the flue. He refilled her glass with a smile. 'Better to be a landlubber tonight.'

Kriega. Hearing the name she'd been avoiding enunciating seemed to bring a chill. Her skin had come over *chi-pi*.

She looked at the American. 'Throw in the Prawn Club?'

'It's a done deal,' said The Mouth, chuggalugging his bottle of beer.

Lutzi brought over two plates piled with a sumptuous selection from the smorgasbord. Holly ordered more wine. Mikaluk stuck to beer.

'I thought HUMINT could eavesdrop on any conversation on the planet. Why do you need me?'

'Straight answer is, we don't. The technology's all there. Sure, the Surabaya's difficult to penetrate but it's perfectly do-able.' He added with a shrug, 'And no doubt the Chinese'll bring along their science whizz-kids with their latest toys of bafflement. Don't worry, we'll still hear, and to some degree, see, everything that happens during the Convention weekend. But that's not enough. It's only half the picture. For truly successful surveillance, in the end, you'll always need what Graham Greene called "the human factor".'

He must be asked to lecture the trainees, thought Holly, watching his huge finger slice the smoky Prem bar air.

'Espionage isn't about proving physical realities,' he

went on. 'That's kid's stuff. It's about deep-diving the cerebral.'

'Better put by James Brown,' Holly cut in. 'You need me *to tell it like it is.*'

'Precisely!' said Danny, his giant frame bouncing about with such enthusiasm that Holly worried for the Prem's old wooden chair. 'See, with your *guanchi*, your specialist skills, your bearing of witness to the real-time events, means you can put the inner expressions on the blank faces. You can join up the dots. You can make the whole goddam movie. Soundtrack, cast, script and all. Holly-Jean, you can give us the *epistemology*.'

Holly-Jean knew when to strike. With the wide-eyed joy of the newly converted, she gushed ecstatically, 'Like, I can tell you why Sammy Yeh of the Four Seas won't let Richie Chiang of the Flying Eagles have the Zurich heroin contracts—'

'He won't? Why not?' Danny almost yelled.

'Because Richie's second cousin Ah-chen slipped Sammy's sixteen-year-old niece, Precious Jade, a mickey at the Golden Cow KTV on Chi-lin Road, Taipei and not only had his way with her, but announced to the world that the prized virgin's Jade Portals were about as intact as a revolving door.'

Danny the Mouth actually clapped his hands.

'Let's get one thing straight, Danny boy,' Holly struck. Her voice was hard. 'If I'm to spy on the Societies in return for your help in nailing him and any others involved, I'll require guarantees in the shape of sworn affidavits from the DIA: extradition to UK or US with hard time of not less than five years. That's my price. Take it or leave it.'

Danny looked at her with a roll-mop herring poised on his fork. 'Why not Delete? If it's what you want.'

Holly didn't speak for a while. Concentrated on the food. When they'd both finished, Mikaluk having a further two

178

more piled plates, Lutzi cleared away the mess. They moved to a carved bench worn by the bums of time into soft curves.

Watching the glowing embers, Holly said, 'Tell me about him.'

By the log-fire of the Hotel Prem, Daniel Mikaluk, also known as The Mouth, used that instrument to hack into the HUMINT data-base and lay bare before Holly-Jean the damned soul of one Holger Pfeltz, aka Kriega.

Born in Flensburg in 1955 of bourgeois stock, his father was a dentist, his mother a school-teacher. They were Catholics, a minority in the Lutheran North, but that was no serious handicap in the New Germany that was steadfastly rising from the ashes of defeat. Holger was an excellent student, well liked, good at games, a Boy Scout leader, a chorister in the Catholic Church.

Germany's education system beat the hell out of Mikaluk, seems you don't get to graduate from University till you're about thirty, but anyway Holger spent a year at Kiel Technical College, before, at twenty years old, joining the Jesuits who promptly sent him to a seminary in West Berlin.

'Now don't forget this was around 1975,' explained Danny, nursing his beer. 'Cold War's chilliest depths. Berlin still divided by the wall. And West Berlin the mecca for drop-outs, free-thinkers, hippies, anarchists and any other freaky what-have-you's of the Western world.'

Mikaluk stopped to drain the bottle. 'There's an inevitability at work here that you get used to when reading these kinds of files. Really, believe me. Human nature's so goddam predictable – opposites attract, that sort of thing. Time and time again.'

Mikaluk suddenly stood up, apologised and went to relieve himself. Holly sat locked into a particular pattern the flames were making as they raced to extinction. Noticing the fresh bottle of Alsace on his return, Mikaluk commented, 'You don't worry maybe you drink too much?'

Holly looked at him. Impudent cretin. What'd he know about grieving? Then she thought, Probably quite a lot, actually. And maybe he was right, she *was* drinking a bit too much. She quoted, '"Come, come, good wine is a good familiar creature if it be well used".' Adding, 'Just panel-beating the dents.'

Danny winked. '"What wound did ever heal but by degrees"!'

'Blimey, another cultured cop!'

'Anyway, predictably, one sunny day, Holger bunks off the seminary, and finds himself at the Free University of Berlin which in those days was a permanent political sit-in, love-in and Mad-Hatter's tea party. If I told you the number of middle-class bombers who got their first taste for blood at Berlin Frei, you'd be amazed,' said The Mouth.

'Suffice to say, our devout young Jesuit, finding himself confronted not only by other equally committed species of zealots, but half-naked female ones to boot, is launched into free-fall.'

'Day-glo body-paint and all.

'Not much is known about our Holg for a few years, till he turns up on a Shin Bet Israeli intelligence trace-request. Spotted in the Bekaa Valley, they want to know if we know whether he's there to buy hashish or train with the PLO. That's the point at which our file on Holger Pfeltz is first opened.'

Mikaluk paused while Fiedler brought fresh beer, and they both complimented him on the dinner. He insisted on fetching them a thin slice each of the smoked pig's knuckle. They pronounced it succulent and sublime.

Tamping down a fresh pipe, resting one foot on the fire-guard, their kindly host looked like staying for a while, so Holly casually suggested a post-prandial stroll.

'In this storm?' Fiedler was incredulous.

But Danny and Holly were soon out of the Prem and heading in a force-seven gale towards the south shore of the fiord as the second chapter of the life and times of a major shithead was relayed over the banshee wind by the giant voice-box of The Mouth.

'About this time, Holger apparently makes two discoveries. First, that he doesn't give a toss one way or the other about Jews, Arabs, capitalism, Communism or any other kind of ism – and two, that once in, you can't just drop out of the urban terror club. So he did what any gun-lovin' guy on the run would do. He walked into the Légion Etrangère barracks at Calvi, Corsica and asked to wear the white képi.

'The sadist drill-NCOs ran him ragged for nine months in the freezing Pyrenees, the cruel tearing Maquis and the burning El Djouff sands of Mauritania, same as the Foreign Legion does with all its new recruits.

'By the time he was passed out in May of '82 and sent to join the Second Regiment to fight the rebels in Chad, Holger could live naked and survive on twigs. Oh, and they'd also taught him photography for surveillance purposes. Five years of African war made that body into what you see today and which caused a sensation when he showed up at Milan recently with a portfolio of African atrocities interspersed with Nubian nymphets to use on some fashion campaign – withdrawn, naturally . . .

'The rest, as they say, is just more history,' said The Mouth as they turned at the eastern end of the south shore harbour wall and felt the full force of the gale at their backs, hurrying them along.

This side of the fiord was dark and silent, a complete contrast to the bright-lit boozery across the wind-whipped water.

'The terse single moniker, Kriega, didn't hurt either – Krieg means "war" in German,' mused Holly-Jean. 'Nor, I

181

bet, did the nipple rings, the Berlin SM leather outfit, the fuck-you attitude you knew for once was really real. *Ai-yo*, those fashion fluffies must have wanked at first sight.'

'Oh, he's a smart one, all right,' agreed Danny.

'I don't know why I loathe him, but I do,' said Holly. 'Trouble is, so far I've only got rumour, guesswork, gut-feeling and the fact that he owns a residence in the Philippines, to condemn this man. Tell me, Mr HUMINT know-it-all – is there a proven connection with the paedophile Prawn Club and Mr Pfeltz? They recently featured "borrowed" dirty pictures of Elfa Ericksson as a child, with whom, at the time of her death, Pfeltz was having some kind of deep personal relationship.'

Mikaluk had marched a few paces ahead to take a piss down-wind. He held up his hand till he'd finished and zipped up. Then he spun round.

'You're a real beaut, you are, Holly-Jean Ho, y'know that?' His voice soared above the howling wind. 'So it was all done on feminine intuition. Amazing! Well, you're right,' he bawled. 'The Prawn Club is all his. Your man Pfeltz's got a beautiful house on a tiny island in the Visayas. Takes two hours to fly his Rotax ultra-light into what used to be Clark Airbase, and five minutes by trike-taxi later, he's on Fields Avenue, Angeles City – one of the easiest places in the world to buy young kids.'

'What's a Rotax ultra-light?' said Holly, catching up with him as fresh snow began to tamp down the wind.

'Micro-light airplane – kind of a hang-glider with a seat and a propeller powered by bolted-on lawnmower engine. Rotax are the top of the line. Austrian-made. Pretty safe if competently piloted. The problem is novices who think they're toys. Very dangerous.' He paused. 'Very dangerous indeed.'

Holly-Jean looked at Mikaluk as the snowflakes fell like candy-floss and the wind ceased its wailing.

'Are you thinking what I'm thinking, Holly-Jean?'

'Doubt it,' she grumbled. 'Since he left the Jesuits our boy's never been a novice at anything.'

Danny started singing a tune. Holly recognised it – 'Magic Moments'. The Mouth's adaptation: 'Fuck-ups, hap-pen, when you least expect them.'

They walked back to the Prem. At the entrance to the cobbled lane, Mikaluk stopped. 'I'll be in touch. Here's my cellphone number. Always available.'

Holly shouted at his retreating back, 'Whatever happens, you be in the Philippines from the fifth of March onwards. Deal?'

'Done deal!' came the voice from the swirling snowy dark.

Chapter 13

The Friends of Chinese Opera Convention went fairly smoothly, depending upon which point of view you were positioned to receive. Holly-Jean's might differ from the general consensus on this.

Of all the aggravation she endured, it was probably not the gambling, girls or golf, nor the underlying tensions and hatreds that might at any moment erupt into automatic gunfire.

It was seating.

Yep, the seating arrangements proved the most troublesome obstacle to a peaceful atmosphere between the rival factions, and proved the irritation which got furthest up Holly's nose.

In Chinese society, where you are placed to sit takes on the deepest significance. Especially at dinner.

Face and *feng-shui* – two obsessions the West does not share.

Faction heads had to sit at the most powerful position: that is with their back to the front entrance. Strange, eh? Not the common or garden mobster's preferred choice! But with each *lao-ban* gang boss bringing his own fanatic protection, safety was less of a concern than gaining face.

Thus, every night there had to be a rotation not just of seats at the individual tables, but of the tables themselves, to ensure no one was offended by lost face. In addition to which, no one could be allowed to feel threatened by dangerous Geomancy positioning. No self-respecting *lao-ban* would travel abroad without his personal *feng-shui* (wind-water) geomancers. And this lot were no exception. They'd all brought one along.

These guys, dressed as oriental wizards, all sported long thin white goatees, walked around with their geomancy compasses in palm of hand, muttering arcane formulas and sprinkling magic water here and there with tiger-hair whisks. Their purpose: to preclude any possibility that the positioning of a dinner-table seat, or bed, or conference table, or the choice of door through which to make an entrance and exit, or bathroom facility, or parking space, or who knew the frock what! would irritate the slumbers of the Earth Dragon.

Yep, the Earth Dragon must not, *under any circumstances*, be disturbed, or not only would your ancestors be made to pay and thus take it out on you and your good fortune, but also any wayward ghosts, lost souls, unhappy dead, or just plain non-RIPs who refused to rest in peace, would be sent from the Underworld to punish and torment you.

Not too cool a prospect, at this time of intense bargaining, negotiation and jockeying for pole position amongst one's deadly peers.

Typically, therefore, Holly-Jean found herself faced with endless requests for the re-positioning of items of furniture. Such as the change Joey Lin's *feng-shui* master insisted upon, within thirty minutes of the Hong Kong-based 14K faction head's arrival at the Surabaya. The problem: the king-size bed in Joey Lin's master suite was positioned, apparently, precisely above the Earth Dragon's left-side fourth leg's funny bone and would thus cause grave irritation.

It took six able-bodied but highly mystified hotel staff to

shift the damn thing a few inches skew-whiff. Not only that, but the bathroom mirror in Joey's suite was also entirely wrong and had to be completely removed because it directly reflected the moonlight when the bathroom door and the curtains of the bedroom were open at the same time. This moonbeam would then in turn be refracted and could cause bad *feng-shui* in the bathroom, which might then filter down through the earth to disturb the dreams of the Earth Dragon below – and we wouldn't want that, would we?

No sirree, added Holly-Jean, thinking, You guys should move to LA. Her previous suggestions that Joey's staff should just make sure that both curtains and door were shut after nightfall in the unlikely event of the moon just happening to peak out from behind the snow-clouds ... or failing which, drape a towel over the damn thing, had been met with Mandarin derision of the type: What do you expect of an Unmarried Miss of her age? Typical female stupidity. *Shao-jye*, please keep your mouth shut and expedite our wishes without further comment.

These difficulties notwithstanding, from others' point of view, the Conference went fairly smoothly.

From what Holly could gather, it seemed that most allotting of turf went to plan. Trade agreements were chopped (signed) that included the distributive rights and tariff deals on various commodities such as narcotics, prostitution, illegal aliens (bonded labour), and Chinese medicine, including endangered species' contraband – tiger penis, rhino horn, Panda-bile etc, and legal products such as ginseng, desiccated sea-horse and cordyceps (dried caterpillar larvae). The most thorny problem appeared to be the allocation of the rights to the protection business in certain disputed border areas, and this led to the lengthiest renegotiations of all.

Holly wondered if the EU leaders knew that the Surabaya

Peace Plan was a *de facto* Balkanisation of the entire North of Europe by a bunch of low-life Chinese warlords.

On the last night of the Conference a special outing was planned. Following the afternoon's golf at the wind-swept sand-dune course of the Zeeland Country Club, the Conference attendees, dressed in variations of black tie formality, including one Taiwanese chap memorable in solid-gold tuxedo lapels, were herded aboard two luxury coaches for the drive to Roosendaal.

Roosendaal looks just like any other sleepy town of the flat Brabant. Prosperous, quiet, a confident burgh. It's seen usually by travellers through the windows of trans-European trains standing at the huge railway station crossroads. In fact, Roosendaal is a surprise. Behind the nondescript glass office buildings are casinos. Twenty-four hours a day the dice tumble, the croupiers call, the wheels turn and the drinks come *gratis*. It's always been that way.

Though legal in Holland now, gaming is still illegal in the staid countries to the north, and gamblers will drive from as far as Stockholm and Oslo, while other punters just like the special historical atmosphere of Roosendaal, and par-ticularly, Damstraat with its discreet row of casinos.

Certain that the Society members were well catered for, and leaving them happily dispersed into various localities, Holly-Jean felt that with just this one last night to get through, she deserved a celebratory drink.

She was sitting at a small Dutch-Mex bar called Hot Stuff, relaxing with a quiet series of clear Genever shots when a voice in her ear said, 'Saw you on telly the other day.'

She looked up at the mirror behind the bar to see Kriega. Raised her shot glass and smiled, 'Telly? *Moi?*' with an exaggerated look of puzzlement before she said, 'Oh right, *Flensburg*, of course. Yes, I was just taking you up on your invitation to visit. Found the door open and wondered if you might be home.'

Kriega hitched himself up onto the stool beside her. 'Finding no one, you naturally stayed to look around. Though in my opinion, Ms Ho, you're rather a nosy guest.'

'My natural curiosity. Can't help it. Always been a problem.' She nodded to the bartender who re-filled her shot glass. 'In *my* opinion, it was rather unnecessary to have your biker friends beat me up.'

'Biker friends? *Moi?*' mimicked Kriega.

Holly turned to look at him face-to-face. 'I'm still on for the photo shoot. Let's pencil in the Philippines for around about the twelfth?'

Kriega was momentarily nonplussed, but soon recovered. He pulled out an electronic notebook. 'Twelfth of March, you say? Sure, no problem. As promised I'll handle all your travel.' He looked up at her. 'As you get to know me more, you'll find I always keep my promises.'

'No need,' said Holly. Then she did a mental about-turn. Nearly forgot the golden rule: a first-class air-ticket was to be accepted without prejudice. 'Ah, wait, yes, you did say first-class airfare, right? I'm not completely finalised about dates, so messenger an open-dated ticket over to my London address, would you?'

'It'll be there within forty-eight hours.'

Holly swallowed her shot and climbed down from her bar-stool. 'Sorry. Got a lot of guys in town.'

'Oh, I know all about your guys,' said Kriega. 'I'm here on a little business myself. But, you, tiny Tiger Ms Ho, you fascinate me more and more. Your connections are, shall we say, quite "specialist", aren't they?'

Holly buttoned up her coat and adjusted her beret in the mirror. 'Nah, just a bunch of Chinese tourists need babysitting. I'll look forward to the Philippines.'

189

'So will I.' Quick eye-contact butting of *chi*s before Holly-Jean left Hot Stuff to go and round up her charges.

She drove back to Rotterdam from Schiphol Airport in Amsterdam after the last of the guests had been seen off safely. Arriving in the afternoon, she met Rita from work and they went to Sint Jacobs Kirk, the church where Ed's ashes had been laid to rest. She stayed Monday night at the apartment on Van der Helm Straat. It was a time-out, a no-fire zone. Neither mentioned work the whole time. Pure bliss. Back in London Tuesday, she had lunch with Mr Hua. He wanted to check the AIA invite had gone through. Holly confirmed it had.

She hedged her bets by saying she might require some assistance at the upcoming AIA gathering in the Philippines where her membership application would be put to vote.

Mr Plum Blossom's reply was not altogether reassuring. 'Naturally, since your undertaking is on our behalf, you will constantly be under our watchful eye.' She recalled being shadowed by one over-enthusiastic Society soldier during her stay in Taiwan the year before.

'Not too watchful, OK? Like when I'm taking a shower, for instance. By the way,' she asked, 'you have any dealings with a German called Kriega? Showed up on Damstraat in Roosendaal the other night. Said he had business with some of your boys.'

The Chinese gentleman's reply was completely devoid of scrute. 'Applying oneself totally and with diligence to the job in hand is the safest path to success.'

Back at Camden Lock Holly-Jean spent a couple of quiet days with Ma and Mrs Howell-Pryce. The Commons free vote had gone through, though it still had to pass further readings in both Houses before it became enacted.

Meanwhile, Ma was amassing further evidence specifically aimed at banning the Prawn Club from UK cyberspace. COMSEM had proposed the formulation of a list of proscribed organisations operating on the Internet, proven access to which would be an offence. How you went about proving the accessing was going to be a whole different story.

Friday afternoon, the three women were sitting drinking Oolong *cha* – Ma had got Mrs H-P hooked – when the telephone rang. It was Soapy Ponds, an old journo *guanchi* of Holly's networking acquaintance. He specialised in software and among other publications did a column for the *Guardian* in which he would slip the occasional exposé of some pirated software which Holly fed him. He'd covered all the copyright infringement trials Holly'd been involved in and by mentioning her role in his writing had definitely given her career a boost.

'Hi, Soapy.'

'Holly, now listen. Nothing to get too worked up about, I hope, but I thought you ought to know what I just heard from an ex-cellmate of Delly Barker.'

Delvin Barker, the copyright buccaneer whom Holly had nailed last year for the fake Windows holograms from Guangdong.

'What's the story?'

'It seems that Delly was just a little bit obsessed with his yacht – you remember the single traceable asset the judge was able to track down and confiscate—'

'Right, the *Copycat*.'

'Yeh; always a wag, our Delvin. Anyway, this cellmate, who just happens to be a good old snitch of mine from way back, happened to mention that Delly Boy was starting to come apart at the seams. Kept talking about the sailboat non-stop, drove my snout mad, and in the same breath, this is the bit I didn't like, he kept going on and on about what he was going to do to you when he got out.'

191

Holly didn't say anything.

'Well, friend Delvin's been out for a couple of weeks already, so my advice to you is watch your delectable rear.'

'What? I thought he wasn't due out for a month yet.'

'You can thank the bleeding heart parole liberals for that.'

Holly cursed silently. Oh well, join the queue, Delvin. Everybody and his Uncle Tom Cobbleigh seemed to be out to get her.

'Uh, thanks, Soapy.' She added, 'You don't take Delly seriously, do you? He's just a lovable rogue, right?'

'Hadn't taken him seriously before now, no,' said Soapy. 'But who knows what a bit of pokey will do to a man. Don't forget he'd never done time before. And Delvin Barker was always a man who savoured his freedoms. Fancied himself as an epicure, a connoisseur, a lover of the good life. Might have done his head in, being banged up with a bunch of petty criminals instead of cavorting in a tower room at Eden Roc.'

Holly sighed. 'Suppose you're right. Oh well, if you see him, tell him to take a ticket from reception and get in line. I'm apparently flavour of the month for revenge-seekers, just for a change.'

'Take care, ace. And stay in touch.'

'Will do.'

The doorbell rang. Holly went out into the corridor and looked through the spy-hole to see a man in a dark bowler hat and formal dress. She called back, 'Ma, go and check the electric meter in the closet under the sink!' When she heard the affirmative reply, she opened the door.

'Our gravest condolences, Madam. May we come up and ah collect the ah?' he said in the sepulchral tones of the professional. Down on the cobbles waited a Daimler hearse

with its back gate open. Three other black-tied men stood at
the bottom of the iron staircase with a coffin. Holly quickly
shut the door behind her.

'There's been a mistake. Could you get those guys out of
here immediately? Don't worry, I'll settle up whatever you
need right away. Tell them to wait for you on Chalk Farm
Road. Just get that thing away! Please!'

She didn't want Ma seeing the traditional Chinese final
warning of threatened death to come: the delivery of a coffin
to the house of the proposed victim. Back inside the house
she pretended to write down the figures Ma was coming up
with from under the sink. Mrs H-P, meanwhile, looking out
the window, was giving Holly very strange looks. Holly
signalled fiercely with finger to her lips.

'Thanks, Mum,' she said, and hurried off to write the man
a cheque.

Later, when Ma was off getting fresh vegetables from a stall
at the Lock, Holly informed Mrs Howell-Pryce a little bit,
not too much, no point in scaring her unduly, about the
campaign apparently directed against her.

'Since I'll be away for the next couple of weeks, I hope
you'll keep an extra eye out for my mother. It's probably just
a local nutter being a damn nuisance, but maybe it's
someone with a grudge. Our agency has had its successes,
and along with the good-will generated, there can't help but
be some ill-will.'

Noticing a certain pallor about the Welsh widow's face,
Holly added hurriedly, 'You're not to worry, Mrs H-P. It's
bound to be me they're after. Problem is, finding me
unavailable, they may just decide to take it out on Ma.
Anyway, you can imagine I'm getting a bit worried, what
with one thing and another.'

'Don't worry,' said Mrs Howell-Pryce, 'I'll have her over
to stay at my place while you're gone.'

'You will?' said Holly, greatly relieved. 'That's wonderful. You really are a brick, Mrs H-P. What would I do without you?'

Even so, Holly took the precaution of informing both Inspector Mick Coulson and Mr Hua of her fears, and exacted their assurances of extra vigilance before she presented herself at the Philippine Airlines first-class check-in counter at Gatwick on 4 March. She was feeling a bit under the weather, hardly in the mood for an intercontinental flight – a mood not helped by the fact that just as she was about to leave Camden Lock, the strangest thing happened. She received a phonecall from a highly distraught Epifania Pangalina, Elfa Ericksson's housemaid.

'*Akaw-lalang!* I dreamed of you last night, Madam. You're going to the Philippines today, aren't you?'

'I am,' said Holly, startled.

'I saw you in grave danger! Serpents! Locusts! Curses! May the Birgin Mary, Soledad, Salvacion, Inmaculada Concepcion protect you!'

'Uh, thanks,' said Holly. But Epifania had rung off.

'*Mabuhay!* Welcome to Philippine Airline first class!' said the counter-clerk, presenting her with a fresh frangipani blossom. 'Your seat has already been reserved.' Holly didn't need to ask by whom. 'May I have your bags, please?'

'Just hand-carry, thanks,' replied Holly. She never checked in baggage. If it couldn't be squeezed into her expandable multi-zippered airline standard travel bag, then she'd buy it at the other end. Bound to be cheaper anyway. Her boarding pass was presented immediately, and she was escorted by a young airline employee to the VIP lounge on the second floor of the terminal building. Francisco Frank Goya, President-for-Life of the AIA was waiting with a small group of three males and one female. His long, thin tongue darted in and out as he said, 'Holly-Jean Ho, welcome, welcome! Here, drink this down!' He handed her a flûte of Krug champagne, and introduced her all round.

'Sorry we couldn't wrangle a private charter. Just couldn't be done this trip, so nothing for it but to fly jolly old FlipAir. It's a bloody inconvenient airline, stops at half-a-dozen Godforsaken airports before reaching Manila sometime next week, so suggest you follow the general policy which is, get immune as quickly and deeply as you can!'

Stops at Frankfurt, Rome, Abu Dhabi and Bangkok made the flight considerably longer than the scheduled fifteen hours twenty-five minutes. Thankfully the brand-new, improved first-class seats were fully convertible into beds with curtains to draw round and sheets and pillow-cases. There were only eight seats in first class, and the other two remained empty until Rome, where they were taken by the Philippine Ambassador to Italy and his wife. The service was faultless and the food surprisingly good.

Needless to say, Frankie Goya had ensured in advance that supplies of chilled Krug would be unlimited.

Needless to say, during the dark hours, Holly made damn sure her curtain was fully drawn and hooked in place.

Consequently, Holly felt pretty good, all things considered, when they finally touched down at Ninoy Aquino International Airport in Manila. There was, however, just one discordant note.

If the Philippines' gift to the world is anything, it is music. The disproportionately high number of talented Pinoy musicians working around the world from *Miss Saigon* on Broadway to jazz bars in Tokyo attests to this fact. In keeping with this proud achievement there has always been a traditional folk-music band standing at the entrance to the arrivals lounge at NAIA ready to strike up a song of welcome whenever a plane discharges its weary passengers. Today was no exception. Sadly, when Goya's

195

party, Holly-Jean among them, was passing by, one of the guitar players fell down dead of a heart attack.

From Manila it was just a short hop by private charter plane to Mactan Island off Cebu in the Central Philippines' scattered Visayas Isles. When the little plane touched down on the bumpy airstrip and the sealed door was opened, the tropical heat came on board like a clanging bell announcing time to sweat, and the party trotted at the double across the spongey tarmac to the waiting limos of the Shangri-La Paradise Resort.

'Thank God for air conditioning!' was Holly's only comment.

Chapter 14

Heeding the maxim as laid down in the Lonely Planet travel survival kit to the Philippines – 'Believe half of what you hear, half of what you see and half of what you do' – an old joke she'd heard applied to countless places from Taipei to Turkey, Holly let the dangerous languor of the islands slip over her like the seventh silken veil.

From the first scent of the tropic air as she stepped out onto the wooden verandah of her individual luxury wooden palm-frond *nipa*-roofed hut on the landscaped hillside of the resort, and watched the surf break out on the distant reef above the sea of palms, she was already seduced by the Philippines, the sheer beauty of the people and the place. Holly was no fool, however. She knew very well this was a man-made paradise. The infamous rubbish-tip community of Manila's Smoky Mountain was a more realistic picture of the grinding poverty of ninety per cent of the citizenry.

Holly-Jean Ho was duly voted in, alongside ten others including a Croatian, a Latvian and a Quebecois Canadian, as a member at the first official meeting of the AIA gathering the next afternoon, after the delegates' jet-lag had been fully expunged by glorious banqueting and widespread pampering.

Holly herself didn't waste time sleeping indoors, preferring to doze and bask in the tropical sun amid palm-frond luxury, either on her verandah or by one of the numerous

197

lagoon-landscaped swimming pools complete with water-falls and lotus blossoms, or sometimes, by slipping away to reality and having a coconut-oil massage down on the beach by a local woman.

Throughout the scheduled meetings and subsequent festivities, Holly carefully avoided contact with the two opposing delegations from the People's Republic and Taiwan. She neither knew nor wanted to know whether anyone else at the Shangri-La was aware of her particular agenda.

She assumed that Society members were keeping a close eye on the proceedings, but whether as participants or not, she couldn't care less. In fact, it wasn't all frolicking in the tropical sun, either.

Real business had to be dealt with.

There were genuine meetings where genuine discussions took place with various sub-committees posted up on the boards or announced over the paging system. Also, there were countless planned social activities which old boy Goya apparently expected her to participate in as his companion.

It was during one of these, a trip to Lapu-Lapu and the memorial to the local hero, Chief Lapu-Lapu, who killed the great explorer, Ferdinand Magellan, in the battle of Mactan Island on 27 April 1521, that Holly-Jean broached the subject of Taiwan's participation under her own flag and name.

'No memorial for Ferdy, then?' she remarked.

Goya, a Spaniard, said, 'He was only a Portugoose mercenary in the employ of the King of Spain.'

'Still, every nation deserves its heroes, wouldn't you say?'

'Absolutely, and today, thankfully, with the concept of global wars becoming increasingly outdated, sport has become a healthy outlet for nationalist fervour. That is why our mission is so vitally important. To keep the ideal of honourable, fair and non-violent competition between nations alive!'

Enough with the speechifying, thought Holly. 'How about Taiwan, then? Why should they be denied their chance to wave the flag?'

Goya looked at her with narrowed beady eyes, tongue darting in and out. Oh, okay, thought Holly, the old Komodo knew all right.

'Taiwan is a problem of twentieth-century Chinese history which the Association cannot be expected to solve.'

'I absolutely agree, Mr President,' said Holly, reaching for the volume control as they climbed back into the air-conditioned bus. And while the bus rocked and skidded across the bumpy jungle roads to the rich harmonies of loud Pinoy music, she spoke *sotto voce* in his left white-hair-tufted ear. 'However, unfortunately, others are less inclined to take the historical perspective. And though I personally abhor any idea of underhand persuasion influencing the democratic ideal upon which your Association is founded, it is my unpleasant duty to pass on to you, from these less-enlightened types, a crystal-clear message: that unless you get an unequivocal ruling from the Association, before the end of this gathering, that Taiwan will be allowed to compete under its own flag at the Asian Games, your ass, as they say, will be grass.'

Francisco Frank Goya's only visible reaction was the rapid darting of his tongue as if to monitor the environment for the presence of predator.

Or prey.

Holly wasn't sure which.

Two nights later, after breaking her vows yet again and stuffing herself with gross quantities of lobster-tails, and after the floor show had finished and all the fire-eaters and parallel-stick dancers had packed up and gone home, Holly was paged by the concierge.

She made her excuses to the table of delegates at which she sat – for once Goya was elsewhere – and walked over to the nearest house-phone.

'Meet me by the fives court,' said Daniel Mikaluk.

She wandered off to the elevators and took one going up. Got off at the third floor of the resort's main building and ran down the fire-escape stairs to the exit, rear of the kitchen area. Keeping to the shadows, skirting the pools and tennis courts she crossed the big sloping lawn to the sea, zig-zagging through the water-sprinklers and the coloured lamps.

Approaching the open-walled fives court, beautifully garlanded with live oleanders, hibiscus, bougainvillaea and frangipani, she heard a charming tenor sing, 'In the blue-skied jungles of Visayas, in search of the lonely palm.'

Holly responded, 'I spied a friendly face, winking out at me.'

The tenor added, 'From behind the frangipani tree!' Then Danny the Mouth stepped out from the darkness and slipped an arm round her waist.

Holly flicked him off. 'Don't get any fresh ideas, Buster. Just because we like the same old songs, it ain't no big thang!'

'Just being friendly,' said Mikaluk, sounding hurt.

'Listen,' said Holly good-naturedly, 'if you'd spent half last night trying to fend off the semi-tumescent advances of a seventy-year-old man in Calvin Klein Teen Spirit under-wear without destroying the old fart's feelings, then you'd be a little touchy-touchy about feely-feely, okay!'

'Got you.'

At first, Holly couldn't figure out why she hadn't just unmanned old lizard-lips when he'd entered her hut with a card-key at three in the morning and begun a surprisingly ardent grope-attempt. Was the Tiger finally mellowing in her old age?

Nope. It'd been gut-instinct. Far better to have the most powerful man in world sport as a doting lap-dog rather than a Rottweiler foaming with the hate of hurt male pride.

They wandered down towards the beach, just a couple of guests out for a stroll.

'First thing first,' said Holly. 'Did you bring the affidavits?' He showed them to her. She studied them under the moonlight.

'Let's go to that little beach bar down there and drink some Tanduay rum and Coke,' suggested Danny the Mouth, pointing to some coloured lights flickering through the palms fringing the beach.

The palm-frond *nipa* hut bar was busy with international back-packers, Aussie surfers and local men trying to chat up the Western girls. From time to time the power would 'brown-out' – a typically Philippine euphemism, and while the generator was being started up, kerosene lamps lit the open-walled bar. The sound of the surf battering the beach competed with the raucous crowd and the battered old speakers relaying Santana's 'Samba pa ti'. The smell of weed mixed with French fries and the sweet scents of tropic ocean night.

After Holly had checked the Defense Department-sealed documents thoroughly, she answered the HUMINT agent's many detailed questions about the Den Haag Triad Convention. He muttered all the answers into a micro-recorder. When she'd finished, she said, 'Now for my pieces of silver. In case you've lost interest, I think you might want to know friend Pfeltz aka Kriega is somehow involved with the Triads. He showed up in Roosendaal one night.'

Mikaluk snapped his fingers at the stunning young bar-girl, pointing at their glasses. '*Dalawa Tanduay at cola, hindi po yelo.*'

201

Big show-off. '*Yelo* is ice – "hold the ice", right?' said Holly. She'd been studying her phrasebook. Still, The Mouth's linguistic talents impressed her. His Mandarin tones were perfect, and here he was speaking Philippine Tagalog. Interesting. Holly'd always understood James Bond was a myth. That the wet-work rough stuff was handled by squaddies or grunts, while the spies were highly cultured individuals who stayed in their hotel rooms having their nails manicured. The Mouth, on the other hand, was smart, highly educated, yet an adept of *Capoeira* Brazilian martial art who didn't mind getting down and dirty.

When the angelic girl brought the drinks, she said to Danny in perfect English,

'Here we speak Cebuano or Visayak, not Tagalog.'

Holly chuckled, '*Mayabang*. Braggart!'

Danny said to the girl, '*Ako hembugero*?' To Holly, he said, 'Cebuano dialect: am I a braggart?'

'*Ambot lang*,' replied the angel, with a smile that displayed rotten teeth, peppered with holes. 'I don't know, Mister, but you sure don't look like a hamburger.' They all laughed. When the waitress had gone, Holly told Mikaluk of Kriega's unexpected appearance at the Hot Stuff bar on Damstraat.

The Mouth was sanguine. 'We know about it. He's trying to expand his operations.'

'Drugs?' mused Holly. 'Wonder if he's renewed his life insurance? Doing business with those boys is about as benevolent to one's general well-being as snogging a snake.'

'Our lad's not scared of snakes, he's got quite a collection on his island.'

Holly digested that along with her Tanduay rum and Coke. *Efifania's dream.* That took care of the serpents. Whither the locusts?

202

'Let's get down to business,' said Holly. 'I've got a date with him at Clark Airbase on the twelfth. Seems like I'm going to be taking an ultralight flight out to his island hideaway. Got any plans?'

'I figure you got two options. Legal or lethal. Legal, we try and extradite him on child pornography and suspected drug-smuggling. The Department can put enough pressure on the government here to ensure that the charges stick and extradition can go through.' He sipped his drink. 'The other way is much more interesting. Bust him doing business with the Triads. See, he's got this new operation. Got coca and opium being produced on Samar Island – the poorest place in the whole goddam country. The NPA Commie rebels run most of the island and Kriega's been developing commodity production with them which is just beginning to produce decent quality product. Our boy Pfeltz's latest career move is flying in the raw material to Clark Airbase in the middle of the night. They don't even have radio on at night, let alone radar. Biggest airfield in the world outside the US is now overgrown with weeds. Anyway, he drops down by ultralight at some distant corner of the airfield, hands over the bags of raw coca-base and raw opium-base, the Triads drive off in a van to some other distant corner of the industrial development zone – don't forget there's ten thousand hectares of factory and warehouse space in which to hide their processing labs. When the product is refined to heroin or cocaine it goes out with the Taiwanese cargo charters from Subic or Laoag along with the cheap shoes, the computer mother boards and what have you's from the factories of this newly developing economy.'

'So where does the lethal bit come in?' asked Holly.

'Easy. Have the locals arrest a couple of the Chinese in the act of handover, but leave friend Kriega free to go. The Triads will assume he's either an informant or an incompetent; makes no difference, they'll mete out their usual

203

unpleasantly prolonged capital punishment, and Kriega goes big bye-byes. Just to make doubly sure he's a goner, if by some fluke he managed to escape them, the NPA would be quietly informed of his apparent treachery and he'd either be dead by the following dawn, or at the very least he would never be able to set foot in the Philippines again, for fear of the NPA's reprisal.'

Holly had listened to all this but she finally shook her head. 'No, that method might implicate me and compromise my position with the Societies and I can't allow that. For the obvious reasons. Besides, Mikaluk, you know this is personal. I want him for myself. Either legal or lethal.'

They talked for more than an hour. Scenarios and options. By the time they were ready to turn in, the bar was much quieter. The locals had long succumbed to the soporific effects of $C_2 H_5OH$ and stumbled off into the cicada-deafening dark. The surfers had gone home to wax their boards or broads or something, and only a handful of travellers staying at the huts lining this end of the beach remained.

Before he left, Danny showed Holly two identical plain black wafer-thin cellphones. Handing her one, he explained, 'This is a special gift from the Department. Fine-tuned. Local airwaves are a complete mess. You'll see plenty of fat Flips showing off their Motorolas and Nokias – they're the big status symbol. Whether they're actually reaching anyone at the other end is a different story. These are about the only things that're absolutely guaranteed to work in the vicinity of Angeles without you hauling around a massive battery-operated transmission unit. Of course, they're totally un-secure, so we use only when absolutely necessary. Passwords?'

Holly thought for a minute. 'You're "Orifice" – The Mouth. I'm "Tigger" from Winnie the Pooh. He'll be plain "Shithead".'

204

Danny said goodbye and disappeared into the palm-grove night.

Holly-Jean decided to stick around for a while to take in as much as she could of the relaxed vibe of the *nipa* hut beach bar.

Tomorrow was the last full day of the Shangri-La shindig and tomorrow night was the crucial vote on Taiwan. Despite the fact that she had repeated her warning to Francisco Frank Goya, she had absolutely no idea which way he would play it. And though she'd discharged her responsibilities as best she could, as far as the Societies were concerned, she knew that failure to produce was not an option in their irrational discourse.

Beyond all of which loomed the menacing shadow of Kriega.

So, all things considered, she reckoned the action was going to get decidedly less laid-back from here on in. She waved at the angel, and when the girl came, asked her for a refill, and to join her with something for herself.

'May I eat, please?'

'Sure. Have anything you like.'

The girl came back with the drinks, sat down, and they chatted.

Riza said she was twenty-three years old, although she only looked about fifteen, and had worked as a bar-girl in Cebu City servicing Japanese tourists since she was eleven years old, when her mother could no longer afford school fees. Her papa was killed a couple of years back, fishing from his tiny *bunka* boat when Typhoon Dolores abruptly changed course. Riza had spent two years in Saudi as a maid, sending the money home to feed her nine brothers and sisters. She quit that when the grandfather with Alzheimer's repeatedly raped her.

After they built the International airstrip and the big hotel, she moved to Mactan Island. Like all Filipinas she'd learned to speak English at elementary school, and had become fluent through contact with the tourists.

'Why don't you work up at the hotel?' asked Holly.

'I've no high-school diploma, so I'd only get low-class jobs like chambermaid.'

'Don't they have training programmes? I could put in a word for you.'

Riza shrugged. 'The money's better here.'

Holly looked incredulous. 'You own the place?'

'Of course not,' giggled Riza as the young male cook brought out a plate of Pancit Bihon, fried noodles with meat and veg. She looked at her plate, and shouted something out. 'No prawns,' she explained to Holly.

'Tell him to cook a full side order,' Holly said.

'I did,' said Riza, with a cheeky grin. *Prawns*. Holly decided not to push the girl further on the subject of money. She had a fairly good idea how Riza supplemented her income down on the beach. Confirmed when Riza said, 'The tourists are kind to me.'

They talked for ages, and by the time the last of the tourists had gone, Holly had already made a decision. She'd need an interpreter, someone local she could trust. She would recruit Riza as a temporary employee of the H-J.H. Agency on very generous terms – the *peso* being what it was, she afford it. First, however, she thought very carefully about exactly how to put the proposition over. A simple cash offer, however bountiful, might be interpreted wrongly.

'If I had your teeth fixed, payed for tuition and living expenses for a full course of study at a local academic institution of your choice and opened a savings deposit account in your name at the Hong Kong Bank, would you come and work for me for a couple of weeks?'

'You drunk too much Tanduay?'

'I'm serious, Riza.' Holly went on to explain what might be required.

Riza said,' Show me something real and I'll consider it.'

'Come with me now.'

Riza shrugged and said, 'Why not?'

Holly waited while she got her bag. They walked back through the dark to the beach entrance of the resort. The guard brandished his sub-machine gun and switched on a powerful light. Holly showed him her card-key. He opened the gate. 'Your guest?'

Holly confirmed it, feeling embarrassed. But the guard obviously knew Riza well and judging by their easy conversation in dialect as he entered her name on his clipboard, this nocturnal access was neither new to her nor of much interest to him.

In the abrupt contrasting luxury of the scented-wood room, the first thing Holly did was to show Riza her name cards, some photos and other proof of identity. She explained that her passport and other valuables were locked up in the concierge's safe-deposit. She then handed Riza 5000 pesos – about 200 US dollars as a gesture of goodwill.

Riza pocketed the cash and said, 'Okay, we'll see when we get to Manila if you're really truthful. But as from now I'll stay with you.' She added over her shoulder, bending down to open the fridge, 'I'll just have to go back in the morning and sort out things at the bar.'

'I didn't expect ... I mean, you don't have to stay tonight.' Holly realised she hadn't really thought this thing through.

Riza looked puzzled. 'You don't want me to stay?' She was already chewing on a Cadbury's whole-nut bar from the fridge.

Holly looked around at the beautiful wall-hangings, the elaborate rattan furniture, the air-con, the fan, the marble bathroom off, the fresh flowers, the fruit bowl, the fridge

207

and wet bar and said, 'Of course, stay. And help yourself to anything. E.M.G.'

'E.M.G. ?' said Riza.

'Everything must go.'

Riza gave her a thumbs-up, opened a can of Coke and clutching her chocolate bar, grabbed the TV remote, found MTV and laid back on the bed under the mosquito net.

Holly was taking a shower when she felt coarse-worn hands soaping her back. She froze. For a long moment. Unable to move a single limb, to breathe even. Tried to speak but words wouldn't come. Unable to resist as a hand reached from behind her and turned the shower to a fine light spray.

Holly exhaled, closed her eyes as Riza's fingers began to lightly knead her bruised ribs, then with infinitesimally gradual movements of soft insistence, the foamy touch moved up and down her ivory back to tease her parted behind. In unbroken motion that relentlessly stoked and sparked flash-fire peaks, the hands moved under Holly's arms and cupped her tiny breasts. Fingers of one hand played with her thick, purple, intensely erect Chinese nipples – so sensitive that they stung at Riza's pinching, rolling, tender milking – while the other hand slid slowly in descent over Holly's belly and with the barest of feather-light touches lingered at her navel before reaching down at last to part the soft long black Chinese fur of her mons. With sublime stealth the fingers uncovered the most hidden stamen and administered to it with an insistence that released a gush of hot oil as Holly-Jean cried out and bucked again and again in spasms of release, joy and violent shuddering pleasure.

Holly lay immobile on the bathroom floor for a long time while Riza stroked her body, wiping the tears from Holly's cheeks, as she cooed a Visayak lullaby. At last Holly opened her eyes and turned to the mahogany-skinned island girl squatting beside her. Craning up she reverently kissed each of Riza's nipples.

Just before dawn, Riza called out in her sleep, half waking Holly.

'What's wrong?' she mumbled into the musty nape of the other girl's neck.

'Nothing. Nightmare,' came the murmured reply.

Chapter 15

Holly woke early in the morning on the last day of the AIA gathering. She was scheduled to go on a *bunka* trip to a deserted tropical island with President Goya and party, where they were to skin-dive a pristine coral-reefed lagoon and have a luncheon barbecue picnic.

With some difficulty she woke Riza and managed eventually to get her up and dressed. They arranged to meet back at the beach bar at sunset. Holly reckoned she'd just have time after the boat-trip to catch the horizon show before she'd have to return to her room and get fully togged up. Tonight was the grand finale of the AIA gathering in the Philippines, with a crucial schedule of tabled motions to be put to full membership vote followed by a dinner-dance and speeches.

She told Riza she should pack a bag and then if she wanted to, she could spend the evening in Holly's room and have a sumptuous room-service dinner. They'd be leaving first thing in the morning for Manila.

Giddy with sunstroke or something – anyway, an over-whelming inner turbulence – Holly stood at the bottom of the steps to her verandah and watched Riza sway down the hillside, through the purple-orange bougainvillaea and the hibiscus groves to the beach.

She didn't hear the cellphone's trilling. Could hardly be expected to, being so distracted. Indeed, she'd completely forgotten that before going to sleep last night, she'd concealed the thing inside a box of panty-liners in a locked suitcase inside the closet of her room.

After a buffet breakfast, the skin-dive *bunka* boat-trip party was driven in four mini-mokes the few hundred metres of beach road to the long narrow wooden landing jetty built on stilts over a channel blasted through the reef. It was low-tide so the party was held up while folks had to make a difficult climb one by one, down the steep, seaweed-slimy steps to the bobbing narrow outrigger boats with their colourful painted names like *Jonathan, Merly, Sherrileen.*

Holly was lingering at the rear of the group still on the jetty, hoping to give Frankie the slip when it came to sharing which *bunka.* But Goya, as usual, was sticking fairly close to her. He was just chatting to the senior Australian swimming coach, a man most had tipped to replace the President-for-Life once he shuffled off this mortal coil, when Holly heard the sound of running feet and her name being called.

'Holly-Jean!'

She turned to see Riza racing down the jetty towards her. In a flash, she ran back to meet her halfway. She hoped the other delegates wouldn't notice and ask awkward questions.

'What is it, Riza?' she gasped.

Breathless reply: 'Saw you from the beach. Last night's nightmare – don't get into the *bunka* called *Maxinea*!'

Holly walked back and improvised a story to the others: the girl thought Holly had dropped some keys. She called out to the delegates already sitting in *bunkas*, 'If anyone's lost some keys, they'll be with the guard at the beach-road gate.' She looked down; only two boats remained to be filled, one called *Jonathan*, the other *Maxinea.*

What with Epifania's dream, and now this, Holly was getting used to the Filipino mania for superstition. Still she

212

grabbed Goya's elbow and said, 'Let's go in that one. I've got a big fat friend in London called Jonathan, and he's unsinkable!'

The mysterious explosion which completely obliterated the *bunka* boat *Maxinea*, four Saudi delegates and two locals – the *bunka*'s owner and his twelfth and youngest son – just as the outrigger was rounding the north-east point of an uninhabited island called Santo Nino, cast rather a pall of gloom over the last night of the AIA gathering.

A two-minute silence was held before the proceedings formally began. Then President Goya stunned the assembly in his key-note address by vociferously denouncing the People's Republic of China for continually meddling in the Association's work, and particularly for its intransigence over Taiwan's participation under her own flag and name.

His announcement that he would resign his Presidency-for-Life should the vote go against Taiwan once again, was met first with a shocked silence, and then by the scraping of chairs as the PRC delegation rose to its feet and walked out *en bloc*, leaving behind only their most junior delegate who marched up to the podium, grabbed the microphone and warned the entire gathering that China would boycott the next Asian Games if the vote went for Taiwan.

Chapter 16

Just off the MacArthur highway into Angeles City, a rutted strip lined with fading American Legion Post Homes, Amvets, McDonald's and Pizza Huts, in leafy Lizares Street is the Woodland Park Hotel – formerly an officers' club with an Olympic-sized pool and the only surviving forest in the city. Holly booked a room on 11 March for one week. Cash in advance for discount.

With Riza as a guide at some ten paces distance, she toured Fields Avenue at night, picking up as much information as she could. It was while walking down a Boys Only side-street known as Blow-Job Alley, that Holly ran into a familiar face. Nick from Taiwan was doorman outside the Sunrise Lounge. Inside the unshuttered chicken-wire windows, old fat white men could be seen necking with very young local boys. Beautiful drag queens and transsexuals were draped on chintz-covered sofas, their arms around iron-pumped foreign leather-jocks.

'Thought you ran a bank, not a paedophile bar,' said Holly disgustedly. To think the guy had been a hero when the chips were down in Taipei the year before.

'The bank got bought out by Chase, I got down-sized. Honest-to-God, I'm just here for twenty minutes minding the shop for the owner, Andrew Mitchell. What about you?'

'Missing person's trace. You don't think I'm here as a frocking customer, do you?'

'Look, don't hang around,' said Nick nervously. 'It's not healthy. Tell you what – catch you later at Gilley's Roadhouse.'

'No way,' said Holly. 'And if anyone asks, you never saw me.'

'Saw who?' said Nick.

'Whom.'

Telling Riza she'd meet her back at the hotel, Holly entered a tiny bar called Private Dancer at precisely nine o'clock. The girls dancing on the narrow stage were clean, happy and dressed in bikinis.

'The acceptable face of Third World sex industry,' said The Mouth, introducing Holly to the owner, a Swede called Wolf who was married to a local with three kids, had his girls checked every week by a doctor, forbade drugs and told Holly, 'None of my girls has to go with a customer if she chooses not to. But if she does, the rule here is, anyone who takes my girls must first promise me personally to use a condom. Any girl found violating the rule for extra cash or whatever, is fired on the spot and the customer is eighty-sixed for life!'

Holly was unimpressed. Sure, he was doing his bit. But Fields Avenue was ancient evil in her book, old Sodom and Gomorrah in the new Dark Age global village.

'By the way,' said The Mouth, 'I read in the papers that old man Goya retired from the AIA Presidency-for-Life. Apparently he needn't have bothered. Suffered a fatal heart attack in the first-class section of Philippine Airline flight 712 just before its scheduled landing at Frankfurt.'

'Sad. He wasn't really a bad old man, just greedy, perhaps. But not real evil like some we know.' Holly was sorry in a way. But she had real evil on her mind. 'Why this place? This dirty old town, dirty old men, dirty old trade?' she asked.

'Clark Airbase was the United States Airforce's biggest airfield in the world outside mainland America,' explained Mikaluk over the din of Private Dancer. 'In continuous use for seventy-odd years, except during the Japanese occupation, till the Aquino opposition toppled the dictator Fidel Marcos and voted in 1991 not to extend the Military Bases Agreement, the MBA, thus effectively ending the peppercorn rent. The leases of Clark, Subic Bay and all the other US bases were raised to a realistic rent and renewable for five years only. At which point the continued presence of American troops in the Republic of Philippines would come up for another vote.'

Holly watched a hugely fat Australian wearing a T-shirt emblazoned with the slogan *Official Fat Bastard* ask the mama-san to tell a girl among the dancers on the stage to join him for a drink. The girl climbed down and sat on the fat customer's lap. The girls on stage screamed as The Cranberries 'Zombiew' came on. They had invented a dance routine and were singing the disturbing anti-war message at the top of their voices. Holly figured that though they might not understand the words completely, they understood the anger of the song and shared it. A group of fuzz-cut US sailors came in and took up seats at the stage.

'The Navy's in town. Only visiting. These lads are on shore leave – up from Manila Bay,' shouted Wolf.

The girls screamed out their welcome at the handsome young boys. Holly was shaking her head in amazement, but Wolf leaned over and said into her ear, 'You might be witnessing the very first moment of marriage. Believe me, it's happened a thousand times before.' The bikini tops came off and some girls tugged open their pants for a quick glimpse an inch in front of the noses of the bemused boy-ratings.

Holly played pool with Mikaluk at the quieter end of the bar. 'So you were telling me why this dusty old town

217

survives. I can understand some paradise beach place like Boracay or Phuket, but here – crummy old Angeles?'

Mikaluk potted a brown ball. 'This place, right? You see, the USAF reckoned on keeping its favourite Asian asset, hoping that by a combination of Washington carrot-and-stick pressure and covert cash contributions to the notoriously corrupt local politicos, they could get the vote to kick the US forces out overturned before the new leases ran out.

'Then on 15 June 1991, after six hundred years of dormant slumber, Mount Pinatubo burst a blood vessel and sent vast amounts of molten earth forty kilometres into the stratosphere at exactly the same time as super-Typhoon Archie roared into North Luzon and the surrounding areas. This twin-pronged attack by Mother Nature resulted in a landlubber tidal wave of rain-dampened volcanic emission called *lahar*, a wall of white mud which buried Clark and the surrounding provinces of Pampanga, Tarlac and Zambales.

'When Pinatubo calmed down in September, more than forty thousand homes had been destroyed, three hundred thousand people left homeless, more than twelve hundred were dead and the US armed forces had gone for good. They'd decided to cut their losses. Y'know, it's reckoned that Pinatubo's ejaculation was the biggest volcanic eruption this century and that it directly affected the world's weather for more than five years.'

'But the bars of this hellhole are still full,' pointed out Holly.

'There's nothing else out there, Holly,' said Mikaluk. 'This is a Catholic country in the middle of Asia. No birth control allowed. Huge families and grinding poverty, and what's the alternative? Subic Bay is a Taiwanese fiefdom nowadays with charter flights in and out, casinos owned and managed by the Societies and locals normally allowed inside the duty-free zone only to work for very low wages in the factories. The poverty surrounding is kept at bay by the

218

electric fences. Over the road there, Clark Base Duty-Free Industrial and Commercial Development Zone is on the way to becoming just such another Taiwanese-backed enterprise. In the end prosperity should trickle down. Least, that's the theory.'

'But I still don't get it: why does Fields survive?' said Holly stubbornly.

'You're asking why the oldest profession is still thriving,' said Mikaluk. 'It's always going to be somewhere. This place or another. Vice came to Angeles during the prosperous years of US tenancy. Vietnamese R&R caused the place to explode, drawing every poverty-struck kid from the provinces. Those days, Fields Avenue was a by-word among the US military. Then Pinatubo smashed it all. Fields would have died a natural death if the mayor of Manila hadn't made a deal with the Chinese to close down the red-light district of Ermita and evict the white-skinned owners so that the Triads could take over. Trouble was, it backfired. The white bar-owners moved up here to Fields overnight, and the foreign trade came with them.'

He added with a shrug, 'The talcum-powder dust of Pinatubo may get up the nose, but now it is the international tourist who patronises the girly-boy bars and sex-shows.'

'And this is where Kriega gets his raw material,' said Holly grimly.

'Like your friend Riza.'

Holly looked at him. 'Just what are you implying?'

'Nothing at all,' he said, chalking his cue.

'I'm employing her as a guide and interpreter. In return, I'm going to give her a fresh chance in life. Education, health and savings.' The words hung hollowly. She was also sleeping with the girl.

Mikaluk shrugged cynically. 'Good for you. I'm sure your motives are purer than the driven snow.'

Wo-dr Tyan! My God, thought Holly, he was right. Fixing

219

teeth, paying for education, opening bank accounts –
weren't they just another form of payment for services
provided? In the end wasn't she doing exactly the same as
the 'Official Fat Bastard'?

Downing her Tanduay rum and Coke, she vowed never to
sleep with Riza again. When she got back to Woodland Park
tonight, she'd pay for another room. Riza would have to
wait here anyway while the Kriega business was dealt with.
It was far too dangerous to risk her further involvement.
And when it was all over, Holly would take her to Manila
and set her up with her chance of education and new
opportunity.

Later Danny asked, 'Have you decided whether to go the
legal or lethal route?'

'Not yet,' replied Holly.

Chapter 17

The Rotax ultralight looked just like a hang-glider with a tiny nose cone that only protected the pilot's feet and a tiny twin-seat behind pilot's tiny perch. It whined noisily as it taxied out of the hangar of the Angeles Flying Club. It was nothing more than nylon wings, metal tubes and a propeller engine strung together with wires.

'You're expecting me to go up in that?' asked Holly incredulously.

Kriega jumped down. '626/4T's Federal Aviation Administration Aircraft Standard aluminum tubes. Safe as houses.'

'Oh, yeh? What happens if we run out of fuel? Are we supposed to glide home?'

'See that?' he pointed to a fat cylindrical object attached to a v-bar running from the tail above the wing to the pilot's open seat. 'Gas-powered parachute canister. This baby cannot crash-dive. If the engine dies, the wings fall off, and the wheels drop, we just hit the cable to release the parachute and glide gently down to earth.'

'Or shark-infested ocean?' said Holly, strapping herself into the passenger seat behind Kriega with great misgivings. The innocent-looking little Nike back-pack Mikaluk had provided was a wee bit bulky and she couldn't lean back on the seat, making her crouch forward uncomfortably.

Then they were rollicking across the rough grass meadow of the airstrip and with a deafening scream of the Rotax engine were suddenly up, soaring above Angeles and Fields

221

Avenue, heading due east, leaving the dark looming shadow of Pinatubo behind them to the rear.

Holly didn't like to look down since there was nothing between her seat and the earth below. She crouched, clutching the back of Kriega's seat with white-knuckled intensity, her stomach heaving. Eventually she released her neck muscles and looked about her.

'So that's *lahar*?' remarked Holly, as the tiny plane flew across the great white moonscape. Recent rains had unleashed further mud-flows and the cross of a church spire was just visible above the smooth cheesecake surface. Kriega couldn't hear her. His helmet was fitted with radio so he could keep contact with the flight controller at the Angeles Flying Club.

After an hour they were out of the desolation and flying over thick tropical jungle. Few habitations and no roads here. Riotous forest country. As they glimpsed the blue sparkle of ocean ahead, flying towards the east coast of Luzon and the Pacific Ocean, Kriega turned to her and shouted, 'That's where they filmed *Apocalypse Now*!'

They crossed the coastline above the town of Baler, and headed south across the sea. Twenty minutes later they landed on a tiny strip of cleared land on a perfect little tropical island surrounded by a white fringe of reef-breaking surf and velvety with palm trees.

'Treasure Island,' said Holly.

'Welcome to Los Confites Reef,' said Kriega.

The ostensible reason for the trip, to shoot a series of pictures of Holly, took place that afternoon before the sun went down. In the evening, during a dinner made by the two or three locals who seemed to be live-in staff, of fresh red snapper, soused in coconut juice, barbecued and served on banana leaf with lots of chili-hot side dishes, and after Holly had been to see his collection of snakes, Holly began her lure.

222

'You were the visitor on Elfa Ericksson's last night?'

Kriega nodded. 'Yes, I was. I came up from Cornwall especially to see her.'

'And either by accident, during an attempt to heighten sexual sensation, or with malice aforethought and intent, you suffocated her by smothering her face in clingfilm.'

Kriega looked at Holly with a smile. 'You're going to have to endlessly wonder which, as there's simply no proof connecting me with that night.'

'Why that particular night?'

'I was just returning a possession of hers.'

'And why did you want her dead?'

'Dead? Who said I wanted her dead? But even if this were the case, well, let's put it this way, hypothetically – let's assume that young Elfa decided she no longer approved of certain of my activities and was getting hysterical, talking of going to the police.'

'You mean the child pornography on the Internet.'

Kriega bowed his head in acknowledgement. 'I knew all along it was you and your meddling old Ma who'd been bandying my organisation about the halls of Westminster. That's OK. The heat was getting intense anyway.'

Holly went on, 'So there were two ways to silence her. One by threatening to ruin her career by publishing pictures taken by her stepfather when she was just an eleven-year old, or two: permanently. The perfect murder. No physical evidence such as DNA, hair or fibre samples. No finger-prints, nothing – except traces of clingfilm which led to the conclusion of accidental death following an exotic brand of contemporary sexual practice.'

Kriega's eyes glittered in the tropical night. He chuckled, 'Yes, ingenious, wouldn't you say? Rather proud of that, what with the alibi in far-off Cornwall and all. But to tell you the truth, ironic as it may seem, in the end I didn't have to do the dirty deed.' He mused. 'Well, depends what you mean by dirty, I suppose...'

'What are you saying?'

'Believe me, Elfa was really into all that stuff. The S&M, the bondage. Surprised even me, sometimes. For one so self-assured, she just couldn't control that side of her appetites. And whatever I might or might not have planned for her, that particular night, she took the lead. Urging me into the scene. Maybe she'd already decided it was to be the last time we would be together. Maybe she had made up her mind to go to the police – who will ever know? Whatever, it really was to be our last time. But not by my intentional doing. You could say, she died because we went a little too far over the top, I'm afraid.'

'You're not trying to tell me she committed suicide? I won't buy it,' scoffed Holly, trying to maintain control. She wanted him lulled. She forced back her rage, bottled it for later use.

'No, no. Not suicide. Rather a miscalculation. You know how she loved to push to the very limits. The triathlons, the incredibly hectic schedule, the fledgling business empire. Elfa Ericksson died because she was into the extreme. Extreme sports, extreme sex, extreme everything.'

'So you want me to believe that it was just an exotic sex-scene that went too far, and she died unintentionally. How very convenient.'

He chuckled again. 'Yes, it was convenient, wasn't it? A perfect ending, so to speak. Couldn't have composed it better myself. Anyway,' he added, 'you can choose to believe what you like. I'm telling you Elfa went down in a blaze of sheer ecstasy. A lovely thing. I miss her ... Ah well, so be it.'

Holly had to look away. Focusing on the silver palm-fronds waving in the cool breeze. Breathing deep, calm, forcing the body to stay put and not leap forward to grasp that neck and strangle the shithead right there and then. She watched a shooting star fall out of the Southern Cross. Could it be that Elfa's death was just that? A sordid little tale of over-indulgence and kinky predilections?

Holly thought about having to tell that story to her mother and friends.

She turned back to her host. Her determination to bring him retribution was stronger than ever. Whatever the real truth about that night, there was no doubt in her mind: he had meant to silence her friend. The intention to harm her was there. *He would have to pay.*

She swallowed the bile and smiled at him. It was time to further finesse that colossal ego.

'How about that trip from Cornwall? Some amazing feat. Just how did you manage it?'

'I've got an ultralight in England. Fucking freezing, you have to wrap yourself up well, I'll tell you. Ninety-five minutes later, landed on my lawn in Surrey. Then it was astride my trusty BMW motorbike up to Holland Park in thirty minutes flat. Induced orgasmic slumber in my young lover, just made sure the clingfilm didn't tear as she slipped deeper and deeper into the Big Sleep. Then reverse trip back to the party in Cornwall. They were all so out of it, nobody'd noticed I'd been gone for four hours.'

Time for the bluff.

Holly said, 'But you made just one mistake.'

Kriega looked up from the sputtering candle. 'No, I don't think so.'

'You left behind the envelope of negatives.'

'So? You can't prove any link to me.'

'Oh yes, I can,' she lied. 'Your fingerprints.'

'Nonsense! I wore surgical gloves and wiped the negatives clean.'

'Yes, but they have electron photonics at the Defense

Department's HUMINT laboratories, and the envelope has produced a superb set of matches.'

Kriega's eyes flared in the candle-light. 'You're lying, Ms Ho.'

'No, I'm not,' she said, taking out the cellphone, stabbing in a number and when someone answered, saying, 'Orifice, this is Tigger. I'm at Shithead's place. He wants to talk to you,' she handed Kriega the cellphone.

Looking hesitantly at the object in his palm, Kriega weighed it for a moment, then with a shrug, held it to his ear.

'Is that so? Uh-huh ... Uh-huh ... Right.' He handed it back. 'He wants to talk to you.'

'You okay, Tigger?'

'Yep.'

'I think you ought to know that your friend Riza has disappeared from the Woodland Park Hotel. Could be she's gone walkabout. Could be Shithead.'

'Roger that.' She flipped the cellphone shut. Stared at Kriega across the bamboo table, at the palm fronds waving in the night wind silvery under the Pisces half-moon.

'Oh "Roger dear". Real pros, are we?' sneered Kriega. 'I s'pose old Mikaluk told you I've got your girl here. You know I always like to take out extra insurance.'

Holly stilled her raging and spoke calmly. 'What's the deal?'

'You go quietly home tomorrow. Riza stays, until I receive assurances that no case for extradition will be brought against me, nor charges of any kind levelled either here, UK, Germany or the US – don't quite know how you're going to achieve that. But till you do, delectable young Riza stays here.' He paused and drank from his bottle of San Miguel beer.

'You know she's a natural. Already given me some very provocative poses. Should make me a final killing on the

Internet. Told you she's twenty-three, did she? With only three lone pubic hairs, you might have got your maths a bit wrong, don't you think? Or did you just turn a blind eye? An eye blinded by desire, perhaps?'

Holly stood up and walked around the little compound, breathing her *chi* technique of control. 'May I see her?'

'Later, maybe. She's little tied up right now!' he giggled.

'You harm her and I'll kill you,' said Holly.

'You mean you'll *try* and kill me. You're forgetting, Madam Ho, that I've been through five years of desert war. I've been shot at thousands of times. I've killed many men and women in my lifetime. So far no one's got close to killing me. You can try, though. Go on, give it your best shot, won't you?'

Holly walked away to the edge of the palm-grove and flipped open the cellphone.

'Be my guest,' called out Kriega. 'Can't think what you'll be able to achieve by phone. Tell the old fart Mikaluk I'll need hard-copy guarantees just like those Defense Department-sealed affidavits he was showing you at the beach bar on Mactan.'

Kriega then burst into hysterical laughter. 'I've been tagging you all along, you little amateur. You didn't really think you could come up tops against someone like me? Ha-ha-ha! I'm a modern-day Professor Moriarty, a Dr No, a Karla – every evil genius you can think of rolled into one. Yi-yi-yi-yi!' He laughed till the tears were rolling down his face.

Holly used the cellphone. 'Orifice?' she muttered. 'Tigger here. Shithead's got Riza. I'm going with the lethal.'

Holly spoke to Riza in the morning before they left.

Kriega had her locked up in an upstairs bedroom of the large wooden *nipa*-style bungalow he'd had built. It was a lovely room, in fact. But there were iron bars across the window and the doorframe was metal.

Riza was understandably frightened and mystified by events, but she said she was being treated well and Holly told her not to worry. 'I'll get you home safe, Riza, I promise. You understand?'

Riza looked at Holly and said, 'Promise?'

'Promise.'

In the brief cool of early light Holly found Kriega feeding the snakes. He was holding a brilliant emerald and ivory diamond-patterned serpent by the head coaxing bloody raw entrails past its fangs. Holly watched from behind a thick clump of banana, transfixed by the gentle almost tender ministrations. The man and his snakes. Outcasts together, reviled like seeking reviled like.

He must have sensed her presence, and without turning he said, 'She's a lethal beauty isn't she? The Green Mamba, imported from Mozambique, one of the most poisonous snakes in Africa. I call her Elfa. You know why? Because she's an extreme one too. You know I always felt Elfa could have done anything if she fancied. Anything at all. Even if the circumstances were right, killed another person. Taken a human life. Crossed the most extreme border.' He gently placed the Green Mamba back on its perch. Turned to face Holly. 'Now the big question: what about you, Miss Ho? Could you cross that line? That's the one we're all losing sleep over. *Not*!' Kriega chuckled and ran his fingers over his skull.

A *carabou*, water-buffalo, trudged slowly past on its way to the rice paddies led by a little boy in bare feet wearing only a pair of tattered shorts. The solid cloud of flies above the horned head was black and whining like a power-drill. The beast of burden's tail flicked lazily at the pair of birds hitching a ride on its black leathery rump.

Kriega chuckled again. But Holly had heard the hollow reed within the pipes of that chuckle.

'And this harmless-looking one,' he picked up another, 'is called the Thousand Pacer Snake. Looks deceive, however, and though, if she bites you, you might at first think you've got away without harm, you will die unless you can reach a serum within a thousand paces.'

Holly stared at him. His sculpted body looked magnificent in the low rays of the early sun. His eyes sparkled with affection for his deadly collection.

The question seemed to hover in the morning air.

Did she really have it in her to step across the line?

Kriega stroked the snake's head, 'This one hasn't got a name.'

'She's an unlikely harbinger of death. Perhaps you'd better call her Holly-Jean.'

Kriega raised his eyebrows and looked at her. And for a flicker she saw his fear.

The ultralight took off into early morning sea-mist and they soon crossed back onto the mainland of Luzon and the thick tropical jungle below. When they'd reached the *lahar* swathe, the soft dusty mud blanket that stretched for fifty miles around Angeles, Holly reached down with the nail scissors she'd brought for the purpose, and snipped the fuel line. The Rotax engine immediately began to stall. Kriega turned round, saw the severed fuel splashing in the wind.

'What the fuck have you done!' he screamed.

But Holly was already out of her back seat and crouching ready to jump, one hand hanging onto the wire wing-strut. 'You've forgotten about the parachute!' he yelled reaching for the cable.

'Just want you to know we already disabled the gas-canister the night before we left the Angeles Flying Club!

Adios!' She toppled forward and dropped into the wind. Waiting for the mandatory seven count Mikaluk had insisted on, in order to prevent any entanglement with the ultralight, she pulled the zipper of the Nike bag and was tugged up as the purple parachute ballooned open above her. From her hovering eagle vantage point she watched the Rotax ultralight and Kriega frantically tugging at the gas-canister atop the wing on its final descent to crash land on the white *lahar* and burst into flames.

Holly-Jean's mind was a blank as she floated gently to earth like the stray down from a sea-eagle's neck. Two thoughts flashed up just before her parachute hit the ground and her head smashed down onto a large rock: I've killed someone and over there looks like an approaching sandstorm.

Her body had landed some 200 metres down-wind of the black-fiery smoke of the Rotax fueltank's burn-off. A passing Jeepney, the folk-art adorned customised Willey's Jeep taxis that are the main form of public transport in the Republic of Philippines, stopped to watch her land. But then a distant roaring sound distracted the driver. From his raised vantage of what passed for a road – it was just a banked-up dune of *lahar* running in a straight line across the ravaged wasteland – the driver turned to the east, the direction of the roaring and crossing himself, cried out, 'Santo Cristo! *Ano-bayang!*' and jumped out of the Jeepney.

He raced down the bank of white lava to where Holly lay, disentangled her body from the parachute, threw her across his shoulders and stumbled back to the Jeepney.

She came to and opened her eyes as he dumped her unceremoniously onto the passenger seat.

'W-who are you? W-whats going on?' Had she woken in the middle of some lucid dream?

The driver was already tying a rag around his head, leaving just his eyes exposed. His foot slammed down on

230

the accelerator and he spun the Jeepney forward gesticulat-
ing and pointing to the east.

Holly looked out of the window to see a dark brown wall
of cloud rolling across the *lahar*. 'Sandstorm?' she asked, as
the cloud darkened the sun and cast a shadow over the road.

The driver screamed, 'No sandstorm, madam! Locusts!'

Then the wall of clacking, whirling, crawling insects was
upon them, filling the Jeepney and smothering Holly from
head-to-toe. She felt them in her ears, her nostrils, her hair,
down the back of her shirt. She panicked and began to try
and fight them off, flailing her arms about and screaming at
the top of her lungs.

'Thank you, Epifania, you silly old bitch! Faster, for
frock's sake, driver, faster!'

Her voice soared above the horrible chattering din. The
driver forced the Jeepney on through the solid writhing wall
of locusts, the diesel engine smoking and whining as the
insects got into the system and fried. Suddenly the Jeepney
began to tip and slide down the steep *lahar* slope of the road.
Inexorably it began to topple over and Holly managed to
throw herself clear diving into the whirlwind of locusts. The
Jeepney spun over and over a few feet in front of her, foul-
smelling diesel fumes mingling with the scream of the over-
revved engine.

She lay face down, burying herself in the white mud,
fearful of a coming explosion. She prayed to both the
Chinese pantheon and the Christian God of her split-race
upbringing. Then the lawful screeching began to ebb and
fade. The air lost the acrid smell of burning fuel mixed with
the excreta of a billion panicked locusts. The sky suddenly
cleared, the plague of locusts had passed by and moved on to
the west. Holly raised her head and looked around. A few
feet away the Jeepney lay on its side and the driver was
squatting by the engine with Asian resignation. It was going
to be a long afternoon. She began to extricate the trapped

stragglers of the swarm of creepie-crawlers still stuck inside her clothing, matted in her hair, mashed into sticky goo on her skin.

Suddenly the unmistakeable sound of an ultralight could be heard. She looked up and saw a tiny blue dot get bigger and bigger. She got up and waved with her Nike bag; the pilot dipped his wings, did another pass before landing on the *lahar* road. 'You Holly-Jean?' he shouted.

Mikaluk was waiting at the Angeles Flying Club where an unofficial enquiry was already being held into the tragic accident. Everyone congratulated Holly on her foresight in bringing along her own parachute. No one could understand why Kriega's had not opened, and an immediate check of all the gas-powered canister chutes was ordered by the Club Chairman to take place forthwith.

Mikaluk offered to drive Holly back to Woodland Park for a rest, but she wouldn't hear of it. 'You got a licence to fly one of these?'

'Yep,' said Mikaluk, 'but I weigh two hundred and forty pounds and with you and Riza on board we won't get up. I suggest you book Brian – he's the best ultralight pilot in the Philippines.'

That night Mikaluk and Holly hosted a celebration party at the Woodland Park Hotel.

Everyone was invited who wanted to come. Riza and Brian were asked to choose the menu and they went with two roast suckling pig – *lechon* barbecue with crispy *pata* crackling and many cases of San Miguel. The Angeles Hash House Harriers (not those animals again, thought Holly), showed up to help drink the beer and frolic drunkenly in the swimming pool. It seemed no one had really known Kriega, he had kept to himself. Not unusual in a place like Angeles – which was a well-known sanctuary for runaways, criminals and bail-jumpers. But for those legit residents, an expat community like the permanent members and pilots of the Angeles Flying Club, the German's reticence and aloof attitude hadn't gone down well. There was a single RIP raising of San Miguel bottles by the assembled crowd and then it was on with the festivities into the night.

Holly kept all her promises, and by the time Riza saw her off at the departure lounge of NAIA Manila she not only had a new set of teeth but was enrolled in a computer-programming course at the San Juan Technical Institute of the Philippines. The little matter of her missing high-school diploma was easily solved by a few thousand pesos.

Before she left for the boarding gate, Holly asked to see Riza's brand-new passport. Her age was given as twenty-three years old.

'Come and see me in England. I'll send you a ticket for next Christmas!'

'I will,' said Riza, hugging Holly with tears in her eyes. 'Thank you for everything, Holly-Jean. I love you.'

'I love you too.' And she knew they both meant it. If in different ways.

Chapter 18

There was no reply from Camden Lock when Holly finally
got down at Heathrow on Tuesday at dawn. With no
checked-in baggage to wait for she was first in the line for
Customs and was waved through and quickly outside to just
a short queue at the freezing-cold taxi rank.

She called home again. It was early, but she'd promised Ma. No reply. She tried Mrs Howell-Pryce's home
number. Also no reply. Warm, cosy feelings of homecoming
were rapidly receding with the freezing wind of still
night-time Heathrow and she was getting a little bit
worried. It had been impossible to get a call through
to the UK from Angeles City, and the two nights spent in
Manila had been the weekend, so getting no reply then,
she'd assumed the two ladies had gone off on a trip
somewhere. Mrs H-P regularly went home to Wales at the
weekend.

As she was waiting for the taxi line to move forward, she
pressed the code number which activated her trestle-top
answer-machine at the Lock, and heard the following message by an electronically distorted male voice: 'You want
the fucken old biddies? Prepare 100,000 clean ones. Call
01271 865553 on Thursday March the twenty-third at 5.07
a.m. Not a minute later. Not a minute earlier. And no police.
You understand that, don't you?'

* * *

Holly had reached the front of the taxi queue. 'C'mon, lady! Ain't got all day!'

She shook her head free of the panic. Jumped in the back of the cab and said, 'Camden Lock.'

On the way back home she called Coulson to remonstrate. He was in bed, still asleep. Good. The bastard useless shithead!

'What?' came the sleepy voice.

'Coulson, you frocking cretinous turd, you promised to keep an eye on Ma – she's been kidnapped!'

There was a short silence, followed by an unpleasant clearing of throat and muttered oaths before Coulson finally responded, 'Tell me.'

She told him.

'Right, I'll have a trace put on that number.'

'And that's all you do, till I tell you. Got that?'

'I'm really sorry, Holls, I'm—' She cut the connection. Called Hua to similarly complain. Gave him some instructions.

By mid-morning, Holly-Jean received the news that the number had been traced to a public telephone box on the pier at Ilfracombe in North Devon. She spent the rest of that day in careful preparation trying hard not to panic, or let the dam of tears burst.

Wednesday noon, driving the Discovery across Exmoor, Holly went over her vague strategy. Beside her on the seat was a Sainsbury's bag full of fifty-pound notes.

Her accountant, Lily Chung, had been busy since Tuesday morning trying to liquidate Holly's paper. The request for a short-time loan had been laughed at. When it was explained what the cash was for, her bank manager, a *wan-ba-dan* schnorrer typical of the breed, had point-blank refused to even consider it. 'More than my job's worth, Miss Ho.' Frock you too.

Luckily, Lily Chung knew some venture capital types in the City and for a private piece of the Holly-Jean Ho Agency the money was raised and brought over by the accountant late last night.

'You realise you just lost control of the ownership of your agency,' pointed out Lily.

'For Ma, I don't care what happens,' said Holly. 'Anyway, who says they're going to get the loot?'

'Sure, sure, I know, I know,' said Lily, just trying to be polite.

Holly thought: Don't believe me? Wait and see.

'The problem is, Holly-Jean,' explained Lily Chung, 'you look very attractive on a spreadsheet—'

'I should hope so too!' Holly was keeping her spirits up, come what may.

'And I doubt they'll want to sell the shares back to you. I couldn't get a stipulatory clause on buy-back built-in at such short notice.'

Holy sighed and with a grim look said, 'We'll fight that battle when we reach it.'

The sun settled in the west as she tooled down the foothills of Exmoor towards the craggy outline of the North Devon cliffs and the Atlantic beyond. She stopped and had a pint of Devenish ale and a cheese and onion roll at the Black Horse Inn at Challacombe.

She reached the ocean at six o'clock. It was pitch dark; lashing rain and raging winds swept the deserted promenade as she looked for a welcoming light.

237

Chapter 19

Ilfracombe, that once world-renowned Victorian seaside resort whose landscaped tunnelled arrival by rail line was the favoured route of Kaisers and Kings, had long since been the victim of Lord Beeching's bloody axe.

Since the Sixties it'd been far cheaper to holiday in the sun of the Med than in this faded splendour full of inner-city migrant dole-queue junkies and thieves. Holly had booked in at the Dilkhusa Grand Hotel, the only place open on the Promenade in early March.

She scouted out the pier Wednesday night and made her preparations for Thursday.

The pier at Ilfracombe was a circular jetty on the outer harbour built out into the battering ocean with three concrete levels for embarkation according to the tide height. Testimony to the resort's swansong heydays in the Fifties, when the White Funnel fleet of paddle-steamers still plied the Bristol Channel from the Gower to Clovelly and back to Cardiff or Bristol. The days when Ilfracombe had four major theatre companies operating each summer.

Nowadays the pier was cracking up, and the only people using it this wintry night were hardy local sea-anglers with their rods and reels and flasks of hot Ovaltine. In the lamplight Holly-Jean read a tattered notice tacked to the Angling Club shed, advertising an Easter trip on the last remaining steamer, the *Balmoral*, for twitchers – bird-watching fanatics

239

– to offshore Lundy Island, the bleak wind-blasted slab of granite in the Atlantic, home to the puffin.

Overlooking the inner and outer harbour was Lantern Hill and the ninth-century St Nicholas Chapel, perched on the cliff peak, its red-light still a sign of safe haven for those in peril on the sea.

Restless, Holly walked about the town till the pubs kicked out their punters and the street-lights were finally extinguished.

Back at the Dilk, Holly couldn't sleep at all, waiting for the time to phone. She'd double-checked her watch, got a negative from the front desk for wake-up call – not surprising since she was the only guest – and set the radio-alarm to come on at the five o'clock news.

At 5.07 she placed the call.

'Don't say one word.' The same distorted voice. 'Listen carefully: it'll be said only once. You're to park your car at the last parking space before the bollards at the walkway onto Ilfracombe Pier tomorrow at 3.35 a.m. *exactly*. You're to carry the money and walk up the paved path on the seaward side of Lantern Hill to St Nicholas Chapel where you will find further instructions. We have the vantage point. You will be watched from arrival. Police radio is already being monitored. Any unusual activity will have inevitable results. You do understand?'

Holly said, 'Who are you? Why are you doing this?'

But only the eerie moan of the same electronic ghost answered from the ether.

She pressed the button on the cam-corder she'd attached to the mouthpiece, and spent the rest of the day in feverish energetic wandering of the beautiful old town, listening over and over again to the distorted voice, and placing

240

various calls. There was a mania to her jet-lagged no-sleep angry fear.

She knew that.

She nurtured it.

She was gathering all her negative and positive *chi* for this final battle with the still-unknown enemy.

She went to the library and the Museum. Saw photos of the town in its salad days. The Victorian bandstand with hundreds gathered to watch the Punch & Judy Show and then attend the afternoon tea-dances.

The world-famous Tunnels Beaches, hewn through the cliffs so that horse-drawn bathing-carriages could access the Ladies in their modesty to the pleasures of ozone and the ocean. The enormous Gothic edifice of the Holiday Inn where Kaiser Bill had stayed before the Great War and where Eddy the cigar-lech lounge lizard Prince of Wales had dirty weekends with Lily Langtry. The Gaiety Theatre with the George Thomas Variety Show and the glass-roofed Crystal Palace-style Winter Gardens of the Victoria Pavilion and 'Palmararium'. All gone now.

But at low-tide, she discovered you could still walk down to the bottom level of the pier, if you dared risk the rusted old steps and the broken concrete walkway. In the evening she looked into the pubs but found most were empty and those that were busy were full of threatening Liverpool/Brum accents and heroin eyes.

At 3.35 a.m. on 24 March, Good Friday, Holly-Jean Ho parked her dark-blue Discovery at the last parking bay up against the bollards to the circular pier jutting out into the Atlantic Ocean at Ilfracombe, North Devon.

It was a pitch-black night.

The wind was howling and the rain spitting. The tide was

rising up, but the waves weren't yet breaking over the car park.

She locked the door and, clutching the Sainsbury bag full of cash, she struggled against the hammering gusts of Atlantic cyclone and headed up the pathway of Lantern Hill to St Nicholas Chapel.

At the top of Lantern Hill, under the red light atop the tiny stone chapel, she caught her breath. Tried the door to the chapel and found it locked. Looked around. Nothing but a penny-operated telescope; rusting and useless. But then, as the red light illuminated the scene, she noticed the leather binocular case hanging from the telescope. She lifted it off and tore open the button. A piece of paper fell out and was caught by a gust of wind and began to dance madly before her flailing arms. It would be blown to oblivion in a second and Ma with it!

Desperately, Holly-Jean dived into the air and just managed to slap the paper down and tag it to the marine grass-tufted cliffside. Almost vomiting with panic, she uncrumpled the paper and in the red-beamed glow she read:

Leave the money under the large granite stone at the base of the telescope in front of you. Use the bins to focus on the lowest level of the pier on the windward side, closest to Rapparee Beach opposite. Do you see the tiny light? Your old biddies are down there. However, the key to unlocking their chains is to be found under the last lobster-pot on the far end of the stone fishing jetty back in the inner harbour.

Hurry now, the tide is rising. At 3:51 it will cover both the old hags! PS When you hear the toot of a horn, cast the bins across the water to Rapparee. You might glimpse yours truly. If you want to.

242

Holly-Jean lifted the huge granite rock and placed the Sainsbury's bag underneath, making sure it was secure from the banshee wind. She jammed the binoculars to her eyes and focused on the bottom level of the pier. Saw a tiny flickering light. Checked her watch.

3.42!

She raced down the pathway, sprinted across the hundred metres of parking space, screaming at the top of her lungs, 'Don't worry, Ma! I'm coming to save you!' – exited the gates of the outer harbour and turned left onto the stone fishing-wall jetty of the inner haven.

Down at the far end was a great pile of lobster pots. She tore into them, hurling them aside in her frantic scrabbling to find the key.

There it was!

She grabbed it and ran back to the outer harbour, her frame bursting with the pain of cracked ribs and icy lung-constricting wind. She veered to the right inside the outer harbour, and when she reached the circular pier, hurdled the rusting chain fence and scrambled down to the lower levels of embarkation. On the lowest level her feet entered the frozen water before she reached the bottom. Steeling herself she plunged on down. The ocean tide was already up to her chest as she fought her way against the heaving pull and tug of the giant Atlantic breakers. Where was that light? A wave engulfed her. She choked and spat. Salt in her eyes and nostrils.

'Ma! Ma! Where are you?'

No reply to her echoing scream.

She began to swim; it was easier to make progress that way than treading the uncertain floor below and fighting the Atlantic. Swimming in a circle, following the pillars of the pier to her left she finally spotted the flickering hurricane lamp hanging from the embarkation level above one of the crumbling barnacle-covered concrete stanchions.

243

Chains were draped around the pillar. And there, just before the pitching water, were the drenched heads of Ma and Mrs Howell-Pryce!

'Ma! Mrs H-P!' she yelled.

No sign of life!

Holly thrashed her arms, powering aside the waves as she ripped through the sea. At last she reached the two women as the waves began to completely cover their heads.

'It's okay, Ma! I'm here, hold on!'

No response. Both ladies looked unconscious.

Grappling frantically with the chains, Holly managed to locate the lock deep under the water. Tried to pull it to the surface, but it was tightly attached and she had to feel blindly, under the crashing icy waves, to at last insert the key, to turn it and finally loosen the clasp of the steel hasp, fling off the lock and begin unravelling the chains.

The water engulfed her as she worked, but she didn't care. She was beyond worries like breathing, choking, for she had spent twenty years fostering her *chi* for this one moment.

The chains were finally freed and as she picked up the floating frail bundles, she felt one woman respond and begin to struggle up with her to the roller-coaster surface of the ocean.

On the surface she turned on her back and began to kick with her feet, both women's heads clutched under their chin in her hands, desperately trying to keep their mouths in access to oxygen.

'Made it!' she screamed as she finally reached the rusting stairway and pulled them out of the water. Then she dragged the prisoners up the steps, their weight heavy-laden with the soaking of saltwater.

She got to the top and managed to set both of them down on a dry section, before she suddenly doubled over and threw up a great gush of seawater.

244

* * *

She struggled with all her might to lift both women – Mrs H-P now apparently fully conscious, but Ma yet to respond – back up to the harbour floor and laid them down to wait while she raced across the parking area to the Discovery.

She jumped in, turned on the engine, reversed the thing with a scream of burning tyres, and skidded across to where the women lay. Heater full on, she dragged them inside one by one. Hugging Ma close to her body right next to the full blast of the car-heater, she rubbed and squeezed her *chi* energy into the old lady's frozen wet frame. They needed an ambulance.

She used her cellphone.

Then heard the toot of a horn.

The bins provided by the kidnapper had been lost somewhere in the ocean, but she had her own set of Nikons in the glove compartment. Keeping her hug tight on Ma, Holly-Jean focused across the water to Rapparee Beach and saw the interior light and the unmistakeable outline of a dark Jaguar illuminated for a moment.

Glimpsed the curly dark hair and thick moustache of a familiar face. The fool was dead!

There were only three roads out of Ilfracombe, she'd got them all covered and the one he'd chosen was his worst option.

Holly made another call. 'Dark Jaguar, heading out on the Old Barnstaple Road. Should reach the crossroads at Lynton Cross in five minutes.'

Mrs Howell-Pryce had regained her faculties and began to help Holly with Ma. They flicked the front seat back, and while Mrs H-P pumped Ma's chest, Holly began to blow air on the 'One-and-Two-and' rhythm into Ma's mouth. The ambulance arrived then and the medics took over.

Holly-Jean waited anxiously as two nurses wrapped both

245

women in silver foil, fitted an oxygen mask over Ma's face and began resuscitation procedure. Intravenous drips were fitted and Ma was put on full life-support.

'How is she going?' Holly finally had to ask.

One of the nurses looked up and said, 'She'll be fine. Her heart's pumping away like billy-oh, just got to stave off pneumonia and the effects of the cold. We're leaving now. Are you going to be all right?' She looked worried. 'You ought to get out of those wet clothes yourself.'

The ambulance careened off into the night with both the old women on board to the sanctuary of the North Devon Infirmary twelve miles away. Just as the lights of its tailgate disappeared and Holly was tugging on her dry sweater and zipping up her clean pair of jeans, a police Range Rover with DI Mick Coulson inside skidded to a halt next to the Discovery.

'Which way?' he yelled.

'You're too late,' Holly told him. 'But if you want to see a show, follow me!'

She threw the crate into Drive, and with Coulson's sirens wailing to wake the quick and the dead following on behind, she drove the Discovery back across the inner harbour, up through the one-way system of the town and out onto the Old Barnstaple Road to reach storm-swept Lynton Cross up on the high ground of Exmoor's foothills some ten minutes too late.

At least for the legal option.

Holly-Jean stopped the car and got out, slowly taking in the scene.

Once again her life had reached the end of a rocky road. She was ragged, but intact; her Ma would survive, but she herself had probably lost control of her life's achievement, her passport to a life of free motion – the Holly-Jean Ho Agency.

But what was this work she had achieved, she stopped to wonder, as she stared at the scene confronting her: because this time there'd been lethal consequences for two of those who'd crossed life's tangled paths and encountered her.

The burning remains of the Jaguar flared in the spitting rain and gusting wind. There was no sign of Mr Hua's soldiers who'd set up the road-block of steel spikes. They'd be long gone on their way back to London by now.

'Who was he?' asked Coulson, scratching his head as some junior Constables used foam fire extinguishers to put out the blaze. The body in the driver's seat was a foam-dripping charcoaled cinder, totally beyond salvage, and so was the melted Sainsbury's bag on the Jaguar's carpeted floor.

'Him?' said Holly-Jean, ungluing the Sainsbury's bag and pulling out the silver-foil fireproof safety-pack inside. 'Oh, he was a once-lovable rogue called Delvin Barker.'

'The software pirate? What'd he got against you?' asked Coulson as the wind howled down from Dunkery Beacon and the Doone Valley.

'Delly?' mused Holly, as she began counting the fifty-pound notes inside the Nike sportswear safety bag. 'It was just business. But he took it too personally.'